Amber's AWAKENING

ISBN: 979-8-89454-103-7 (Paperback)
ISBN: 979-8-89454-104-4 (eBook)

Editing by Ava Anderson
Cover and layout design by Lance Buckley

First Edition

10 9 8 7 6 5 4 3 2 1

Amber's AWAKENING

STEPHANIE WINKEL

THE FACTIONS 1

In loving memory of my mom.

*This book is dedicated to Carol Mae Lucasey.
Thank you for teaching me how to get
through the hard times. You did it first.*

CHAPTER 1

Amber

At first, all I saw was a beautiful, lush green forest that looked completely untouched. The smell of pine after a light rain brought the forest to life. In front of me was the Lunar Tree with its wide, twisting trunk and thick roots that stuck up from the ground. It had a soft glow, as if it was alive. Beams of moonlight rained down from its branches, beckoning me closer, trying to tell me something.

I watched the tree's moonlight dim as smoke slithered down the branches, suffocating each leaf. Eventually, the light went out. The tree was dark, and standing next to me at the base was the most beautiful white wolf I had ever seen.

She stood tall, illuminating the surrounding darkness. Her light filled me with hope. I knew I had nothing to worry about as long as this wolf was alive and well. She was the White Luna, the mate of the legendary White Alpha. The wolf turned her piercing emerald green eyes towards me as I heard her voice in my head.

"Wake up, Amber. Your people need you."

I gasped as I sat up in bed; the safety of my dream was gone. Fires outside my window cast an orange glow in my room.

The sounds of fighting on the other side of my door combined with the screams from my pack filled the air of our once-quiet territory. We were under attack.

I picked up my phone, which lit up with a picture of my dad and me on the lock screen. There was a text from Caleb Dawson. A man I have felt drawn to since I was fifteen. He sent a message at midnight, that was five minutes ago. When this is over, I will call Caleb instead of waiting for him to contact me. Hopefully, this will finally get him to visit. I haven't seen him in five years.

I put on my shoes and grabbed my crisis pack. Bullet-point arrows were in the outer side pocket, and I kept my recurve bow in a compartment on the back. I can only get to it if I unroll the pack itself. Inside the bag were hand warmers, gloves, a first aid kit, protein bars, and anything else I might need for the hike to our family's cabin outside our territory. Out of habit, I zipped my phone into the front pocket of my winter coat.

My name is Amber Cahill; I am the daughter of the Forest Moon Alpha and Luna. During an attack, it's my responsibility to get the children, or pups as we call them, to safety until my father comes when it's all clear. Even though I won't merge with my wolf for another year, I can hold my own against some of our best warriors in hand-to-hand fighting, and no one has better aim than I. Once ready, I opened the door and raced across the hall to my little sister's room.

Willow isn't your average five-year-old. She's smarter than she looks and has a tender, sweet side that charms everyone she meets.

Placing my hands on her small shoulders, I shook her gently, "Willow, wake up!" She jumped, opening her eyes in a panic.

As she looked around and heard the sounds of combat, she began to cry. "Amber, what's happening? I want Mommy!"

I hugged her quickly, saying, "I know, I do too, but you're safe with me."

Willow continued to cry as I wrapped her little body in her favorite blanket and put her boots on her feet. Next was her crisis pack. Only Willow would have a crisis pack that was pink and gray camo with a fuzzy white bunny keychain on the zipper.

We ran to Ryan's room and discovered that his bed was made and his pack was gone. He had left some time ago. I only hope that my brother would meet us in the tunnel. Ryan is our future Alpha; he was supposed to be the first person I got to the tunnels.

As we made our way from the third floor to the second, we were met by my best friend and cousin, Olivia. She was wearing the same clothes I saw her in yesterday: designer black jeans and a light blue sweater, her leather coat, and snow boots. She even had her crisis pack.

Olivia is the daughter of my father's beta, second in command, and our mothers are sisters. Olivia had been away at college but came home for my birthday.

When we were little, we looked alike with our blonde hair, even though my skin was slightly more olive than her peach color. Olivia also has blue eyes; mine are like emeralds. Olivia's hair is now a deep red, and mine is the color of chocolate.

"Amber, Willow!" Olivia grabbed my hand, and we went down the hall to get the twins. Tyla and Tyler are the children of Jorden Clark, my father's gamma, or third in command. Gamma Clark met her mate, Morgan, later in life than most wolves, so the twins are closer to Willow's age.

We heard the children screaming as we reached their open door. I didn't have time to get my bow out of my pack, so I left Willow with Olivia and hurried in, ready for a fight. I found a man in a gray uniform trying to carry them out of the room.

"Let them go!"

The man sneered as he sized me up. "Or what?" He didn't think I could stop him. I knew he was human, which meant I was stronger and faster.

I clenched my fists as I got closer. "I won't tell you again."

He smirked, then set the twins down. They looked at me and then moved out of my way. The human came at me, and I planted my feet. Once he was close enough, I head-butted him, giving myself a minor headache and the human a major one. Then I used as much strength as possible without killing him to land a hard right hook to his ribcage, just under his arm, and a left hook to his cheek. The human was out cold.

I held my hand out to the twins. "Come on, kids. We need to get out of here."

They kicked him as they grabbed their bags from their bunk bed and came to me. I held their hands, and we left to meet Willow and Olivia.

The entrance to the secret tunnel was in the Alpha's office, but the hall was now in complete chaos. One of our warriors shifted into his gray and brown wolf. The shift was so complete that you wouldn't have known the four-legged wolf was a man if you hadn't seen the change. His wolf advanced and took out the human intruder.

Olivia pulled me in the opposite direction of my dad's office. "This way, or we won't make it in time!"

I pulled out of her grasp as I put the twins behind me. "No, I can get us through these guys."

"Amber, I know you're used to being in charge in these situations, but you need to trust me right now! We'll be fine, trust me." Olivia wouldn't fight me on this if she didn't have a good reason. I have faith in my cousin, so I did as she instructed.

"Fine, but I'm going first." I switched places with Olivia so she was still protecting the kids from the rear as I led the way back in the direction we came. As I started to go up the stairs, Olivia stopped me. She grabbed my shirt and pulled me flush with the wall as a man tumbled down the stairs, head over heels.

Trent Walker, a warrior visiting from the Royal Pack, came down after him, picked up the human, and repeatedly slammed him into the opposite wall. Olivia and I covered the eyes of the pups we were protecting.

Trent was a friend and my trainer. The human didn't stand a chance against him. Both Trent and the human had soot and burn marks on them. I knew there was no going up there. Down was our only option, and I was dreading it. The ground floor was where most of the fighting would be. I looked at my cousin as I realized what I had forgotten.

"It's too dangerous for the kids to go down there. I will meet you in my dad's office."

She made eye contact with me as she gave more instructions. "Look in the third crib on the left. Hurry, you're running out of time."

I thought that was a bit specific. I'd ask her about it later. Trent dropped the unconscious human and cleared the way as Olivia ran with the three pups through the hall back the way we came.

I ran down the stairs, heading to the pack nursery. No one should be in there. All the omega pups would be in their own homes by now. As I made my way to the room, it was complete chaos. A fire was blazing where our kitchen should be and spreading fast. Our warriors fought in wolf form, and human men used silver blades.

As I approached the nursery, a human kicked my stomach, knocking the wind out of me. The human's eyes were wild and full of hatred as he came at me with his blade raised.

I dodged to the side, grabbed his arm, and pulled it down while bringing my other palm up against his elbow, breaking his arm and forcing him to release his blade. When it landed on the floor, I stepped on it, turned him away from me, and used my foot to push him into the wall.

Drake, the wolf of my dad's head guard, Ian Baxter, grabbed the man with his teeth and dragged him away from me. Once he had the man away from the nursery, Drake nodded to me. I took the opportunity to pick up the blade and sheath it in the side pocket of my pack. Then, I entered the nursery before something else happened.

As I made my way into the room, it was quiet. I went over to the third crib on the left, and found an infant sleeping through the chaos. As soon as I saw her lying there, I understood what Olivia had been trying to say. Alice.

Alice is Drake's daughter. Her mother, Rose, is a night nurse at a human emergency medical center in town. He must have been on night patrol and brought her here before the attack.

I reached into the crib and swaddled her up, making sure to keep her head covered. "Don't worry, Alice. I will keep you safe until I get you back with your parents."

I saw a worn pink bunny, and at the last minute, grabbed it. As I left the room, Drake came up to me and whined. I showed him his daughter as I rubbed the bunny on his fur. "I promise, Drake, I am going to take good care of Alice. She will be waiting for you at the cabin." He licked her face and nudged me to get going. I left him as he returned to fight off the threat to our pack.

The smoke was starting to get thick and it smelled different from before. There was something else in the air, too. It was odd and hurt my nose, giving me a headache. My vision was blurry at times. I only hoped to get back to the office before this worsened. I ran down the hall, dodging wolves and men. The fire was getting bad down here. I hoped Ryan made it to safety. Once I reached the second floor, I ran to the office.

There were several times when I was shoved against a wall by humans and wolves as they paid more attention to each other than to me. I turned so that I could protect Alice, who was now screaming.

One of the human's silver blades scratched my arm. The cut wasn't deep, but it was painful. A wound from silver is like a mosquito bite, except instead of itching, it burns, and it will burn for a long time after the silver is removed. I wanted to cry out, but I had to focus if I was going to get us to safety.

I kicked a few more men out of my way. The air was getting thinner; there was a strange yellow smoke in the hall that burned my lungs, as well as my eyes and nose. I was beginning to feel lightheaded. My whole body felt like it was now on fire. I had to stay focused, but the burn and smoke made it difficult to move forward.

When I reached the office, Olivia was coughing, and Willow and the twins also struggled with this strange smoke. There was still no sign of Ryan.

I couldn't tell if the tears coming down my cheeks were from the yellow smoke in the air or the burn on my arm. "We…." I began coughing and covering my mouth and nose didn't help anymore. "Have… to go."

The door to the secret passage was along the wall of book-shelves. When my dad designed the wall, he wanted a way to hide the entrance to the passageway. What better way than a bookshelf? The lock was hidden in a small safe with a false wall in the back that I lifted to insert my key. The shelf slid halfway behind the one next to it.

After Olivia and the young pups entered the tunnel, I pulled my key out of the lock, giving me ten seconds to get in before the door closed. Now, going out into the forest was the only way out. The air wasn't much better in here. I could feel the heat of the fire. We needed to move quickly down the stairs into the underground tunnel.

My heart broke as I worried about my brother but I knew that I had to leave to protect the others. With secure in my arms, the five of us descended the wooden stairs past the basement and into the hidden tunnel under the packhouse. It was cooler here, and the air was better. I was still a bit disoriented from the strange yellow smoke that had been lingering in the pack house. I held Alice close and shielded her when I stumbled a few times.

We walked through the tunnel and came to where it split. One tunnel went to the forest, the only way out, and the other was from the garden shed near the Omega houses. That was where I found my brother.

"Ryan!" I gave him a big hug while keeping Alice from getting squished. I had been so worried about him. "Don't scare me like that." I knew I sounded upset, but really, I was happy he was safe.

"Let's just get out of here," Ryan began, but then he saw my arm. "Amber, you're bleeding."

I looked down and shrugged. "It's just a scratch. Come on."

Behind him, I saw the omega pups from the surrounding houses. Ryan saved their lives. I squeezed his shoulder, proud of the alpha he's becoming.

I took a breath of the stale air inside the tunnel. At least it was free of smoke. I swayed a bit before handing Alice off to Ryan so I could myself. I took another breath and was able to find my footing again. I still had a headache and the burn in my arm was more painful than I let on.

I wouldn't let myself cry in front of the pups. They needed to see me as a strong leader right now. I made my way to the front of our group and pulled out my phone out of my front coat pocket. I tried to turn it on, but the screen was damaged, and I couldn't get it to light up. It must have happened when the human kicked me outside the nursery. I placed it back in my pocket. "It's broken."

The others checked for their phones. Ryan patted down his pockets.

"I must have forgotten my phone in my room."

"Mine's broken too." Olivia held up a warped phone. "It must have happened just before we split up, or before I found you."

Olivia's movements were slower than Ryan's as she placed her phone in her back pocket. She was still suffering from the effects of the yellow smoke.

I reached into my pack and pulled out a flashlight. As we walked farther away from the packhouse, the air in the tunnel became colder. I looked behind me, and saw Olivia bracing herself against a wooden beam. I stopped the kids from moving and went back for Olivia. I took her hand and waited until she was ready to move on again. When she nodded, I let go and turned around.

"Hold on to my pack."

She grabbed the top of my pack and held on as I ushered her ahead of the group. Ryan handed Alice to one of the older kids then moved to the back of the group. It's instinct for warriors and guards to know that being at the back is just as important as being in the front. We kept the children surrounded by the strongest in our group to better protect them. Even normal wolf packs will travel like this.

We walked a few more steps, before we heard something strange. Olivia tugged on my pack, forcing me to stop and look at her. Her eyes flickered, but I couldn't see the color of her wolf's eyes.

"Stop, no one move." Olivia's eyes stopped flickering and began glowing bright lime green. Slowly, Olivia let go of my pack and moved in front of me. I had followed to give her the support she needed when the beam of my flashlight revealed hundreds of long, slender, moving figures. One of them lifted its head, and I saw the slanted eyes and heard the distinct buzz of the rattle. Then another, and another rattled until all of them were shaking their tails. The sound was so loud in the tunnel that it was like white noise with the volume up all the way.

In a voice I didn't recognize, Olivia's voice resonated louder than the snakes. "Let us pass."

This must be the voice of her wolf. Her eyes continued to glow lime green. The snakes then slithered over one another to the dirt wall of the tunnel. There was a small path along the wall we were standing closest to. I returned for the kids; they all looked as scared as me. I hate snakes.

A young blonde girl, Ellie, clutched onto my sister's shoulder and peeked around her as I approached. "What was that sound?"

Josh Morrison, a thirteen-year-old know-it-all, couldn't help himself. "It's called a hibernaculum."

Willow's curiosity overpowered her fear. "What's a hiber… hiber…nac?"

"Hibernaculum, it's when hundreds of…"

"Don't finish that sentence, Josh," I warned. "Everyone, we are going to walk single file; put your hand on the shoulder of the person in front of you. Close your eyes, and I'll lead you out. Ryan will protect you from the back."

Ryan nodded, and I held Willow's hand as I walked them through the tunnel. Olivia was still keeping the snakes on their side. At least the buzzing stopped. We made it to the other side of the hibernaculum. Olivia returned to us, and thankfully, we made it to the exit without any more obstacles. I hoped my dad was waiting for us at the cabin.

CHAPTER 2

Amber

The tunnel exit was in a shallow cave, hidden from natural eyes. The door was shaped like a giant rock and helped soundproof the tunnel. My grandfather found this cave when he was young and often camped inside. My father and his command agreed it would be an excellent place to hide a tunnel.

I told the others to wait inside while I scouted for any more dangers. I held the door open and stepped into the cave. The only sounds of life were the wind blowing through the trees and an owl screeching in the night. Thankfully, there was nothing threatening so I waved for everyone to follow. "The coast is clear; you guys can come out."

Everyone entered the cave, and took a deep breath of fresh air. "We'll camp here for the night and make our way to the cabin at first light." The pups sat down where they were. Some of the boys, like Michael and Josh, huddled together. Many of them were shaking from fear, adrenaline, and the chill in the air.

Alice cried every time I tried to place her on the bed of coats Willow and Ellie had made for her, but She only calmed down when she was being held. I didn't blame her. Finally, Ryan walked up and held his hands out. I gave Alice to him so I could take off my pack.

Olivia found a place for her things, then unzipped her bag and pulled out a medical kit. "Let me see your arm." I removed my pack and coat and showed her the still burning wound.

She inspected my cut and opened the kit. Then she grabbed antiseptic spray, gauze, and a linen wrap. Olivia cleaned my cut, placed the gauze on my arm, and wrapped it with the linen.

When she was done, I looked at the damage to my coat. I stuck my fingers through the hole in my sleeve. "I think I can fix this, but we may have to wait until we return to the packhouse."

It was going to be a cold walk to the cabin, so I pulled some duct tape from my pack and tore a piece off to cover the hole. The blood on the sleeve had dried, so it would do for now. I put the coat back on, careful of the bandage on my arm.

While Olivia settled the pups, Ryan handed Alice to Josh and shook the tension out of his arms. He helped me gather wood for a fire. We worked in silence, not knowing what might be close by. Every crack of a twig we stepped on made us jump. My heart skipped a beat whenever I heard branches being moved out of place. We made it back to the cave where Olivia already had the kids set up to sleep, though no one wanted to. We were all thinking the same things: What was happening with our pack? Were our families okay?

The cave felt warmer once I got the fire started. I looked over at Josh, who had managed to fall asleep with Alice tucked in close to him. She was content enough with his body heat to sleep.

Olivia, Ryan and I sat by the fire. We were silent as we thought about what to say next. We were all still in a state of shock.

Ryan was the first to recover enough to say anything. He held his hands near the fire as he looked at our cousin. "Olivia, thank you for the warning to get to the omega pups early. We barely made it to the tunnel entrance when the attack started. We couldn't have gotten them out if it wasn't for you."

Olivia had been so composed during the attack. But now that we were away from the fight, she cried. Tears streamed down her cheeks as I moved to put my arm around her. She sat up and wiped her face with her sleeves.

"It wasn't supposed to happen like this. We were supposed to have more time. Uncle William said we would have more time."

"What do you mean?" I asked.

I thought all the strange behavior had been because of party preparations. Everyone, especially my parents, had been acting strangely. I knew something was up when my dad had ordered all the elders in the pack to be evacuated.

Olivia wrapped her arms around her stomach. "When I arrived, I spoke with your parents and the rest of the command. Your dad said we should have 48 hours to get out."

I remembered seeing her in my dad's office yesterday morning. It had been the first time in years that I wasn't included in a meeting.

"I'm one of the evacuation leaders. Why was I left out of the preperations?"

Olivia turned her head to avoid eye contact. "Uncle William didn't want you to know everything yet. He knew how you would react. He also said that you deserved one last normal day. This morning, Trent and Ian were supposed to escort us north to the Royal Pack. We should have had more time." A tear ran down Olivia's cheek as she sniffed.

How I would react? I would have pushed for a full evacuation before sundown.

"How did you know what was going to happen? Did you know about this whole attack?"

Olivia's smile didn't reach her eyes. The mixed emotions of joy about merging with her wolf and the fear from the attack were warring on her face. "You know that I merged with my wolf a few months ago. Like I told you before, her name is Sage, but what I didn't tell you is that she's blessed. Ever since that night, I've been having dreams of the future. They're nothing more than glimpses and I didn't know what they were. I don't always understand what I'm seeing, they can be really vague. A few nights ago, I dreamed about the attack. I didn't realize it was a prophetic dream. I'm still new to this; I didn't exactly know what I saw. I remembered seeing Ryan with the omega pups already in the tunnel. I saw Willow, me, and the twins being taken to the office by Trent. The last thing I saw was Alice in a crib in a smoke-filled room."

Ryan looked at her over the fire. He moved his hands to his pockets. "Sage didn't give you any guidance? That's what our wolves are meant to do."

Olivia nodded then wiped away another tear. "Sage had been trying to convince me that my dreams weren't normal and that I should return a week before I did, but I didn't listen. I still didn't understand my dreams. When we arrived she told me to instruct to Ryan meet us in the tunnels with the omega pups." She looked at my brother. "That's when I approached you after dinner."

My frustration was reaching its limit. I knew something big was happening. I faced my cousin and ran my fingers through my hair, interlacing them behind my head in an attempt to calm down. It didn't work. My heart was still racing and my chest felt like it was going to explode.

"Is that why my parents began acting so weird? Why didn't they send us into the tunnels at dinner? We could have gotten more people out! At the very least, you should have told me about your dream and Sage's instructions. Why didn't you?"

Olivia once again avoided eye contact. "I didn't think you would believe me."

"But you told Ryan?"

"He was in the dream; I had to tell him first."

Ryan looked slightly guilty.

"Livy, everyone was acting weird, and my mom told me that they moved the elders up to Idaho in the morning. Of course I would have believed you! Besides, you've never been one to tell wild stories."

Olivia smiled, and another tear ran down her face. I had to know more.

"What about the guy on the stairs?"

Olivia tapped her ears. "Wolf hearing. I heard him hit the wall at the top of the stairs."

Our conversation came to an end as the kids became more restless. They didn't want to sleep, making it hard to continue talking without scaring them more. We decided to discuss it further once we got to the cabin.

Periodically, we'd hear crying; sometimes one of the younger ones would come and sit in our laps. It was cold, and everything from that night was still fresh in our minds. It would be a long hike in the cold with so many kids and little sleep.

We decided to take shifts on who would keep watch. I volunteered for the first shift since it was clear that neither Ryan nor Olivia had slept at all. I picked up my pack and walked to the mouth of the cave.

The forest was so different at night. The animals were active, letting me know that no danger lurked close by, but I still didn't want to let my guard down too much. My body felt stiff, so I shook my arms to loosen up in case I had to fight off an intruder. As the minutes ticked by, my mind raced after everything that had happened.

Olivia and I are practically sisters and tell each other everything. So why did she tell Ryan about the danger to the pack and not me? This was my responsibility. It's my job to keep them all safe, especially Ryan. How can I do that if I am left out of vital information? We could have gotten more people out.

This was the worst night of my life. As I looked over at my crisis pack, the moonlight's reflecton on the silver blade caught my attention shifting my thoughts to my family. How many had survived? What happened to my parents? I closed my eyes and took a deep breath. I could ask them when I got to the cabin.

I thought about the last things we said to each other. Mom was trying to hide her concern. She told me to be true to myself and that she loved me. She hugged me and kissed my cheek. It was strange, I should have pushed for her to tell me what was going on.

Dad told me to remember everything they had taught me. He hugged me and told me he loved me. My dad called me his Emerald Princess, a nickname he gave me when I was ten.

My parents knew. They raised me to be a strong Luna, then kept me from defending our pack when it was most important. I wiped an angry tear off my cheek and suppressed a sob bubbling up from my chest.

An Alpha and Luna are supposed to protect the pack. If they had told me, we could have acted sooner and rescued more people. I won't let them do that to me again. He knew better. Why did he wait until the last minute?

I knew who was behind the attack; I had seen a patch on the human's shoulder outside the nursery. It had two bold letters, CB, with a black border. Charles Balor and his soldiers also use specially designed silver weapons. I pulled out the blade I picked up by nursey, and studied it. It was light, and the hilt had polished wooden sides, so I could hold it without burning my hands too much.

We all thought we were safe from him since our pack was small. We were well hidden. The only way to find us was if you had been there before. If the humans found us, then someone betrayed us.

Balor may be human, but he's a monster. He's the reason humans now know about shapeshifters. Because of him, other humans have joined his army to exterminate our kind just because we have abilities. Humans are afraid of what's different.

It doesn't matter that we are faster and stronger than humans. Until we merge with our wolves at the age of twenty-one, we share the same characeristics as humans. The only difference is that we heal faster, and our bone density is stronger. When we merge with our wolves and gain the ability to shapeshift, we become what humans call 'Werewolves' or 'Lycans'. It's insulting, just because something is more common or easier to say doesn't make it less hurtful.

Call us by what we are: shapeshifters. Werewolves are fictional monsters born from the imagination of humans. They look like giant,, furry men with the head of a wolf, fangs, claws for hands, that stand on two legs. We are not monsters.

We are shapeshifters; we can shift from a wolf to a person. When we shift, we become giant wolves. We can't walk on two legs in wolf form, and our hands don't look like claws.

We can't turn anyone into one of us with a bite; you must be born to at least one shifter. We don't have hybrids, either. The strongest gene will determine if you are a shapeshifter. You're either a shifter or you're not.

The same is true if on the rare occation a person has a mate from another faction. The strongest gene determines what shapeshifter you become.

Humans don't understand, nor do they try to, so they created their own version of us from their imaginations. Humans fear what is different, and they allow that fear to create lies that lead to prejudice. It's why our kind has remained hidden from the human world for centuries.

Balor preyed on that fear when he proved our existence. That was the day everything changed for my kind. Humans and shapeshifters lived in fear of each other. The violent nature of the video Balor used and the lies he told the public sparked chaos in our country. No one knew who they could trust. I would never forget the day I saw that news report with my parents when I was ten years old.

TEN YEARS AGO

It was just the four of us in our cabin. I was chasing Ryan around the house, playing tag.

"Take it outside, you two," my mom yelled. I ran out the front door and waited for Ryan.

"That's cheating! Mom, Amber's cheating."

Mom smiled, then winked at him. "Then I guess you will just have to outrun her."

He stood inside the door, looking for ways to get around me. The back door wouldn't do him any good because I could just run around the portch and catch him.

Dad came up and distracted me. Ryan took the opportunity and ran by me, making me chase him again. Our dad laughed as he watched us, then snuck up behind me and held his hand out to me. I tagged him, and he ran after Ryan. My brother squealed in delight as our dad picked him up; he set him down and then winked.

"You're it," my dad said and ran away. Ryan has always been fast, but he still couldn't catch our dad. Ryan almost tagged me, but I climbed up a tree next to the woodshed.

"No climbing!" Ryan complained again. I stuck my tongue out at him.

"Amber. Get down from there. Play fair," my dad instructed.

"Fine." I jumped down and ran away from my brother. We played for another hour until my dad's phone went off. He checked it and got a stormy look on his face.

"Get inside, both of you."

Ryan and I knew that tone, so we didn't argue. We ran inside with our dad close behind. He went straight for the TV and turned it on.

Ryan jumped on the couch and waited for whatever we were going to watch. "Can I have popcorn?"

Dad ignored him, which was odd. This must be serious. Mom came out of the kitchen when she heard the noise. "Liam. We agreed, no TV on this trip." She is the only person who can call my dad that. I tried once and got in trouble.

"Shh," he said to her.

I walked over to the couch to sit with Ryan. Mom joined my dad in the center of the room as we watched the news. A red strip with bold letters shown at the bottom of the screen read 'Breaking News'. The reporter's eyes were red, and he kept fidgeting with the papers in front of him as he gave his report.

"We have recieved a report of a new threat to our nation. I need to inform you that this video is live and nothing has been edited. There are no special effects used in this video. What we are about to show you is graphic, so if you have a weak constitu-tion please leave the room. We take you live to the scene."

The screen changed to a video of a man I didn't recognize. His eyes were wild and glowing a briliant red. They reminded me of rubies. He took his shirt off and even through the TV screen I could see a vein in his neck as it moved. His arms were up and he pointed at the other man on the screen.

The other man was in a suit and kept looking behind him. It was blurry and too dark to see anything besides the men. The man in the suit kept shouting for the other man to get back.

My mom placed her hand on my dad's back and pointed to the man with the glowing eyes. "Isn't that Ethan Harrison? He's one of the most gentle wolves we know."

My dad wrapped his arm around her shoulders as they kept watching. "I worked with him and his pack last year. You won't find many Alphas like Ethan. He doesn't get angry like this unless his family is threatened."

"What's going on, Dad?" I asked.

"I don't know, baby."

On TV, the man kept telling Alpha Harrison to stay back as he pulled out a gun. Ryan jumped and looked up at me. I had a dreadful feeling, so I put my hand over his eyes. He pulled my hand down and watched with us.

Alpha Harrison screamed as his eyes flashed. In an instant, he shifted into a large, snarling, black wolf and charged as the other man pulled the trigger. We all heard the bang of the gun as he shot the wolf.

"No!" My mom screamed, and my dad turned her into his chest. I couldn't pull my eyes away from the TV. I couldn't believe what I just saw. I didn't want it to be real. How could someone do that? The small red letters at the bottom left of the screen that read 'Live', told me this was happening. The news anchor's voice was heard over the video, "Did that man just… His eyes were glowing! What is that thing?" The wolf lay there motionless and then shifted back to look like a man in tattered clothes. The camera zoomed in on his face. The light was gone and his eyes were open. The vein in his neck was pumping blood onto the floor where it pooled around his body.

Ryan turned away from the TV and I held him tight. My heart was pounding and it was as if time stood still. A tear ran down my cheek as I tried to understand why the man on the TV killed that alpha in cold blood.

The picture went back to the reporter. "I am just as shocked as you are." The reporter's voice trembled. "There it is. We can no longer deny the existence of werewolves. We will keep you updated as the story develops about these murderous creatures."

PRESENT DAY

Murderers or killers, werewolves or monsters, that's what they called us. Some still call us that. I have never killed anyone; I'm not a monster. After the news release, Olivia and I made a vow to never ever kill anyone, no matter the circumstances.

Rumors about our kind spread, and there was nothing but chaos for more than two years. Balor had begun handing out rewards to anyone who killed a shapeshifter. He gained favor with the federal government and they gave him his own agency. It was more like an army, but it didn't matter. Innocent people were being murdered.

My dad had instructed anyone with a wolf not to shift outside our small territory. It was a year before we had any more pack runs. Members could no longer roam the mountain in wolf form because humans were hunting us. Our guards had to stay in human form while on duty.

Keeping the wolves from being allowed out was hard on so many. The wolf would get restless and demand to run, or they would make their humanoid side go almost insane. My father had to work at keeping our guards from getting too aggressive, as they would sometimes take on the personalities of their wolves.

Some pack members couldn't handle the pressure. Many felt as if they were locked in a house and not allowed to leave. Only, the 'house' was their bodies. It was too much. Some would shift anyway and go into the mountains.

Just when we started to think we could go back to normal, random pack members would let out that awful scream that let us know their mate had been killed. Some just disappeared. Then, months later, their mate would scream and cry, letting us all know the unthinkable had happened.

That man! That one human! He is the monster. He's the reason so many innocent people are dying. Ten years later and he is still hunting us.

I felt a tear run down my cheek. I wiped it away quickly before anyone noticed. A light touch on my shoulder startled me out of my thoughts as the sun started peeking over the horizon.

"Sorry. I didn't mean to surprise you." Ryan whispered to me.

I nodded to him. "I was just remembering the day humans learned the truth about us."

"What made you think about that?"

"When a human tried to attack me by the nursery, I saw a patch on his shoulder. He worked for Charles Balor." Ryan's body became rigid. I handed him the weapon I was holding.

"Why use a silver blade?" he asked, "This would hurt us for sure, but it would be difficult for a human to kill us with one of these."

I remembered the human Trent was fighting; the blade he used didn't help him. I saw a gun holstered on the one who attacked me. Ryan was right; it didn't make any sense.

"I don't know; they had guns, but they weren't using them."

"At least we know Dad will meet us at the cabin. Dad is the strongest wolf we know," Ryan sounded hopeful as he returned the blade to me, and I put it back in my bag. "Our pack has been so careful. For as long as I've known, no one knew our location. Dad made sure of that. Not even in our own town. What changed? How did Balor, of all people, find us?"

I rested my elbows on my knees as I played with a piece of grass. "The only way the humans could have found us is if someone led them to us."

"Who? We didn't have many visitors."

I shrugged. "It had to be another wolf. Dad doubled up on our security measures a few years ago when he came home from helping the Northern Colorado Pack."

Ryan looked at the blade of grass in my hand then back up at me. "Do you think they will help us?"

"How are we supposed to call them?"

"Right, I forgot."

I dropped the piece of grass and put my arm around my brother's shoulders. We sat there until the sky began to change colors.

"We should head out; the pups need to get out of the cold," I said as I stood up.

Ryan and I walked back into the cave to wake those who had fallen asleep. We gathered everything we had and used dirt to smother the fire. I put on my leader's voice and addressed the group.

"We all need to stay together and walk as quietly as possible. Those of you who are older need to help the younger ones. We'll only get to the cabin if we work together."

Josh nodded when he saw me looking at him. We cleaned up the cave, and I made sure the fire was safe enough to leave. Josh handed Alice to me so he could walk with a few of the little omegas. Then we headed out into the chilly morning to hike up to the cabin, where we would wait for my parents to bring us back home.

CHAPTER 3

Amber

The hike was more challenging than we anticipated. What should have been a twenty-minute hike took more than an hour. At least most of the pups had shoes. The omega kids had gotten out early enough to be dressed for this weather. The twins only had coats and slippers, and Willow only had boots because I had to get them out quickly. It was early April, and the air was still cold.

Olivia shifted into Sage and carried some of the younger kids who struggled the most. Sage was able to keep the animals away, too.

Willow sat up front. Behind her was her best friend, Clella Mae. She goes by Ellie for short. Ellie was a year older than Willow. Her blonde hair was as bright as she was, especially at math.

Sitting behind them were Tyla and Tyler. The two dark-haired twins were never apart. They clung to each other more than anyone I know. Sage walked slowly and gently to make sure no one fell off.

Ryan, Olivia, and I were used to this hike, but the young ones weren't. Not even Willow had hiked to the cabin; she usually rode with Mom or Dad.

We made frequent stops. Ryan and I took turns with Alice. She often cried because she was tired and hungry, like the rest of us. She also needed a clean diaper, but we couldn't do anything for her until we reached the cabin.

The uncertainty of what happened to our families had the pups whimpering often. We would have to stop when we could to shuffle the kids around, carry some while they sobbed, or try to get them walking again.

Josh was a few years younger than Ryan. He was dark-skinned with curly dark brown hair and brown eyes. He helped carry some of the younger pups when they struggled to keep going.

Michael Romans was the opposite. He was a ten year old boy with light-skin, with freckles on his face, green eyes, and red hair. His fear made him anxious and he would often make comments that upset the pups or complain about the walk.

When the cabin came into view, the sun was shining through the trees. The thought of a roaring warm fireplace, a shower, and decent clothes quickened our pace.

The cabin was quite large. It had three bedrooms with a bathroom in each. The outside looked like your standard log cabin with a wrap-around porch, but the inside was a different story. The living room was big enough to fit a couch, two recliners, a coffee table in the center, and an entertainment center without a television.

My dad was so enraged when Alpha Harrison was murdered that he ripped the TV off the wall and threw it outside. We never replaced it.

Instead of a TV, we had a radio and a lot of board games. The living room opened up into the dining room and kitchen. We had a large dining table with a row of four country-style light fixtures, the kind with one bulb in a black cage that hung down over the table. Those same lights were over the center of the kitchen, too. The kitchen had a nice stovetop built into the counter, facing the dining table. The walk-in pantry was fully stocked.

Inside the pantry is a hidden door to the basement. Ryan and I were the only ones with the lock combination. I need to give it to Olivia as well. That was where we stored anything we needed in an evacuation. Clothes of every size, shoes, towels, blankets, cleaning supplies, detergents, and ten sizable first aid kits.

There were four shelves of food. Two shelving units had mason jars of food like green beans, carrots, peaches, beets, jams, and anything else we could could preserve. There were two shelving units with large cans of powdered milk, pasta, dry beans, rice, potato flakes, and dried powdered eggs. We had one shelf of store-bought items like peanut butter and cereal. There were two freezers with meat and loaves of bread.

The basement also contained other necessities and the keys to the truck parked in the shed out back. This cabin had everything except a washer and dryer, which should keep us fed for at least two months.

When we walked in the front door, we all found a place to sit until we were ready to move. Once I cleaned Alice up, I found Olivia in the kitchen looking through the cupboards. She had peanut butter and a jar of jam on the counter.

"I found the baby formula," she said, pointing to a container by the fridge.

"Thank you," I responded. Ignoring the burning pain in my arm, I searched the cupboards for a bottle. Thankfully, I found them on the top shelf of the pantry. I quickly made a bottle for Alice.

She was so hungry that I had to work at slowing her down before she made herself sick. Once I had her fed and burped, she went right to sleep, so I laid her down in the makeshift nursery in the main bedroom. I left the room and found Ryan starting a fire in the fireplace. In my room, I found socks for Willow and the twins. I would worry about shoes tomorrow. We were all tired after the restless night and cold from our hike. We sat together by the fire while Olivia brought us sandwiches.

This cabin initially belonged to my family. However, when our existence was exposed to the human world, my dad offered it as the first evacuation point. Our ranked members have kept this place stocked with everything we might need, like hand-me-downs from pack members, tools, and full gas cans for the truck.

Once I had finished my sandwich, I went into the basment to get the pups dry clothes from their familys' boxes, then brought up the boxes one at a time. The items had their families' scent, enough to comfort them. We all started feeling a little better with the dry clothes, food, and the smell of those we missed.

It was lunchtime when I began to worry that no one had come for us yet. My dad and Uncle Colin were supposed to come for us when it was over. I looked at the clock on the wall. The attack was twelve hours ago. Why hadn't they come yet?

We played games with the kids to keep them occupied, but soon we were all worried. Someone should have come by now. Dinner was silent. No one wanted to voice what we were all thinking and it was all any of us could think about. After we were done eating, my sister was the one to break the silence.

"Amber, will you tell us a story?" Willow asked. I thought about it, and only one story seemed appropriate.

I sat on the floor by the fireplace, and Willow climbed into my lap. The other pups joined us out of curiosity. Ryan sat with Alice and fed her an evening bottle. Ellie and Tyla climbed onto Olivia's lap. Once the kids settled down, I began.

"A long time ago, long before any of us were born, before our grandparents were born, there was a meeting between the royal pack and their allies. The moon goddess stood in front of them with a warning.

"There is a threat coming to all shapeshifters. It will destroy the balance of nature, and you will suffer at the hands of this threat."

"What was the threat?" Ellie asked.

"The goddess didn't say. Instead, she told them that there was hope. She chose champions to help defeat this threat. Leading these champions will be two wolves."

"The White Alpha!" Tyler exclaimed excitedly.

"Yes, the White Alpha and his Luna. They're meant to save us all."

"Do you think he could help us?" Michael asked.

Ryan adjusted Alice and brought Michael onto his lap. "The White Alpha will be the most powerful wolf our kind has ever known; if he was here, I think he would help us."

"The White Alpha is said to have many abilities. But he won't get any of them until he finds his mate. Then it's all over for the big bad guy," I said. I had to change a few words since I was talking to small children.

"Why does he have to have his mate before he gets his powers?" Tyler asked.

I smiled. "So he isn't discovered and killed before she can be with him."

"Who's more powerful?" Tyla asked.

I winked at her. "The Luna. Obviously." Tyla and the other pups giggled.

After the story, Olivia and I used the three bathrooms to get all the kids bathed and dressed in clean clothes. We had to adjust the hot water so it wasn't as cold, but it was still uncomfortable to bathe in. By the time the pups were all clean, the hot water was spent. While we were busy, my brother made the sleeping arrangements. Ryan and I took our rooms leaving the master bedroom for Olivia. All the boys went with Ryan and the girls were split between Olivia's room and mine.

Once the pups were clean and asleep, I was finally able to take a shower myself. I went to my dresser and pulled out a tank top and shorts. Then I went to the closet and found a towel. My crisis pack was nestled into the corner of the closet, and my bow was leaning against it.

That wasn't what got my attention. I pulled the blade out of my pack and then my phone. I tried to charge it, but it was no use. Nothing changed; the screen was completely cracked, and the phone was warped. I was more worried about how I was supposed to call for help if we needed it. Wanting to forget about them, I put my phone and the silver blade in my drawer and went to the bathroom.

The water was cold, but I didn't care; I just wanted to wash off everything from the night before. My arms hurt from the fight. I looked down at them and saw all the dark bruises on my arms. The cut had reopened and was bleeding again, but I didn't feel the burn this time. My chest felt tight, my head hurt, and I started scrubbing and scrubbing until my skin started to get red and raw.

If I could scrub away the bruises, I could convince myself this was all a bad dream. The sting was better than the memory of the strange smoke and the battle. Maybe I could convince myself that Balor hadn't found our pack, that I was only here at our cabin on vacation with my family instead of on the run trying to protect the children of our pack.

I had been training for years and knew how good I was. This was still the first real battle I had ever witnessed. I didn't think it would be so horrific.

Unlike the thrill you get from action movies or books, nothing was thrilling about what I went through. It was frightening. The whole time, I was scared that I wouldn't get the pups or myself out in time, and I was afraid that I would never see my brother again.

I wanted the humans to leave. We hadn't done anything to them; why did they think they had the right to invade our home?

I couldn't hold it in anymore. The attack had shaken me to my core. I began to cry and hyperventilate; I was thankful for the water. I didn't want anyone to hear me.

I slid down the shower wall and cried until I had nothing left. My dad was supposed to meet us here. He should be here by now. But he wasn't, and I didn't know what had happened to him. Someone would have come for us if he couldn't. Uncle Colin, Gamma Jordan, or even Ian. But no one had come. I was still afraid that I would never see my parents or pack again.

When I was done crying, I left the shower, rebandaged my arm, and got dressed. My skin was raw, and my throat was sore. I slowly walked to my bed and crawled under the covers. I closed my eyes and let sleep take me.

Amber

Just like my dream from the night before, I woke up in the Forest of the Gods. This place was peaceful. I was warm, even though I had gone to bed cold. The air was clean with no smoke lingering in the air. The only sound I heard was the breeze blowing through the leaves and branches. I didn't see the Lunar Tree this time. I saw more of the forest and I wandered among the other trees until a voice got my attention.

"Hello, my child."

A man stepped out from behind a tree to my right. At least half of him was a man; the other half looked like an animal, and the horns on his head made him appear more like a goat than a man.

He had brown curly hair. His horns were long; they started at the top of his head and curled around back towards his ears. They held all of the different shades of tree bark, brown and gray, with hints of green and white.

His face was handsome; he looked to be in his mid-forties. His eyes were the color of moss, a vibrant yellow-green. His skin was dark brown, and he wore a cream and gold vest that showed off his muscles. His legs were covered in light brown hair, and his hooves were gray, almost black, and smooth like the rocks at the bottom of a river.

When he spoke, his voice was deep and full of compassion. "I know what you and your pack went through last night. Take this time to wander my forest and find some peace for a short while. Rest your mind here. I'm afraid your journey has only begun, and you have a long road ahead."

"Who are you? What do you mean, your forest?" I felt as though I should know him.

He smiled at me. "I am Pan, the keeper of this forest. I watch over the creatures here and in your realm. I created this forest with the help of the moon goddess, Selene. We intended this to be a place of birth and eternal rest for your kind, the shapeshifters."

When I realized what he meant I had a horrible thought. This is where our kind goes when we die. I looked at him wide-eyed as I pointed at myself.

Pan smiled and sat down. "No, Amber, you are not dead." I let out a breath I didn't know I was holding. He patted the place next to him and I joined him. "I brought you here because you have just been through a traumatic experience. You need to rest here so you can handle what is to come and start on your path to become the person, the wolf, you are destined to be. It won't be easy. This is a path only you and your mate can take. Rest now; when the sun comes up, you have much work to do."

I had so many questions, but he was gone. I knew about the Moon Goddess, but Pan wasn't mentioned in any of our history books. I closed my eyes, listened to the birds in the trees, and felt the warm wind blowing across my face. It didn't feel cold here. It was warm, and I could smell the fresh dew on the trees and grass. A smell that brought me peace, which only a sacred place like this can provide.

I did as Pan suggested and wandered the Sacred Forest. In the distance I noticed a familiar glow. When I came across the Lunar Tree, it was untouched. In my dream last night, smoke had taken over the tree and put out its light; but looking at it now, moonlight radiated as if nothing had happened. Its magnificence was enchanting.

"Hello, Amber," a woman said in a voice as gentle as my mother's. She came from behind the tree. There's only one person she could be: Seline, the moon goddess. She walked towards me in a light blue flowing, sheet-like gown. It looked like what the women wore in ancient Greece, complete with gold accents and jewelry. Her dress sparkled as if it were made from the stars. Her hair was as black as night, with skin the color of cinnamon, and she smelled like milk and honey.

I took a knee, bowing my head and placing my fist over my heart. This is how we show respect and absolute loyalty. The goddess placed her fist over her heart, and I stood again.

"Have a seat and rest awhile," the goddess said. I sat on one of the smaller roots.

"Why am I here?"

The goddess smiled. "You are special, Amber. There is more to you than you realize."

"What do you mean? I'm just a small country wolf. There's nothing special about me."

"You don't consider your speed and physical strength special?"

"Not really. They get me in trouble. Not as much as my principles, but I still make people angry."

"You have made prideful men angry. Men who think they are above a Luna. And you, Amber, are more than just a Luna."

As much as I wanted to believe her, it was hard not to picture the looks on their faces and words they shouted at me. I didn't see how that made me special. I brought my legs up and hugged my knees.

"Pan said something about destiny. What was he talking about?"

"You are one of my chosen champions," the goddess said.

I wasn't sure I heard her correctly. How could I be a champion? The goddess gestured to the tree. She pointed to the spot I had stood and saw the White Luna.

"Amber, not everyone dreams of the Forest of the Gods, let alone their wolf, before it's time for their merge. You have a connection to this forest that is unique only to you."

She dropped her hand a looked at me meaningfully.

"Why would I be given a connection to this forest? I know you said I was your champion; but what does that mean? Why me?"

"Why not you? Amber, you're not afraid to stand up for what you believe is right; you stand up for the innocent, regardless of whom you are talking to. You care deeply for your pack, and I know you will take great care of the pups. It's that kind of tenacity and compassion that makes a great champion."

"What if I hurt someone?"

"I'm afraid you will have times when that will be necessary. Like when you protected the twins and Alice during the attack. There is a reason your father trained you in combat as much as he did. You live by the law of the forest, and I know you will use your training wisely. We are at war, Amber. The human threat has made their first move, sparking your journey."

The goddess looked at me the same way my mother would when we talked about important subjects like boys and when she was pregnant with Willow. I knew that there was a lot going to be expected of me as her older sister. I was only fifteen when Willow was born. I thought about the stories I told Willow at night. They were the same ones my mom had told me. Something seemed to click into place and I began to understand what the goddess was telling me.

"I've heard this before. My mom used to tell me the story about the White Luna, 'When tragedy strikes, the Luna will begin her journey.' Wait… you said I saw my wolf?"

The goddess smiled. "Yes. Amber, you are the White Luna. The wolf you dreamt about was yours. You will probably see her again. Emerald, your wolf, will guide you and help you as much as she can from here until you are ready to merge with her."

My eyes went wide with shock, and I fell off the root I was sitting on. The goddess chuckled as she helped me up. We stood like that as her warm hands cupped mine.

"What am I supposed to do with this information?" I asked; I felt like a giant weight had been placed on my shoulders.

"Focus on what is going on in your life right now. Every moment is precious. Your choices will define you."

"How am I supposed to focus on anything after hearing that I'm the White Luna?"

"Amber, you are an exceptional young woman. Just be yourself; you don't have to carry this burden alone. You have your brother and Olivia. You chose well when you decided she would be your beta. You also have a mate out there who is waiting for you. As for your first question, you will come to understand your gift. There is no one I trust more to have a connection with this forest than you."

The goddess smiled. I bowed my head shyly as I processed what she was saying. My mind was spinning and it was difficult to focus on everything I wanted to say. "You have time for one more question," the goddess said.

There were many things I wanted to ask. I decided on the one that no one else could answer for me. "Why haven't I heard of Pan before?"

"You haven't?"

"I learned about him in school, but I didn't think he was real."

The goddess nodded, understanding my confusion. "All the gods and goddesses are real. I'm standing here with you as proof of that. You knew I was real because the wolves and the cats were taught about me from birth. Pan was remembered by the bears and the foxes. It didn't use to be that way. When the factions began fighting among themselves, Pan and I were forgotten by most of our children." Though she tried to hide it, the goddess's eyes glistened with tears. "It will be up to you to change that and bring everyone back together."

The goddess saw my shoulders droop and she placed her hands on either side of my arms to lift me up. "That conversation is for another day. You need not worry about the distant future. For now, focus on what you can do for the pups and for your pack."

"What can I do for them?"

"That is for you to figure out. You are smart, and I know you will make your parents proud. But first, it's time for you to wake up."

"But I'm not ready to wake up."

The goddess smiled and kissed my forehead. "I know you will make me proud." Then she pulled away. The last thing I saw was her warm smile.

I closed my eyes, and when I opened them again, the dim light outside of my bedroom in the cabin replaced the goddess and the Sacred Forest.

I was stuck in place with the sun shining through the window. At first, I thought the weight of my destiny was physically weighing me down. I couldn't seem to move. I looked down and saw several little bodies. All the girls that that had been asleep on the floor of my room were now piled somewhere near me or on me.

Willow was snuggled up to my side with her arm draped over my chest. Each girl had attached herself to me somewhere. It looked a little funny. I sighed to myself, wondering what to do.

I understood the goddess's meaning when she said to focus on the present. Now that I saw each one of these girls. I remembered how much they needed me, not my destiny. That made me feel lighter, and I could refocus on the here and now.

I thought about waking them up, but they looked so peaceful. Willow started to stir, and she stretched, accidentally kicking Ellie in the head. The rest of the girls woke up, and I smiled at them.

"Morning, Willow," I whispered and laughed, as she looked up at me with sleepy red eyes.

"Morning, Amber."

"When did you all climb up here?"

Willow sat up a little bracing herself on one hand. "I don't know. I felt really sad and then I could feel this, peace and I had to follow it. I felt better when I touched you and could sleep again."

The peace and tranquility I felt in the forest must have been so strong that they could all feel it here. Good, they deserved a good night's rest.

"How about I make some breakfast?" I asked, and they all sat up when I mentioned food. "Okay, let me get cleaned up, then I'll meet you all in the dining room." The girls got out of bed and started going through boxes so they could get dressed.

I made my way to the bathroom and started my morning routine. When I was done, the girls were changing and doing their hair. One of them went into the bathroom as I walked out.

When I opened my bedroom door, Tyla and Tyler were sound asleep on the floor. They refused to be separated last night and insisted they would rather sleep in the hall than be apart from each other. They somehow managed to huddle up directly in front of my door, almost completely blocking my path. I held onto the door frame as I stepped around their feet.

I went to the kitchen to start breakfast. I found some pancake mix and decided we needed comfort food, so I grabbed the package, set it on the counter, and found everything else I needed: a bowl, whisk, peanut butter, and water. I made up the batter and let it set as I prepared the long electric griddle.

A little while later, Tyler entered the kitchen, rubbing his eyes and sniffing the air filled with the smell of breakfast. "Yummy. I love pancakes."

I found a ladle and scooped some mix onto the griddle. "Morning, Tyler; since you're the first one out, you can set the table." He didn't seem to mind and brought out the plates and cups. As he was getting the silverware, Ryan walked in.

"Morning, Ryan. Since you are up second, you'll make sure dishes get cleaned in time for everyone to get some food. Starting with your own." I had two pancakes ready to go. I plated them, handed my brother the first plate of food, and placed the second one in front of Tyler.

When I walked back into the kitchen, Ryan was looking down at his plate then set it on the counter. I know I'm not great at cooking, but Ryan approached me about something else.

"Morning to you too, Amber. Happy late birthday, sis."

I just stared at him; I completely forgot that yesterday was April third, my twentieth birthday. I'm now one year away from merging with my wolf. Ryan gave me a small smile and hugged me.

"It's okay. I know." Sometimes, I forget that he's only sixteen. I hugged him back.

"Thank you."

I let go and went back to my cooking. Ryan grinned and shook his head. Then he picked up his plate, found some syrup, and walked to the table to eat with Tyler. Breakfast went smoothly, and it was nice to see everyone satisfied with full stomachs.

Tyler was smacking his lips. "Feesh panchaiches awe shticking cho my mouff."

I laughed as I watched him take another bite. Ryan shook his head at me grinning. "You know the peanut butter is supposed to go the pancakes after they are cooked."

"I was trying something new."

Ryan bit into his pancake and nodded. "You've made worse, but I think Olivia should handle the cooking until we can get back into the packhouse."

I rolled my eyes at him as he chuckled. Then I remembered seeing the kitchen full of flames. "That might be a while."

Ryan looked at me and I shook my head before he could say anything.

"As soon as everyone is done eating, I'm going to scout out the territory and see what I can do to help Mom and Dad rebuild. We may need to stay here until it's finished."

Olivia walked in and saw me holding the spatula, then held out her hand for me to give it to her. I gave it to her then stepped aside for her to finish the breakfast.

Ryan had this look on his face as if he were silently asking me about our home. I shook my head, then said, "We should be good here for a few days."

Ryan got up from the table and brought over Tyler's plate as the kid jumped down from his seat. "I'll take a look at the old truck. Make sure it's up and running for us to use later." Even though we check on this place often, forest critters have been known to occasionally make homes in the truck.

Olivia covered a yawn as she flipped a pancake, "I'll keep the pups occupied." She looked at the spatula as she asked. "What's in these pancakes? They're sticky."

Ryan tried to hold back a smile as he left the room. I left before Olivia could say more.

CHAPTER 5

Amber

I left the cabin dressed in a long-sleeved shirt with a hole in the bottom, jeans that I found in my dresser, and an old wool coat. My boots were a little small, but they kept my feet dry.

I ran down the hill, and as soon as I saw the territory I wished I hadn't. I wished I had paid more attention to the silence in the air. I wished I had walked or not come at all. I began to shake, and I had to support myself on a nearby tree or I would have fallen to the ground. My chest was tight, as if someone had a hold of my heart to keep it from beating.

I clutched my chest as pressure built until I remembered how to breathe again. Every time I inhaled, the air was filled with the metallic scent of blood, smoke, and that sour smell.

What made it all worse was that there were no signs of life. I thought I would at least see my dad talking with Uncle Colin about the attack and tending to the wounded, but no one was there. It was too quiet.

Yesterday, each house was alive with people walking around and talking to each other. Mr. Landry was fixing the rooftop of the old gazebo. Taylor Romans gossiped with Grandma Tate as she helped her with her laundry. Uncle Colin was helping my dad with the electrical system in the garden shed. Everywhere I went I would see people walking, talking, smiling, and living their lives…. Now it's nothing more than a memory.

As I looked down at what was left, it was hardly recognizable. Only a few houses were untouched, others were burned but still standing. I looked up and the smoke was still so thick in the air that not even the birds were singing. No chipmunks or squirrels chattering over nuts. It was as silent as the dead, and the worst of it was the building I had spent my whole life in. The once beautiful, white, four-story packhouse was burned to the ground. My home was now a pile of smoldering ash.

With tears in my eyes, I walked up what was left of the packhouse stairs to the body of Trent Walker, who stared into nothing. He had a hole in his chest, and my heart broke at the sight of his lifeless form. His body was warm only because of his proximity to the embers. I closed his eyes and as a tear fell from my eyes onto the ground I prayed, "Goddess, Selene, please honor this man who gave his life serving my pack."

I realized that when I spoke with her last night… she knew. She knew what I would find today. This was why she and Pan had kept telling me to rest and that I needed to be prepared.

I heard a familiar voice in my head, *I have honored them all; lay your people to rest.* A sliver of peace entered my chest as I took small comfort in knowing that Trent was now with the goddess in her realm. Instantly I realized there were more. He wasn't our only loss. Even though it was our heaven, I didn't want to think of my pack entering the Sacred Forest so soon.

I wanted to fall to my knees and never get up again, but that wouldn't help anyone. Through the ashes and the scarred boards of what used to be our front door, I reached for the eight-inch pack seal that had rested in the woodwork framing the top of our door. The intricate brass work of a wolf's head formed out of willow branches within a circle was now the last tangible memory of my home.

Tears stung my eyes. I didn't know if it was from the smoke or loss of my home and pack. The seal was warm but not hot; or maybe it was, and I didn't care. I needed to hold this piece of my home. I looked up, and all that was left of where I grew up were ashes and memories. The rest was gone; lost because of hatred.

I set it down and walked away from the packhouse to see what else I could find, starting with the homes that looked untouched by the fire. I had been inside of each of them at one point or another growing up. Where was everyone? Panic began to set in, but I pushed it down.

The more I saw, the more my chest compressed. With every burned building I walked by, the smell of blood and seeing my home destroyed made my stomach turn. I'm not squeamish at the sight of blood, but I had never seen a dead body before; I hope I never see one again.

I continued to walk around the destruction. There had to be someone left. They couldn't all be gone.

One of the perimeter houses had its door open but was eerily quiet. This didn't make any sense. There had to be someone here. I couldn't accept that we were all that was left. "Hello?" I was met with silence.

I checked as many of the houses as I could. They were all empty. I didn't like the quiet. The smell of death was everywhere. With every house I entered, I was haunted by what they used to look like. The reality coming through the haze, nothing but black ash and blood on walls. It was like the houses themselves were screaming from the events of the attack. I wanted to leave and run as far away as possible, but if I did that, who would tell the pups what happened to their homes? They deserved hope that we would find their families. Or at the very least, closure.

I approached one of the houses close to the packhouse. The door was hanging off one of the hinges. I heard something inside; it was the only sound of life in the territory. It sounded like wings. Blood coated the walls. I kept walking towards the noise, and soon I heard pecking, too. I wasn't prepared for the gruesome sight.

Blood coated the front room as if it had been painted red. As I looked towards the kitchen, I found the source of the noise. Crows were feasting on the remains of a human. He had the same emblem on his shoulder that I had seen last night. Those were noises I had heard. The human body wasn't complete. The lower part of him was missing. As I looked around, I found bits and pieces strung around the room, probably by her mate.

Lying on the table was a woman from our pack. Her name was Kate; she was the head housekeeper for the packhouse. She had been stabbed through the chest, and the blade was still there. It matched the one I took last night.

It was too much; I felt dizzy, and stepped backward into the wall, which was covered in blood. I thought I saw some on my hands.

My stomach flopped, and I retched as I ran out the door and vomited all over the pavement. I lost everything I had eaten that morning. I couldn't go back in there, but I couldn't leave Kate like that.

It took some time for me to gain control of myself. As soon as I had my bearings, I went into the garage, found a spray paint can, and marked her house with a big 'X' on the side of it.

I spent the rest of the day checking all of the houses. I made four more Xs. Three of the houses had bodies of humans; all of them were wearing gray uniforms with 'CB' on their shoulders.

All I could think about was how this could have happened to us. Where were my parents? Were they coming back? Did they go for help? No, my parents would never just leave us alone with this kind of devastation. A shiver ran down my spine; I was colder than I should have been in this weather. There was only one explanation.

The last house had the remains of our pack doctor. Dr. Brown had been shot through the chest, lying on a wolf I recognized as his nurse, Gina. Seeing how he had died trying to save her brought me to my knees.

I screamed at the goddess, "Why, why did this have to happen to our pack? We didn't do anything to those humans! Why did they have to die?" I leaned on the doorframe as my whole body shook and tears streamed freely from my eyes. I stayed there until my lungs felt as though they were straining to find air, and my eyes felt dry.

When I could move again, my muscles felt sore, but that soon faded, and all I felt was cold. I left the house and looked for a place to bury my pack members.

First, I went to the garden shed and looked for a shovel. I found one in the corner, and when I picked it up, I saw a bow and quiver. My dad always said large garden tools were good places to hide weapons like a bow. There was also a bow staff. I made a mental note to come back for those.

The ground in the center of our training arena was the only place soft enough because of the heat from pack house fire. It made for a suitable burial ground. I dug four holes as deep as the ground would allow.

As the sun sank behind the mountainside, I went back for Trent, lifted him onto my shoulders, and carried his body to the burial ground. I lined up his body with the hole.

"Trent Walker, I lay your body to rest. May your spirit find eternal peace in our goddess's Sacred Forest." I pushed him into the hole and covered it up.

I returned to Kate's house. It took me a while before I could go back inside. I tried several times and backed out. I finally had to close my eyes to walk through the door. Focusing on Kate, I tried not to look at the human remains. I pulled the knife from Kate's chest and threw it on the ground. Then I picked up her stiff, cold body and carried her to the training grounds. I set her down by the next hole and said another prayer.

"Kate, I will miss your stories. I will miss how you used to dance as you dusted. May your spirit find peace in our goddess's Sacred Forest." I pushed her body into the hole and covered it up. The first time with Trent was hard enough; this time was worse. The feeling of the cold, lifeless bodies in my hands would haunt me forever.

As I walked back to Dr. Brown, visions of the past continued to haunt me as they collided with reality. I placed my hand on my chest and felt the steady thrum of the lifeline connecting me to my parents. I realized the humans had taken them as prisoners. That was almost worse. What was more disturbing was that my father and his command were nowhere in sight. An average human doesn't stand a chance against a ranked wolf. None of this made any sense to me. How did this happen?

Gina was easier to carry than Dr. Brown, so I picked her up first and returned to the training grounds. By this time, I was completely numb. The cold no longer affected me.

"Gina, I will never forget how tenacious you were. You kept the pack hospital running and we both know Dr. Brown would have been lost without you. May the goddess grant you comfort and peace in the Sacred Forest." I moved her body into place and buried her.

Finally, I went back for Dr. Brown. I didn't know if it was from exhaustion, or something else, but I couldn't carry him. So instead, I dragged his body from the house to the training grounds.

"Dr. Brown, you will be greatly missed. Thank you for teaching me about medicinal plants. You were always busy caring for the pack. May the goddess reward you and grant you peace." I pushed his body into the hole and covered it up.

I sat next to the graves with my knees against my chest for what felt like hours. I love my pack; I couldn't help but wonder if I could have saved them. The goddess said she made me a champion, so I should have been able to, right? These were good people. I knew each of their names and saw them every day. They deserved so much better.

I finally composed myself and left the graves to check a few more houses for transportation. We needed something that would fit all of the kids in one vehicle. Eventually, I found a dark green Kia in a townhouse that wasn't severely burned. It was the largest vehicle I could find.

I went into the house to see if I could find the keys. My mind raced and my hands shook while I searched the kitchen. I found keys with a little wooden spoon key chain in one of the top drawers in the kitchen. The keychain was a gift I had given to her for her collection. I held it against my chest and prayed that she was still alive; and that we would rescue Greta in time.

Dawn broke as I returned to the garden shed, grabbed the bow and staff, and placed them in the back of the Kia. Then, I drove up to the packhouse, grabbed the brass seal, and put it in the back. I drove halfway up to the cabin; I wasn't ready to face everyone yet. I knew questions about our home would come, and I wasn't prepared to answer.

I pulled over and walked into a grove of trees. I had so much anger and grief that I screamed at the top of my lungs. I started hitting the trees and throwing whatever I could find; I didn't even notice someone watching me. I screamed again, cried, and hit the trees until my hands were bloody, or maybe they already were. Everything was blurring together.

Finally, I couldn't stand any longer. I sank to my knees and felt someone's arms wrap around me and hold me. I sobbed into their shoulders, unable to speak just yet.

After about an hour, when I had quieted down, I looked at my best friend. Olivia just held me. Did she have a dream about what I found? Did she know? It would be nice if she did; I wouldn't have to say it out loud. Would it be less real if I didn't?

Olivia's voice was barely above a whisper. "What did you find? You were gone for twenty-four hours, and you're covered in blood and dirt. We've been worried about you."

I shook my head; I wasn't ready to speak yet. She knows me well enough not to push me to talk. Olivia helped me up, and I motioned to the Kia. She drove us back to the cabin.

We pulled into the cabin's driveway and Ryan came out to investigate. I could see the hope in his eyes when he saw Greta's car, but I shook my head once we made eye contact.

"NOOO!" He punched the nearest beam of the cabin. He then told all the pups to stay inside before he opened the door to the Kia and joined Olivia and me.

I closed my eyes and shuddered as I took a deep breath. Then I told them about the destruction to our pack lands and what I had done.

"These were humans. How were they able to take an entire pack?" Ryan asked. I shook my head.

"I don't know. It doesn't make sense to me, either. Maybe that's why they used blades instead of bullets. At least our parents are still alive."

"I don't know if that's very reassuring," Olivia said as she gripped the steering wheel.

Ryan said, "How did they overpower Dad? A human is no match for an alpha, and our dad is one of the strongest."

Olivia shook her head as if she was realizing something she should have already known. "You missed it, Ryan. You were already in the tunnel. The smoke in the packhouse had yellow wolfsbane. It made me dizzy, and I would have passed out if we hadn't gone into the tunnel when we did."

"I was dizzy too… our parents… everyone is just… gone."

Ryan slammed his fist into the door. "Dad knew that an attack was possible."

"Not like this. This should not have been possible. The attackers were human. Until we find our pack, we are all that is left of the Forest Moon Pack."

CHAPTER 6

Amber

"You have to find them, Amber," Willow sobbed. She continued to cry in my lap until she fell asleep. I placed her in her bed and tucked her in. Ryan walked out with me, and we checked on Olivia and the twins. Tyler and Tyla held onto each other, and neither wanted to let go as they sobbed. Olivia was rubbing their backs as a single tear ran down her cheek.

The other pups had similar reactions. There was a lot of crying and screaming.

"No! This isn't fair!" Michael shouted. His face got red as tears streamed down his face. He began to strike out at us, and Ryan had to hold him to keep him from hurting himself or anyone else. Michael eventually settled in Ryan's arms and cried.

"This sucks," Josh said. "We did nothing to those humans; why did they attack us?" Tears threatened to fall from his eyes, and his whole body shook.

Ellie wiped the tears off her cheek. "What's going to happen to us now?"

"We'll think of something," I said. "Don't worry; we won't let anything happen to you guys."

We held them while they let out their grief. No one was hungry that night. As they wore themselves out crying, they started to fall asleep. We moved them one at a time, careful not to wake them.

Once everyone was in bed, Ryan, Olivia, and I went to bed, too. My nightmares began that night.

First, I was back in the packhouse; I was in the middle of the fight, the sounds of blades cutting flesh, wolves howling in pain, and the smell of blood and yellow wolfsbane filling the air. Only this time, I didn't get out.

The dream changed, and I was standing in the pile of rubble of what used to be my home. I heard the screams all over again; I saw the dead bodies of our pack members scattered around me.

I gasped as I woke up with beads of sweat across my brow. Once I composed myself, I went to my closet and pulled out the pack seal. Something about holding the cool brass brought me comfort. I sat in my closet and held it against my chest.

The beautiful, eight-inch seal depicted the Lunar Tree and the first wolf she created. It once adorned the top of our front door. Now it rested safely in my bag.

I placed the seal back in my bag and walked around to calm myself down. It didn't work very well. I went to the basement and took inventory of our supplies. I already knew what was down there, but it kept me from going back to sleep. I didn't want to relive the attack again.

Even though I had showered and washed my clothes, the smell of blood and death lingered with me. I would never forget it or what I saw. I knew it was in my head, but that didn't make it easier on my stomach. I still felt nauseous.

I came up from the basement when I heard footsteps in the kitchen. When I saw Olivia, she hugged me and asked if I was hungry. I shook my head. My stomach was in knots. Olivia made me eat breakfast anyway. "You haven't eaten in two days, here."

"Thanks, but I'm not hungry."

"Amber, you need to eat," Olivia said. I took the cereal from her, ate one bite, and shuddered.

"I know. Powdered milk isn't the best, but it's better than nothing," she said.

"I'm not so sure about that," I responded. I finished the cereal, and my stomach felt a little better. Powdered milk might stink and taste weird, but at least it's better than the memory of blood.

We struggled to get the pups to eat, too. Some because of sorrow and depression. Others had difficulty with the milk the way I did.

Ryan walked in from outside, and he looked cold. I could tell that he'd been out there for a while. "Where have you been?" I asked him.

"I walked the perimeter. I may not have my wolf, but I can still walk patrol." He had a good point. We should stay on guard. This wasn't over.

"Good idea. Did you cover your tracks?" I asked.

He nodded, "I also took care of all the tracks we left from the cave." I guess I wasn't the only one who couldn't sleep last night. At least I'd had the sense to stay in the cabin. I looked at Olivia, and she had the same thought I did.

"How long have you been awake?" I asked. Ryan shrugged. I immediately got him to sit down, and I started a fire. Olivia brought over a mug with hot water.

"What are you two doing? I'm fine."

"You drink that water, Ryan Cahill, before your body freezes," Olivia snapped. Once I got the fire going, I helped Olivia remove his boots, and Ellie brought over a blanket for him. I started tucking it around him, which irritated Ryan even more.

"I told you, I'm fine! Geez, it's not like you're my mom," he snapped.

All the chatter from before stopped, and I looked at Olivia. I didn't need to say anything because she knew what to do.

"All right, if you are done with breakfast, get dressed and be ready to go outside," she said as she took care of each kid.

"Ryan."

"Shut up, Amber. I don't want to hear it right now."

I sat with him, not wanting Ryan to be alone. But he still had things to work out. I sat on the couch, and Willow hugged me, then glared at him.

"You be nice!" she yelled, shaking her finger at Ryan. He rolled his eyes at her, and she ran down the hall to get dressed. I started laughing at Willow's cute response to his behavior. Soon, Ryan began to laugh, too; then his laughter turned into tears. I held him while he cried on my shoulder.

"Shh, I'm here," I whispered as he continued to cry. After he calmed down, he drank his water. It was still warm, and I could see the color come back into his face.

Olivia wasn't much better throughout the day; in the quiet moments when the pups couldn't see, she would break down in tears.

The next day, Olivia didn't want to leave her room. I found her after breakfast crying into a pillow. I walked over and sat on the bed with her. She leaned her head on my shoulder and sobbed. When she was able to speak, the words that came out of her mouth echoed the questions that had been circling in my head for the last couple of days.

"Where are they, Amber?"

"I don't know, but we'll find them."

"How?"

"First, we need to leave this cabin and get help from our allies."

Olivia shook her head. "Amber, there's only one way those humans found our home: someone betrayed us."

I didn't want to admit it either, but she was right. Balor found our pack because someone who'd been here before told him how to get here.

I sat with her until she was ready to leave the bedroom. We found the pups with Ryan, who had found Dad's guitar. It wasn't Ryan's best instrument, but he was decent. The pups enjoyed hearing him play, and they would sing with him. It was nice to hear music again.

I spent the rest of the day wondering who had betrayed us. It distracted from the memory of the smell that still invaded my nostrils and gruesome visions of our destroyed home. I knew it wasn't one of our allies. My dad only allied with alphas who were loyal to King Verrick.

I have met our closest allies, Alpha Cole Shepherd of Shadow Moon and Alpha Peter Marsh of Table Rock. I've met the king twice. He would never betray us. My dad always said Varrick was like a brother to him, and I felt that closeness when I met him. The king had been working harder than anyone against Balor. It was why my dad would visit the royal pack every month.

As for the other allies, none of them had a reason to betray us. They all know that working with Balor would put a target on their pack, and every alpha we were allied with was dedicated to their people.

So, who betrayed us? Only one wolf came to mind; he wasn't an alpha. He was an omega that was banished from our pack. Last we heard, Carl Gallo was a rogue. He would have nothing to lose… but he couldn't find Balor alone. Someone helped him.

CHAPTER 7

Caleb

"All right, there you go," I said to the little orange kitten in my hand that I had immunized.

"Meow?" she said to me. I chuckled and then gave her back to her owner.

I handed the little boy his kitten. "Missy is ready to go home."

He was gentle as he took her from me. "Are you sure she doesn't hurt? I hate my shots."

"You know what, Jackson? I hate shots too. But they're important and today, we ensured Missy wouldn't get any nasty diseases. The shot acts like a shield."

He hugged his little kitten. She meowed in his arms and tried to climb onto his shoulder. He giggled, and his mom helped him get her back into his arms.

"See? She's good as new and ready to explore. It's like nothing happened."

I opened the door for the boy and his mom. "Thank you, Dr. Caleb."

"You are very welcome, Jackson."

His mom smiled politely as she ushered the boy out of the exam room. "Thank you, Doctor."

I smiled back. "You're welcome." I followed them out, grabbed a new chart, and called my next patient.

When I saw the young woman approach, my wolf, Apollo, alerted me to the predator in the pet carrier. We were uneasy about the python waiting for our care.

I covered my mouth and cleared my throat to cover up my laugh. "What is wrong with… Cuddles?"

"I fed her this morning, and the rat fought back," the woman said.

I carefully lifted the snake from the pet carrier and placed her on my exam table. "Have you owned snakes before?" The woman fidgeted and shook her head.

"Where did the rat come from?"

The woman continued to play with her fingernail. "I found it in my basement. I usually don't give Cuddles live food, but I thought it would be a treat for her."

The snake was big enough that the rat would have been a decent meal. I studied her scales and then looked at her mouth. I studied the red spot on her bottom jaw a little more closely. "Did she eat the rat, eventually?" The snake flicked her tongue out, which was a good sign. I didn't see any buildup either.

"No, not even after I killed it."

"Some of the bite marks are deep. Cuddles will need stitches. That's not my main concern though. How long ago did she shed her skin?"

"Oh." The woman thought for a minute as I cleaned the bite marks. "I think it was a few weeks ago."

I figured as much. Once the wounds were clean I began stitching. "Cuddles is large enough that the rat would have been able to fight, but then eventually become a good meal.

I'm more concerned that she didn't eat it. Was this the first meal she refused?"

"No, she's refused her last three meals."

I nodded. Once the wounds were stitched, I moved on to the snake's mouth. "Take a look at this." The woman came over and I moved Cuddle's head towards her owner. I pointed to the red spot. "Do you see that?" The woman nodded. "Cuddles has what's called Stomatitis, or mouth rot." The woman gasped, and I smiled to ease her worry. "It's not as bad as it sounds, we caught it early. I'm guessing that when she shed her skin, she became stressed. You'll also need to check her habitat and make sure it's set at the right temperature and humidity." I reviewed how to care for Cuddle's wounds with the owner. The woman hung on every word and stood closer than necessary.

As I put away the bandages and cleaned up, I felt something on my leg. I looked down, and Cuddles was wrapped around my ankle. I was sure I had put her in the carrier before handing it to her owner. Weird, the floor was cold and not good for this animal in her condition. Thankfully, the python wasn't very big yet.

"Oh, I am so sorry, doc," the woman said. I thought her voice sounded strange, and I realized she had taken the snake out of the carrier. I smiled and bent down. I got my face close to the snake and let my eyes glow a bright sapphire blue as Apollo's consciousness came forward.

Snakes don't see the same way people do. Pythons use infrared to find their prey; in my case, she can see the wolf within me. When she flicked her tongue out and relaxed, I knew she recognized my authority as a shapeshifter. Like most shapeshifters, I have that effect on animals. I unwrapped Cuddles from my leg and returned her to her owner, who picked her up.

"How did you do that?"

I grinned. "I have a way with animals; that's why I'm a vet."

"I don't see a ring on your finger. Do you have a girlfriend?" The woman asked as she walked to the exam table and placed Cuddles into the pet carrier.

Cuddles didn't want to stay there, so I picked her up and put her back in. My eyes flashed briefly, and the snake stayed where she was.

"I want to give Cuddles some antibiotics, and I will send a topical cream with you." I gave her the instructions for the cream, purposely ignoring her question. I also emphasized the importance of cleaning out the habitat.

"Oh, thank you, doc." I gave Cuddles the shot and handed the box to the woman before holding the door for her.

The woman ran her finger down my arm. "You should let me buy you a drink sometime as a thank you." I ignored her bold invitation and walked her to the receptionist's desk.

I pulled out my phone and was disappointed to see that there were no missed calls or messages. I put my phone back in my pocket and moved on to my next patient.

The rest of the day went by in a blur. There were still no messages, or at least not the one I was looking forward to. I was supposed to call during my lunch break, but I had been so busy that I didn't get much of a break.

At the end of the day, I left the clinic and returned to my apartment. When I arrived, I sat down and rechecked my phone. Still nothing; I was about to call her, but there was a knock at my door. I put down my phone and went to answer it.

My best friend was on the other side. "Hey, wanna go for a beer?"

Lucas Barnes is my beta. If you were to look at us, you would think we were an odd pair. We are as close as brothers, but where I have light brown skin, dark brown hair, and sapphire blue eyes. Lucas is pale-skinned and blonde-haired, with light blue eyes. He's built like a tank and is three inches taller than me. I'm built well, with broad shoulders and toned abs, but I'm not as big as Lucas. Sometimes I wonder if he has a bear in his family line, but that's just a stereotype.

"Yeah, I could use one. Let's go."

I grabbed my phone and coat, and we left. We walked down the street to The Lotus Den, an old building with dark wood siding and neon lights in green and purple. As we walked inside, our eyes adjusted to the dim lights. It smelled of spirits and humans. It was a slow night, and when the bartender saw us, I held up my hand for two beers. Tyrell Newman had them on the counter for us by the time we got seated.

I like Tyrell; he's a friendly guy with a Texan accent who treats his customers with southern hospitality. Tyrell has a thin build, even by human standards, with curly blonde hair and bright green eyes. His nose has been broken at least once, and it shows, but he always smiles when Lucas and I enter his bar.

"There you go, marshal, doc. You two look like it was a tough one today. This one is on the house," Tyrell said.

"Thanks, man." I picked up my bottle and nodded in gratitude before taking a drink.

"What was your day like?" Lucas asked.

I shook my head and grinned. "I love my job; sometimes, I wish I could see my patients without their owners. I had a python today. Cuddles was friendly but not as friendly as her owner."

I took a big swig of my beer and Lucas nearly spit out his drink. "Wait, hold on. You had a python come in named Cuddles?" We both laughed. "Of all the names for a snake, Cuddles is the last thing I would expect."

"I know."

He turned in his seat to face me, "What was the owner like? Black leather, piercings with tattoos?"

I side-eyed him. "For a US Marshal, that was very stereotypical." He shrugged.

I sighed and placed the bottle on the counter, "Black leather, yes; piercings, no; I didn't pay attention to tattoos."

Lucas squinted his eyes at me as I lifted the bottle again, "You didn't hear from your mate today, did you?"

I choked on my drink as I tried not to spit it out. After finally swallowing, I coughed. "What are you talking about?"

Lucas smiled knowingly. "Your mystery woman. You always talk to her on Wednesdays."

I looked down at my beer and then emptied it. I could feel another headache coming on. I get them now and then; it's been daily for the past two weeks. I closed my eyes as I tried to focus. My wolf, Apollo, has tried to help me but it's useless.

"Another headache? Have you talked to a doctor about those?"

"You know I can't; it will pass soon."

"What about your mate?" Lucas teased again. For some reason, my headache got worse.

"First, Apollo hasn't confirmed that she's my mate. We're just friends. Second, no, I didn't hear from her. I was about to call her when you dropped by."

"You act like she is. You are the only man I know that gets almost hostile when someone flirts with you. Also, you would be dating."

"You know me better than that."

"Then call her now."

"I'm not talking to her while I'm at a bar."

"It's not like you're drunk; just go outside."

The more we talked about this, the worse I felt. I took my phone out of my pocket, but it wouldn't light up. I couldn't get the lock screen to glow. I held down the power button and saw an empty battery sign appear briefly before it shut down again.

"My phone's dead; I'll call her when I get home."

Lucas handed me his phone, and I shook my head. He shrugged and then put it back into his pocket. "Who is she?"

It wasn't that I didn't trust Lucas, because I did. There was just more to my situation than I wanted to discuss.

"I'm your second in command; one of these days, you will tell me who your mystery woman is."

My headache started clearing, and I wanted to change the subject. I waved Tyrell over. "We need two more, please." When Tyrell brought over our drinks, I noticed something on the side of Tyrell's middle finger. "What does the purple flower mean?"

Tyrell put his elbows on the counter and leaned in. "It means I'm a member of the Purple Lotus."

Copying Tyrell, Lucas asked, "What is that?"

Tyrell signaled the woman helping him tonight. "Abby, can you cover for me? I'm going on my break."

"Sure."

Tyrell motioned for Lucas and me to follow him to a booth in the back corner. Once we sat down and he was sure we wouldn't be overheard, Tyrell answered Lucas's question.

"The Purple Lotus is the human resistance against Charles Balor. Most of us have been raised by shapeshifters, like me. Some are in relationships with them, and others want to make a difference, like Carole Cawthra."

"Carole is a part of your organization?" I asked. She was the owner of the vet clinic I worked at. She was a sweet old woman who always surprised me with her energy; she was also unbelievably kind.

Tyrell nodded. "That's why she always wears that pendant. Carole is the head of our chapter. All our meetings are either here in the bar or at her house."

"I don't know how I missed it."

Tyrell winked at me. "We wouldn't be a secret organization if we advertised who we were. We mostly work with the royal lines, so don't beat yourself up."

I looked at Lucas, and he shrugged. I felt a slight bitterness. I should have known all of this, but I didn't.

Lucas realized something else I had missed. "I didn't know shapeshifters raised you."

Tyrell smiled, but it didn't reach his eyes. There was a sorrow there I wasn't used to seeing. "A family of cougars took me in and adopted me. The pride didn't think much of me at first, but I was adopted around the time Balor showed his face to the world. Soon, they all realized I was just as scared of them as they were of me."

I felt ashamed. I'd known Tyrell for over a year and never knew he was in the foster system or adopted by cougars. He'd listened to Lucas and me all the time, but I realized how little we knew him. I should have been a better friend.

"I see what you're think'n. Don't worry 'bout it, doc. I didn't tell you because I wasn't sure how you would feel about it. I know relations between the wolves and the cats are strained."

I tipped my bottle to him. "Someday, I hope that changes."

"We have nothing against the cats or you for being part of a pride," Lucas agreed. Tyrell smiled.

"What happened to your family?"

Tyrell sniffed and used his knuckle to wipe away a tear. "Balor happened. Three years ago, I went to New York with my parents. We were supposed to be there for two weeks. We left the city for a couple of days so my parents could go for a run so their cats could stretch their legs, but they never returned. Only one police officer from Jersey took me seriously. He was the one who introduced me to the organization. He located my parents and helped me lay them to rest. I joined the Purple Lotus and was assigned here."

"You didn't go back to your pride?" I asked.

"I stay in touch, and the chief still recognizes me as a part of the pride. But I'm doing more good here."

Lucas nodded towards the door. "Is that why your bar is called the Lotus Den?"

Tyrell laughed once. "Yeah."

"I'm sorry for your loss."

"Thanks, Doc."

My wolf whined, echoing my sympathy for my friend.

He's still grieving.

I would be, too, Apollo.

Lucas raised his bottle. "Well, you have us."

Tyrell's face lightened and his eyes crinkled as he smiled. "Thanks, marshal."

"How did you know we were wolves?"

That really made Tyrell laugh. He used his fingers as he ticked off the facts. "First, there are more wolves than any other shapeshifter faction. I guessed. Second, you two drink exactly three beers each. No more, no less, and neither of you ever gets drunk. I've run this bar and been in your world long enough to know how to spot a shapeshifter when I see one."

We heard shouting coming from the counter. "Hey, bartender! Can we get some service?" A man in a nice suit was trying to get Tyrell's attention. He looked over to see Abby helping another group that had just walked in.

Tyrell nodded to the guy and slid out of his seat. "Looks like Abby could use a hand."

He left to help the man in the suit while Lucas and I stayed at the booth and tried to wrap our heads around the new information. It was a lot to take in.

I broke the silence as I sipped my beer. "How was your day?"

Lucas downed his drink before answering. "I got a call from Jasper. He wants me to help him with a case in Telluride." I tried to hide my shock. I hadn't been able to set foot in that pack in five years, mostly out of shame. My heartrate picked up and I did my best to hide it.

"Who's missing?"

My attempt was in vain. Lucas was too clever not to have noticed.

"You okay, Caleb?"

"Answer my question."

Lucas's eyes widened as a grin spread across his face. "Amber Cahill is your mystery woman."

"Who's missing?" I asked again.

Lucas sighed. "Ian's wife, Rose. She was taken from her car in the middle of the night last week." I let out the breath I was holding.

"Does Jasper have any idea who took her?"

Lucas shook his head. "All he told me was that it was humans. There were no signs of wolves or any other shapeshifters nearby."

"Rose is good woman."

Lucas gave me a suspicious grin. "Now, tell me about you and Amber. I remember what you two were like five years ago. I don't know how I missed it."

"I'm not discussing this with you."

"Why not? Oh, this has to do with Alpha William." He began to laugh. "Of course, the only girl you'd fall for is the one you can't have."

"Shut up. What day last week?"

He ignored my question. "It all makes sense now… well, most of it. You didn't want to tell me, so I have plausible deniability."

He can think that if he wants. It was mostly because of shame. I should have visited Forest Moon a long time ago. I was expected to go to Amber's graduation, but I didn't. Lucas and I knew that no one was more protective of their family than Alpha William, which was why I respected him. When he finds out the truth, I'm wolf chow.

Lucas smiled and let it go. "I leave in the morning. Kade will be here to stay with you while I'm gone."

"I'm going with you," I told him. "This is Forest Moon, our closest ally, we're talking about. I'm not about to let you go alone."

"What about your headaches? They're more frequent than normal."

"I don't care, I'm going."

"Not with your headaches. What if you get hurt?"

"I can handle it."

"They're getting worse."

"So?"

"Our kind doesn't get sick easily; what if it's serious?"

"It isn't."

"Caleb, all I'm doing is getting Jasper to the territory."

"I could order you to take me."

Lucas grinned. "Yeah, but you won't. You respect me too much, and you trust me which is why I know you'll stay put."

I banged my fist on the table. I hated this, I should be there. "Fine, but I want to be updated twice daily."

"Deal, now back to our other subject." Lucas downed his beer and held his bottle up to Tyrell who nodded.

"No."

"I don't see the problem; Amber's nineteen."

Tyrell brought us two more beers and we thanked him. Then I glared at my beta. "She's twenty. Her birthday was on the third, but she was fifteen when we met, and I had to hold myself back because of the age difference. Besides, Apollo wants me to keep my distance for now."

Lucas smiled and then shook his head. "Why, what if she's your mate?"

It's the one thing I had hoped for, but I was too much of a coward to find out. "Apollo hasn't confirmed it; he thinks it's because she hasn't merged with her wolf yet... What?"

Lucas looked as if he wanted to question me more, but he shook his head and faced me. "You're so into her, but you're afraid to tell her the truth," Lucas said. I just looked at him. "Why else would you have put off seeing her? Age gap or not, Amber has been of age for the last two years and you still haven't made a move."

"Sometimes I hate how well you know me."

We finished our beers, then Lucas pulled a few bills from his wallet and I did the same. We always left a large tip for Tyrell since he was such a good friend.

Lucas reached the door before me and held it as I walked out. "I have an early morning. Don't worry, I won't tell Alpha William about you and Amber. Man up and do it yourself, and while you're at it, tell Amber the truth."

CHAPTER 8

Amber

We had been in this cabin for more than a week; it was beginning to feel suffocating for all of us. The longer we were here, the more anxious everyone became. This morning was no exception.

Ellie was upset with Tyla for not washing off her plate and putting it away. Tyler was mad at Ellie for yelling at his sister. Michael would take his anxiety out on the others; normally he was a tough kid but he was fair. Since we've been in the cabin, the smallest things would set him off and he would either start a fight or he will wander outside. This morning his target was Willow because she accidently ripped his drawing. Michael yelled at her and called her stupid. Willow is so sensitive that she ran out the door crying.

"Willow!" I shouted. We had all taken off after her, but knowing Willow, she wouldn't be found until she was ready.

"I found her!" Ryan yelled as he walked back from the hillside with Willow on his back. Willow was giggling as Ryan bounced her and pretended to drop her. You never would have known she was crying a few minutes ago. I wished I could bounce back as quickly as she did. I tend to hold on to things. Not that I meant to.

Olivia's face was white as she sprinted up the path. "Get Willow inside!" she shouted.

My brother and sister stopped playing and ran into the cabin. "What's going on?" I asked.

"I smell someone I don't recognize."

Olivia was panting as she tried to catch her breath; her eyes were constricted. I had to calm her down but I was thinking the same thing. What if Balor had come back for us? My heart began to race.

I placed my hands on her shoulders, "Human or wolf?"

"Does it matter? We were betrayed, Amber. We can't trust anyone right now."

She was right. I removed my hands and pointed to the bushes. "Shift. I'm going for my bow."

I went inside to grab my recurve bow and a quiver of bullet-point arrows. I didn't want to kill the intruder, just scare them off. I strapped my bow to my quiver and threw it over my shoulder.

I ran outside and secured myself in a tree above the shed. The man who came into view had dark hair and light skin. I nocked an arrow, ready to fire if he posed a threat. Sage laid her ears back and snarled at him, placing herself between him and the cabin.

He jumped back and put his hands up. "Whoa! Hold on; I'm not here to hurt anyone. I was following the trail."

"What trail?"

He looked around for me. "I found footprints in the mud."

If I fired now, I would give away my position. "Who are you?"

He moved his hand, and Sage growled at him again.

"Whoa. I am just reaching for my badge," the man said calmly.

"Slowly. Keep your other hand where I can see it."

He pulled out a badge and held it up to Sage. "My name is Agent Jasper Hayes. I'm here on behalf of the FBI. I'm working a disappearance case."

I shouted back, "What does that have to do with us?"

Agent Hayes kept looking around for me. "She was the wife of a friend of mine. Rose Baxter went missing ten days ago."

That was the same night the humans had attacked us. Since Olivia had shifted into her wolf, the only way to communicate with her was through a mindlink. Some people would call it telepathy, but we only comunicate what we want to say and it's only to those we want to link to.

"What do you think, Olivia? Can we trust him?"

"Amber, I don't trust anyone right now. What if some of those guys were cops, too?"

"Is he a shapeshifter or a human?"

"He's a wolf, but I still don't trust him; we don't know who betrayed us."

"What does Sage say?"

"I don't know. She isn't much help right now."

I realized that Olivia was in complete control of her wolf form. That wasn't good. We needed Sage at a time like this.

"What if this agent can help? Olivia, we can't stay here."

"I'm not ready to take that chance."

"It's been two weeks."

"We will last a little while longer."

I wasn't going to get anywhere with her. I needed to get this agent away from the cabin and hope he understood. He was patient while Olivia and I figured out what to do. I'd give him that.

"It's just him; between Sage and my bow, we can take him."

Olivia snorted at him. I took that as her approval.

Agent Hayes reached for something in his jacket. I was worried it was a weapon, so I pulled back my arrow and let it fly. The arrow hit the ground right in front of him. He jumped back tripping over his feet, and nearly fell to the ground. Sage moved forward and continued to bare her teeth.

"I was just reaching for the flyer," Agent Hayes said quickly.

He's not a threat to you.

The voice of my wolf from somewhere within me set me at ease, but Olivia's anxiety warred with the confirmation I had received. I couldn't focus on the agent's intentions with Olivia this agitated.

"Keep your hands where we can see them," I ordered. Agent Hayes now looked annoyed. I had to get him out of here.

"Or what?!" he shouted. Sage looked flustered, and I could feel Olivia's anxiety over her wolf. I had to keep this from escalating. I let another arrow fly, this time hitting Agent Hayes in the rear.

"Ow! Son-of-a… What was that for?!" He tried to reach for it to pull it out then stopped.

"You wanted to know what would happen. Now you do!" I knew the location of the arrow was harmless since he was a wolf. The arrows didn't have silver, so his body would push it out… eventually.

"You shot me!"

"I answered your question."

"You can't last; what happens when you run out of arrows?!"

My best option was a bluff. "I'll use my gun!"

Agent Hayes winced as he tried to pull the arrow out again. I fired another one as Sage advanced. He stepped back and put his hands up.

"Leave, or the next one won't be so harmless," I warned, and he backed off. I had no intention of hurting him. Well… more than the arrow in his rear.

"Fine, I'll leave. Here, take my card." He reached slowly into his pocket. Sage growled at him, and he threw down a small piece of paper.

As he limped away, I jumped down from my tree and followed. I walked him to the cave and then halfway down to the territory.

Agent Hayes knew I was behind him. He looked back a few times, and when it appeared like he was going to double back and try to come after me, I fired another arrow. This one clipped his ear.

"Ow. Who are you?" he growled as he grabbed his ear.

"I'm the one making sure you leave." Agent Hayes put his hands up and then continued to limped down the hill.

Halfway to the territory, Agent Hayes stopped walking. "I'm not a threat to you."

I stopped and stood right behind him, relaxing my bow. "I know, or you would've tried something by now."

"Then why are you still aiming your arrows at me?"

I looked at the arrow still in my hand and realized, I didn't have an answer. "We don't know who betrayed us. I don't trust anyone at the moment."

"You know I'm not a threat, but you don't trust me? That sounds a little contradictory, don't you think?"

"Not really." I still didn't want to lower my bow even if it wasn't armed.

Jasper moved his head to the side as he spoke to me. "How do you know you were betrayed?"

I placed the arrow back in the quiver. "My pack was well hidden; there was only one way Balor could have found us."

"Fair point. Do you have any suspicions?"

"The only person I can think of is Carl Gallo; last I heard, he became a rogue after being banished from his last pack."

"What pack was that?"

"I don't know; somewhere in Wyoming."

"I'll look into him. What is his connection to Rose Baxter?"

"I don't know; she came to our pack after Carl left."

Agent Hayes tried to turn around but thought better of it. "I don't suppose you would mind removing this arrow."

I blushed, reached in front of me, and yanked it out.

"Ow," Agent Hayes winced. He took some deep breaths and then asked his next question.

"Can you tell me anything about Rose?"

"She's probably with the rest of our pack, wherever they are," My voice quivered as I spoke.

"You're worried about them."

"Yes, and I can't afford to take any risks."

"I understand. So are we."

"Why would the FBI care about a pack of shapeshifters?"

"I wasn't talking about the FBI."

"Then who's 'we'?"

"The Royal Pack," Agent Hayes said. I lowered my bow. He wasn't just another shapeshifter; he belonged to the most powerful pack in the world and our closest ally.

"How did the king find out so quickly?"

"I'm going to reach into my pocket." Agent Hayes pulled a folded-up piece of paper from his pocket and reached over his shoulder to give it to me. I lowered my bow and took the paper from him. When I unfolded it, I saw "missing" at the top with a fuzzy picture of Rose and her description.

"King Verrick found this in his email two days ago," Agent Hayes said. He started to turn around. I used my bow to tap his shoulder and keep him from moving. I wasn't ready for him to know who I was yet. It may not be safe for the word to get out that the Alpha's daughter survived.

Agent Hayes sighed. "You can trust me; I want to find your pack as much as you do."

I answered him without looking up from the flyer. "I doubt that."

"I've met your Alpha. He's one of the best I know. Please let me help you."

"Why? The only thing I know for sure is that we were betrayed. You couldn't even tell me that the king sent you; now you want me to trust you?"

"Fair… look, you have to trust someone; you won't be able to find your pack on your own."

"I know."

"I will give you some time to think about it. Call me when you're ready."

"I can't."

"What do you mean, you can't?"

I slung my bow over my shoulder and held onto the arrow. "My phone broke. None of us have any way of contacting anyone."

Agent Hayes sighed. "I'll be at the Courtyard Diner, eating breakfast every morning at seven. Meet me there when you're ready."

"I'll think about it. How did you find us?"

"I'm here with a friend of mine, Lucas Barnes. He was here five years ago."

"I remember Lucas, I believe you." I took a deep breath. "I can keep us safe here for now. Please find my pack."

"You have my word," Agent Hayes said.

"You better leave before my cousin runs after us."

Agent Hayes placed his fist over his heart and bowed his head. "Don't forget what I said. The Courtyard Diner, whenever you're ready." Then he limped down the hillside.

I walked back up the hill, picked up the card from Agent Hayes, and put it into my pocket. I found Olivia waiting for me in the living room. She had shifted and gotten dressed.

"Is he gone?" she asked. I nodded. "What took you so long?"

"Agent Hayes was harmless. We can trust him."

"We can't take that chance," Olivia said.

"He's a member of the Royal Pack," I told her as I handed her the flyer with Rose's face on it.

"What's this?"

"King Verrick sent Agent Hayes to help our pack locate Rose when he saw this flyer in his email."

"Amber, not everyone in the Royal Pack is safe."

I'd heard the stories, too. I knew my dad didn't trust everyone. He never told me who he disliked, only that they were high up in the command. Then again, maybe no one was safe to trust. Except this FBI person.

"We can trust Agent Hayes."

"How can you be so sure?"

"I can't explain. I just know."

CHAPTER 9

Amber

I woke up feeling as if someone had kicked me in the ribs. The pain was enough to jerk me out of my sleep. I looked around, but no one was in my bed with me. Then I felt a sharp pain in my stomach as if I had been punched. The sensations continued over and over.

I groaned as I held my stomach. It was hard to breathe, and I just wanted it to stop. When it did, there was a burning in my wrists.

I sat up in bed, wondering what was going on. I focused on my surroundings. This was strange. I looked at the girls, who were all sound asleep. I didn't know what was going on.

I looked down at my wrists, and there wasn't anything there. My heart raced, making my chest hurt, and every muscle in my neck tightened. What's happening to me? I didn't want to scare the girls, so I quietly got up and staggered out of the room, trying not to trip over Tyler and Tyla.

As I walked through the house, my arms felt tired; they ached as if they had been raised for too long. My wrists began to hurt more and more. The beating sensation started again, and I had to keep myself from screaming.

This was crazy; there was nothing around me. My breathing was rapid, but getting any air into my lungs was hard. What was happening to me?

Out of nowhere, a burn coursed through my entire body. I couldn't move as I tried to hold back another scream. Tears flooded my eyes, and I held my ribs as the pain seemed to stop as suddenly as it began.

Disoriented and worn out, I collapsed on the living room floor and lay there until the pain eased from my body. My face was soaked from my tears, I didn't understand why I didn't have a mark on me. I had never felt so much pain in my entire life.

I was drained from the experience. Eventually, I picked myself up off the floor and was about to return to my bed. Ryan came out of his room with tears in his eyes and rubbing his chest. "Did you feel it, too?" I nodded, not trusting my voice at the moment. Ryan leaned against the wall for support. "What was it?"

"I don't know," I whispered and continued to rub my wrists. The pain was gone, but the memory of the burn still lingered.

Willow came out with her hand on her chest and tears in her eyes. She tripped over Tyla and fell on top of Tyler, who pushed her off as he rolled over. Willow got up and walked over to us. I wrapped my arms around her and sat down while she cried softly in my lap.

Olivia came out with Alice and stopped when she saw us. "What happened to you three?"

Ryan sniffed and shook his head. "That's what we're trying to figure out. Suddenly, my chest hurt, but the pain left as quickly as it started."

Olivia looked deep in thought as she entered the kitchen and picked up the bottle we had prepped for Alice's midnight feeding. Olivia's eyes flickered from blue to lime green as she listened to her wolf.

"What does Sage say?" I asked.

"Did all three of you experience this?"

Willow nodded. My experience was different, but Olivia spoke up before I could discuss it. "Sage says this was one of your parents. We all have a strong bond with our families. Something happened to one of them, and it was enough for you to feel a tug on the bond."

I took a deep breath and focused. The anger and humiliation were hard to separate between my mom and dad, but there was also a tiny relief. I couldn't focus on it before because the pain was so intense, but as I looked back, I realized there was also relief that it was them… no… him, going through the torture and not my mom or anyone else.

"It was our dad; he was being tortured," I said. "We knew something was going to happen; I just didn't think it would be like this."

Ryan got up from the wall and walked over to Willow and me. "I think you're right. The whole time my chest hurt, I kept thinking about Dad."

Willow whimpered, "Me too."

A stray tear ran down my cheek as I realized I had felt everything my dad endured. It was hard to tell the difference between what he had experienced and my body's reaction. I wished this were all a bad dream.

Olivia was somber as she tested the now-warm bottle, walked over to the couch, and began to feed Alice. We sat in silence, not knowing what to say next. The only sounds in the room were Willow's sniffles and Alice drinking her milk. Why did I have a different experience than Ryan and Willow?

Willow looked up at me as if I held all the answers. "Will Daddy be okay?"

I responded with the words I wanted so much to be true. I looked down at my sister and stroked her hair. "Yes, Willow. I can still feel our connection to him. He's alive."

Ryan nodded his head to me, a silent confirmation of what needed to be done. "As soon as we leave this cabin, we'll look for our pack."

"How?" Willow asked.

I looked at Olivia as she sat the empty bottle on the table beside her and adjusted Alice to burp her. "We'll get help from Alpha Cole, and I'm sure the king is now looking for our pack, too."

"Can we leave tomorrow?" Willow asked.

Ryan ruffled her hair. "Soon, Squirt. There are things we have to do first."

"Like what?"

Olivia narrowed her eyes at me. "We need to find out who betrayed us."

I met her gaze and nodded. "We will."

Willow looked at Ryan then back up at me. "What else?"

I kissed the top of her head. "How about you let us figure that out? I think you need to go back to bed." Willow nodded, got up, and left the room. When I heard the door close, I turned to the others. "Willow is right, we need to leave the cabin."

After what I had just felt, I knew we had to find our pack as quickly as possible. Alice burped loudly and fell asleep on Olivia's shoulder.

Olivia stood up, and holding Alice in one arm, she helped me up with the other. "Yes, but now isn't the time to come up with a plan. We should all get some sleep and talk about this in the morning when we are rested."

Ryan stood up and looked at me meaningfully and said, "As much as we can be." Then he walked back to his room.

Olivia smiled. "I'm surprised you didn't have the chocolate out."

I smiled at our little ritual. "I didn't get the chance."

Whenever we would go through something difficult, we'd get chocolate from a special jar. Sometimes, when things seemed impossible, Greta would make us her famous French Silk pie.

A stray tear ran down my cheek. "Chocolate makes everything better…. Except this." We went to our rooms and, surprisingly I fell asleep. It wasn't restful, and I woke up just as tired as when I went to bed. Olivia, on the other hand, was in the kitchen, humming as she made breakfast.

"Hash browns and scrambled eggs?" I asked as I walked into the kitchen.

"The eggs were powdered, but it's still protein," she said. I went to the cupboard and grabbed a cup.

"What has you in such a good mood?" I asked as I filled my cup with water.

"After we all talked last night, I had a dream," Olivia said.

"What about?"

"I saw your dad; we'll save him, Amber. My parents, too."

"What did you see?"

After last night, it was a relief to hear that we still had time to rescue them, but I didn't want to get my hopes up. Olivia might have dreams about the future, but that didn't mean it wouldn't change.

"First, I saw my parents with me in a car. They didn't look good, but they were alive. Then we were on a plane, and I saw your dad, he was alive and talking to you."

"What did he say?"

"I didn't hear what anyone said. Your dad was smiling, though."

"You didn't hear?"

"It was like seeing it all from across the plane."

"Who else was there?"

"I don't know, their faces were fuzzy."

This was good news. We had hope at least. It wasn't much, but it was more than we had yesterday.

"What about my mom?" I asked. Olivia looked deep in thought.

"I didn't see her, but that doesn't mean she wasn't there," Olivia said.

That sliver of hope was enough to get us through the day without drama. Even Alice didn't cry as much today.

As I looked over at the little infant in Ryan's arms, I thought about the flyer of Rose. I wondered if the search for her would lead to our pack. There was only one way for me to find out. I needed to meet with Agent Hayes.

CHAPTER 10

Caleb

I sat at the bar with Tyrell and Kade. It had been a tough day because we still hadn't heard from Lucas or Jasper. They were supposed to contact Alpha William two days ago. I should have heard something by now.

"I hate being left in the dark," I said. Kade tipped his beer bottle toward me, and I tapped it with mine.

"If we haven't heard from them, then it means they have the investigation under control," Kade said. That wasn't very reassuring. All this stress was bringing on another headache.

Kade was my oldest friend. I've been close with him and his twin sister, Piper, since we were in diapers. Kade takes after his mom, with black hair and a lighter skin tone. His hazel eyes are more like his dad's, but Kade's eyes are more green than brown.

"I have a bad feeling about this whole thing. I should have gone with Lucas," I grumbled.

"Me too," Kade admitted.

"What happened to them having it under control?"

Kade shrugged. "I have to tell myself something. It isn't like Lucas or Jasper to not tell us anything."

"That's what worries me." We got up to leave the bar early, and Tyrell handed us both his card.

"What's the Purple Lotus?" Kade asked.

Tyrell looked at me seriously. "If you need help at any time, let me know."

"I will, Ty. Thank you."

"What is he talking about?"

"I'll tell you on the way back." As we returned to the apartment, I told Kade everything I'd learned from Tyrell and my boss, Carole Cawthra, over the last three days.

"So, these humans have allied themselves with shapeshifters? Why didn't we learn about them sooner?" Kade asked.

"According to Carole, they work mostly with the Cats."

"Her son-in-law is one of the founders?" Kade tried to process all of this.

"Yes, Jarom Vickers is the founder and a close friend of the Tiger King."

"The Tiger King hates wolves."

"Do you blame him? You heard what happened." We approached the elevator in our building, and I pressed the button for the fourth floor.

"Yeah, I heard," Kade said. "That still doesn't explain why we wouldn't know about them."

"Apparently, they only work with the royal lines. Carole told me Jarom has worked with the Alpha King multiple times." I said. I was still bitter about the Alpha keeping that from me.

"He didn't tell you about it?" Kade asked.

"No, and I intend to ask him why the next time I see him."

The elevator stopped on our floor, and we walked down the hall. I opened my door and found Lucas pacing inside my apartment.

"You're back," he said. I looked at him closely; his eyes were red and he looked like he hadn't slept.

"I expected you to call. What happened?" I asked. I was glad to see him, but I was also upset that he didn't keep his promise. Then again, if he felt the need to update me in person, this must be worse than I thought. Lucas cracked his knuckles, which he only did when he was nervous.

"Sit down," he said. Kade and I found a spot on my couch, and Lucas sat in my chair, but he was too restless. He stood back up and paced.

"You were right; you should have gone with me," Lucas said.

"What happened?" I asked.

"Forest Moon…" Lucas's voice cracked, and he was now pale.

"Lucas, what is it?" My heart pounded in my chest as I waited for his next words.

Lucas closed his eyes, and his nostrils flared as he exhaled through his nose. "Forest Moon is gone."

I wasn't sure I had heard him correctly. I shook my head in disbelief.

"Forest Moon is a small pack; they probably just relocated," I said. Lucas stopped pacing and looked at me with sorrow in his eyes. My muscles felt tight, and my hands shook. My headache from earlier was now worse.

"What do you mean, gone?" Kade asked.

"The packhouse and most of the omega houses were burned to the ground. Jasper and I found multiple human bodies."

"Human?" I asked.

Lucas swallowed, and his eyes filled with unshed tears. "Somehow, Balor found their territory."

"You're sure it was Balor?" Kade asked.

"The remains we found all had CB patches on the right shoulder of their uniforms."

I knew he was holding back. My heart pounded in my chest, making my head throb "What aren't you telling us?" My beta avoided eye contact. "Tell me, Lucas."

He looked at me with a pained expression; his jaw was tight, and he balled his hands into fists. "There were four graves. I had no way of identifying them; the smell of decay was so strong in the air that it masked the scent of anyone in the territory. I'm sorry, Caleb."

It was as if someone had knocked the wind out of me. Four graves, but the pack was larger than that, so where were the rest? Was Amber in one of those graves? My ears rang. I felt dizzy, and couldn't breathe.

I shrugged Kade's hand off my shoulder before standing up and walking to the opposite side of the room. I ran my shaking hands through my hair as I tried to calm down.

"Don't go there, Caleb," Kade said. "You know as well as we do that Alpha William would have gotten his kids out before the attack."

I nodded; he was right. Still, I should have been there to see this all for myself. I paced as I processed this information.

"I should have been there," I growled.

"I'm sorry. If I had known how bad the situation was—"

"I told you from the start that I should have gone; I am your Alpha!" I balled up my fist, walked over to Lucas, and punched him hard across the jaw. He didn't even move to stop me.

Kade stood up. "What difference would that have made? It sounds like this happened a while ago; there's nothing you could have done."

Lucas rubbed his jaw. "Jasper found survivors. A red wolf and an archer, but he thinks there's more."

"What did the archer look like?" I asked.

"Jasper didn't say. He never saw her. She didn't want anyone to know who she was."

She. It could only have been one person.

I felt a small amount of relief and it helped clear my head a little. "It was Amber, I'm sure of it," I whispered. "She knows she could have called me; why didn't she?"

"According to Jasper, her phone broke during the attack. She had no way of reaching out. Not that they would; they don't trust anyone right now. The archer went so far as to shoot Jasper with an arrow."

Bile rose from my stomach at the thought of her being so fearful. "What do you mean?"

"The archer, Amber, confirmed that they were betrayed. Someone gave their location to Balor, which led to the attack." Lucas explained.

"How bad was Jasper's injury?" Kade asked. I licked my lips, and my mouth felt dry as I processed everything.

"It could have been worse. Jasper couldn't sit down for an hour, but he recovered quickly," Lucas said.

I couldn't believe Amber would do that, or what she must have been going through to cause such a reaction. I shook my head. "I can't stay here when Amber needs me."

"What are you going to do? Amber and the red wolf won't let you near the cabin," Lucas said. I felt my wolf echo my need to be there. His desire to protect our people matched my own.

We will keep watch over them until they are ready to seek help.

"I'm not wasting any more time here," I said. I went to my room to pack and call my boss.

Carole was understanding and offered her help. "Caleb, are you sure? The whole pack is missing?"

"Yes, ma'am."

"I will consider this your resignation; get down there and do what you need to do. I'll contact Jarom, and we'll help however we can."

"Thank you, Carole. I appreciate your understanding."

She ended the call, and I went to my closet and filled a bag with clothes. When I walked out, Kade and Lucas were still talking.

"I don't get it; where's the pack?" Kade asked.

Lucas took a bite of an apple as he answered, "We don't know; we think our investigation into Rose's disappearance will lead us to them."

I dropped my bag by the door. "Then we need to get back there and find Rose."

"What do the local police say?" Kade asked.

Lucas shook his head, and his eyes darkened. "I can't prove it yet, but I think at least one of them was working with Balor."

Kade's phone dinged and he checked the message. "Looks like my dad has been updated on the situation. I need to return to the mansion. He wants me in charge of the rescue team once we locate the pack."

I nodded. "Good."

Lucas finished his apple, and he seemed a little more calm. His body was still tense, but he wasn't as stressed as he had been a moment ago. Kade left the room to pack, but he didn't have much. I could barely look at Lucas; he never should have left me behind.

Kade walked out with his bag and looked at the two of us. "I'll see you both later. Hopefully, by then, you two will have made up." Kade fist-bumped Lucas, then pulled me in for a bro hug before walking out the door.

I looked over at Lucas. "Be ready. We leave before dawn."

"Yes, Alpha."

CHAPTER 11

Amber

Olivia was in the kitchen making breakfast when she saw me walk past. "Where are you going?"

I knew it wouldn't be right if I snuck out. I took a deep breath and told her the truth. "Agent Hayes told me where to meet him when we're ready to seek help. I'm going to find out what his progress is on locating our pack."

Olivia's face darkened. "I don't trust him."

I went to the dining table and sat in a chair to put on my boots. "I do. He had the chance to attack us, but he didn't. It's been two days, and things are quiet. I need to know about the pack and Rose's case. We won't know anything if we stay here and do nothing."

Olivia turned off the stove and walked away from it. She was quiet as she played with a strand of her hair. Her eyebrows were creased, creating wrinkles on her forehead. Olivia shook her head, then went to the top drawer by the pantry and tossed me the keys to the truck. "Don't let anyone follow you."

I caught the keys. "I won't." I gave her a quick hug and left, grateful that she didn't argue more. As I got into the truck, I realized how much it took Olivia to let me go. She still didn't trust anyone, but her curiosity about the pack was as great as mine. We needed to know.

I drove down the path to our territory; seeing my home destroyed like this was still hard. As I went through the broken gate, I saw new tracks in the mud. Those must have been from Agent Hayes.

There was something scary about leaving the territory. It was the first time I had gone outside our pack lands or the cabin since the attack. I couldn't stop my brain from going into overdrive.

What if something happened to me? What if something happened to Olivia and the pups while I was gone? What if I was followed and couldn't make it back? Who would look after them all?

I nearly drove back to the cabin, but we had to know what was happening outside. We couldn't help anyone if we stayed isolated. Eventually, we would run out of supplies. More importantly, we had to get the pups to safety. They needed the protection of an Alpha and his pack.

I continued my drive up the 145 and turned right at the roundabout. Three miles down the road, I turned into the parking lot of the Court Yard Diner, a small restaurant close to the medical clinic where Rose had worked.

A little bell rang above my head as I opened the glass door. I walked down the short hallway to the dining room's opening on my left. On my right, the hall continued towards the public restrooms, and a small meeting room at the end of the hall.

The rooms were painted beige, and black-and-white photos of Telluride's history lined the walls. Close to the register, Jim Oliver kept his treasured Bronco gear and photos of him and his family at one of the games last year.

My family had been here multiple times. The owner, Jim, is a nice man, but this time he didn't acknowledge me when he saw me. He seemed to be avoiding any kind of eye contact with me. I looked around for Agent Hayes, but a waitress saw me first. She was young and must be new in town because I didn't recognize her. Her name tag said Ruth.

"Just one, Miss?" The woman picked up a menu as I found who I was looking for. Agent Hayes was sitting with his back to me in a booth off to my right. The man sitting with him looked up and spotted me. I ignored the waitress when I recognized Zane Ellis and instead walked right for him.

Zane stood up, looking surprised to see me, "Amber?" He opened his arms, but I refused to hug him. I wasnt ready for close contact with anyone outside my family in the cabin. Zane understood and gestured to the booth they were sitting at. I sat down, and he sat next to me. Zane is the king's royal Beta. I know him well; he's been like family since I was eleven and has helped with some of my training.

"Have you eaten?" Agent Hayes asked. He didn't smile; I wondered if he knew I was the one who shot him.

"I'm not hungry." I hadn't been able to eat much since the attack. An older gray-haired waitress came over to take the guys' order.

"I'll have the bacon and eggs special," Agent Hayes said.

"How do you want your eggs."

"Poached, and I would like a pancake instead of toast."

The waitress wrote it down and then looked at Zane.

"I will get the Denver omelet please, and I'd like a refill on my coffee." Zane responded as the waitress wrote it all down and then looked at me.

Something about the waitress made me uncomfortable. I couldn't look her in the eye as I responded, "Just a water, please." This place, the people, all felt different. I had been in this diner many times, but now I felt out of place.

Agent Hayes held his menu up for the waitress. "Can I get an extra pancake?" She wrote down his order and took his and Zane's menus before walking away. Agent Hayes leaned forward with his hands clasped in front of him. "I'm glad you decided to meet me here."

I nodded. "I wanted to know if you found anything out about my family."

Agent Hayes nodded once. "Nothing yet; we just started on the case. I received the caseload from the deputy in charge last night. We'll go over it after breakfast."

I nodded slowly; I should have known it was too soon to know anything. "Who was the deputy in charge of the case?"

Zane looked up when the bell above the door rang. "Speak of the devil." Before the deputy could look our way he hid his face by looking down at his empty coffee cup.

At the door I saw a small built man with blonde straw-like hair. His face was pleasant, but I knew better. David Benson is county's dirtiest deputy I have ever met. I avoid him as much as possible.

The diner owner smiled at his arrival. "David, what can I do for you?" Tina walked up to them happily with a bag of food. I watched them silently, hoping they wouldn't notice me.

"Mornin', Jim. I came in to get my usual burritos," the deputy said.

The waitress handed Jim the ticket and gave Benson the bag. "Here you go, sweetie."

"Thank you, Tina," Benson said. He looked in the bag as Jim rang up the order. "Oh, it looks like I'm two short; there should be six here."

"I'm sorry. Have a seat, and we'll get those out to you," Jim said.

Benson smiled. "That's all right, I'm not in a hurry." then he sat at a table before noticing us.

Zane tensed, and Agent Hayes did his best to stay calm. I kept my head down, hoping he would stay where he was. He didn't.

"Agent Hayes," Benson said as he approached our table, "Have you made any progress on my case yet?"

"Your case?" Agent Hayes asked. "The file you gave me didn't have much in it for the amount of time you've had, I don't think you can call it your case if you haven't done the work."

"I've been busy; you stepping in lightened my caseload."

The confidence in Agent Hayes' tone was unmistakable. "In a small town like this? I can't tell if you're lazy or if you had an ulterior motive for not being more active."

Benson just smirked and looked him in the eye. "You underestimate my job, Agent. I expect an update from you by the end of the day." Benson leaned in closer. "If I had anything to do with those mutts, I wouldn't have let you near the case."

Agent Hayes sat back resolutely, looking Benson in the eye, and calmly drank his ice water as the two of them stared at each other with contempt.

Benson looked away first and noticed me. "I've seen you around, but I don't know your friend." He pointed at Zane. I froze; I couldn't open my mouth. It felt like my lips were glued together, and my mouth was full of cotton.

Zane put his arm around me. "I'm her uncle."

Benson studied me. "What's wrong with you?" The deputy sounded genuinely concerned, but I still didn't trust him. I shook my head as a bell rang in the distance.

"Order up!" the cook yelled. Then Tina, the older waitress, walked up with two burritos and handed them to Benson.

"Here you go, David," she said. Benson held the bag open, and she put them inside. I noticed the tattoo on the inside of his left wrist. I'd seen it before, but it was as though he was purposely showing it off this time. What was so special about a gray sun?

Benson smiled down at Tina. "They're nice and warm; thank you, Tina." He stopped what he was doing and reached into his pocket. "Oh, I almost forgot. Here is your pin. Welcome to the Silver Suns."

"Thank you," Tina took the small pin from him and put it on her collar.

Benson looked at us. "See you around."

When they left, Agent Hayes growled. "Arrogant weasel."

"I caught it, too," Zane said softly.

"Caught what?" I asked then coughed and drank some water to get the cotton feel out of my mouth.

Zane leaned over and whispered, "Benson said 'mutts'. Implying that he knew Rose was a shapeshifter, and that she wasn't the only one who disappeared that night." Suddenly, I felt cold.

Agent Hayes leaned forward. "He confirmed my suspicion that he's working with Balor. But I still can't prove it."

I was shaking even with Zane's arm around me.

Zane moved his arm, still focused on the conversation with Agent Hayes. "Even if you could prove it, working for Balor isn't a crime."

"What Balor did was a crime." Agent Hayes growled and his eyes began to flicker.

Zane raised his hand slightly in an effort to settle him. "The government won't see it that way, and besides, we can't prove anything. Calm down before you draw attention to us."

Hayes coughed and looked down at the seat next to him as the waitress walked over with their orders. We sat there quietly as she refilled Zane's coffee mug. When she left, he looked at Agent Hayes.

"Her pin matches the deputy's tattoo," Zane said. Agent Hayes nodded.

Feeling a little braver, I found my voice. "What are the Silver Suns?"

Neither of them answered me. Agent Hayes pushed his pancakes towards me and set the syrup next to them. "Eat."

I stared at the plate. The last time I'd eaten pancakes was the morning I found my home burned to the ground and found the bodies of my pack members. The smell of the fluffy, sweet bread was replaced with the scent of blood and smoke.

I pushed the plate back. "No, thank you."

Zane brought the plate back to me. "Amber, you need to eat."

I shook my head, as the smell of the pancakes triggered the horrific memories. I closed my eyes but saw Kate's body all over again. My heart pounded in my chest, and there was a rushing sound in my ears. I wanted to throw up right there in the restaurant.

My hand shook as I pushed the plate farther away. I tried to focus on anything but the smell.

"What's wrong?" Agent Hayes asked as he pushed the plate back to me, still not seeing my distress. Did he just ask me that?

I used his stupid question as a deflection. "I thought you were an FBI agent. Did you just ask me, 'What's wrong'? I would think the answer was obvious."

"That wasn't what I meant."

My chest was tight and I felt like my heart was going to explode. "I appreciate your concern, Agent Hayes—"

"Call me Jasper."

"I appreciate your concern, Jasper, but I came to find out if you had any information on my family. Now that I have my answer, I need to leave."

I wanted away from this place. My throat felt thick, and I needed air.

Zane seemed to catch on and moved the plate of pancakes away from me and replaced it with his omelet. Nothing else looked appetizing anymore. My stomach was in knots, and I was so tense the muscles in my neck ached.

I began to move out of the seat, I didn't care that Zane was blocking my way. "I need air." He moved out of the booth, and I walked out as fast as I could. The ding from the doorbell alerted the others of my exit. The cool morning air felt good on my face, but my stomach was still upset.

Leaning against my truck was Deputy Benson, as he ate one of his burritos. "You don't look so good."

Finding the little strength within I addressed him for the first time. "Please get off my truck."

Benson looked back at the truck with fake innocence and stood up. "I'm sorry, is this your truck?"

Benson took one last bite of his burrito and wadded up the trash as he walked over to me. I might be a wolf, but being confronted by the deputy like this made me feel more like a deer without her antlers facing off against a cougar.

Benson smiled at me as he approached. Anyone else would think he was your friendly neighborhood deputy, but this isn't classic television.

I froze as he approached. "I know what you are. Your eyes give you away, werewolf." His voice sounded gentle when he whispered in my ear, "I'm coming for you, and I have the law on my side. Once I prove you're a mutt, I'll lock you up for good."

Benson brushed my arm as he threw away his burrito wrapper and stepped back. He smirked as he said, "All I need is one reason to arrest you."

The bell above the door rang as Zane and Jasper approached us. Their presence didn't help at all. Benson wasn't intimidated by either of them. Zane pulled me closer to him as Jasper stepped in front of me and approached Benson.

"Why are you still here? Don't you have a job to do?" Jasper asked.

Benson shrugged. I felt Zane's breath by my ear as he whispered, "Leave while we have him distracted."

Not needed to be told twice, I left him and Jasper to handle Benson. Using the back roads through Telluride to Mountain Village to the 145. I checked my mirrors to see if anyone was following me. There was no one, so I drove to the cabin.

Once I arrived, I sat in the truck until my heart stopped pounding and my breathing evened. When I opened the truck door, the scent of pine filled my nose, easing my upset stomach.

Amber

I sat at the table with Olivia and Ryan as they processed what I had told them about Deputy Benson. Olivia was silent, and Ryan drummed his fingers on the table.

"I knew Benson was bad news, but did he really have something to do with the attack?" Olivia asked.

"Agent Hayes seems to think so."

Ryan hit the table. "That doesn't make sense; what does he have to gain by invading our pack?"

I looked at my brother, echoing his frustration. "What did Balor have to gain ten years ago when he killed Alpha Harrison? What is he gaining now with all his talk about eradicating the 'monsters'?" I used my fingers for air quotes. "Balor is fueled by his hatred, and he's spreading it like a disease. Benson is just another zombie, infected by the hateful words of a hateful man." I was still shaking from my encounter with the deputy, and all this talk about Balor wasn't helping.

Ryan got up and stood behind his seat, bracing himself on the back of the chair. "Why us?"

Olivia's hand shook as she played with her hair. "We're just another group of people at the mercy of a silver-tongued devil. History is filled with humans like Charles Balor, who are afraid of those who are different."

I couldn't talk about this any longer. The pressure in my chest was only getting worse. "We need to figure out what to do next; we can't stay here, but I'm not sure we can leave either."

Olivia stared at the table as she slowly nodded. "We stay until we know what to do." I nodded reluctantly. I knew the longer we stayed in the cabin, the worse it would be for us, and it wouldn't solve anything. Benson still concerned me.

"Then we need to use our time wisely," Ryan said.

Olivia finally stopped playing with her hair and looked up at us. "We can't underestimate Benson; just because we are staying doesn't mean we shouldn't prepare for an emergency."

My anxiety made me antsy; I had to get up and do something productive. Usually, I would spar, but I couldn't do that right now. Olivia's suggestion gave me the perfect outlet.

"Agreed. Olivia, I want you to go over our supplies in the basement. I want to know how long our food supply will last, and how many diapers and clothes we have," I said. Olivia looked at me defiantly.

"Ryan, make sure the vehicles have everything they need. I know you went over the truck on our first day here, but I want you to review the rest of it, too. Check our fuel supply and go into the basement for anything else that may be useful. I also want you to check our weapon supply."

Olivia looked at me with narrowed eyes, "Why are you giving orders all of a sudden?"

I'm not an official Luna yet, but my instinct to lead is strong. "It's my responsibility. I am still one of the evacuation leaders. My father put me in charge of the children of the pack and until we get them to the safety of our allies or our family comes home; I will obey my alpha."

Ryan leaned in eagerly. "What are you going to do?"

"I'm going to go over escape routes to Grand Junction. There has to be a way to sneak around Benson if we need to."

Ryan nodded and seemed to relax now that there was a plan. Olivia pursed her lips but didn't say anything.

I folded my arms in front of my chest and addressed her. "What?"

"We were having an equal conversation until you started barking orders."

"Do you want me to pull rank?"

Ryan stood up and put his arms between us. "Cut it out. This isn't the time."

He was right, but Olivia's defiance still annoyed me even though I knew it had nothing to do with me, or her for that matter. What happened this morning added to the stress we were already feeling. I didn't say anything else; I just got up and left.

In my room, I began looking for our maps and a notebook. Once I had what I needed, I laid it all out on my bed and began to work. I took out a marker and circled Telluride. The circle I made was faded. I tested the marker in my notebook, and it was drying out. I threw it into the wastebasket and then got up to get a new one.

Back in the living room, Olivia and Ryan were gone. Willow and Ellie were now playing Chutes and Ladders on the floor. I rummaged through my dad's old rolltop desk for another marker.

Willow saw me and walked over. "What are you doing?"

"I'm looking for a way out of here without Deputy Benson seeing us."

"You mean we're finally leaving?" Willow exclaimed. I found a marker and closed the drawer. Willow followed me back to our room.

"Why do you want to leave so badly? This cabin is as much our home as the packhouse was."

Willow shrugged. "I don't feel safe here, and I miss Mommy and Daddy. If we go, then you can find them."

"Me?"

"Yep, you're special."

Her faith in me made me smile. For a brief moment the weight on my shoulders felt lighter.

She's right. You are the White Luna and the daughter of a powerful Alpha.

The voice of my wolf was faint, and more of a feeling than something I heard since I hadn't merged with her yet. The merge would happen at midnight before my twenty-first birthday. For now, I had to be open to hearing Emerald's voice. I was beginning to wonder if I was going crazy.

You're not crazy. Have faith in yourself.

I sighed and took a deep breath. The goddess did say that Emerald would lead me the best she could from the Sacred Forest.

"Amber? Are you okay? You've been quiet for a long time," Willow asked.

I realized that I had zoned out. "Sorry, Squirt. I didn't mean to stare off into space like that."

"Are we leaving to a new pack?"

"We don't need a new pack. We just need to find the one we have."

Willow began to rub her chest, and I felt two familiar stings on my wrists. I knew what was coming and didn't want anyone to witness it.

"Willow, close the door."

She ran to the door, came back, and sat on my lap. Holding my sister eased my shock as I felt every punch to the gut my father experienced. I had to hold back a cry as I felt one of his ribs crack. There was more to this attack. I also felt his rage. The beating wasn't like the last one. There were gaps and spaces of time between it all. At least there wasn't any burning this time.

I squeezed Willow, and she clung to me as tears ran down her cheeks. I hugged her, trying to ease her pain. A five-year-old should never have to go through this kind of suffering.

When it was over, Willow stayed in my lap and sobbed. "You have to find them, Amber."

"I'm just one person, and the Royal Pack is already looking for them."

"No, it has to be you, you're special. I know you can do it, Amber." Willow said.

I kissed the top of her head. She had more faith in me than I had in myself. "I'll do my best, Willow."

She climbed off my lap as she wiped her runny nose on her sleeve. It was gross, but it was her way of telling me to get back to work.

Looking at the map, Willow asked, "Where are we going?"

I pointed to the dot labeled Grand Junction. "Shadow Moon, Alpha Cole Shepherd, and his pack will help us."

Willow nodded and watched as I picked up my marker and drew another circle around Telluride. I drew a line from the roundabout west on the 145, then, north just past Placerville up to Ridgeway. Next, I went back to the junction and traced a line west to Norwood and up the 145, to Highway 90, then 141 where it meets up with the 50 towards Grand Junction.

The first route through Ridgeway was a straight shot on the million-dollar highway. We could drive through Ridgeway and take the 550 highway all the way to Grand Junction, and the Shadow Moon Pack would be due east.

The second route along the 145 was more out of our way. It goes farther west and then meets up with Highway 50 near Whitewater. We could then take the 50 into Grand Junction and, from there, to Shadow Moon.

With Deputy Benson looking for us now, it wasn't safe to travel all together. We could either split up or take several small trips north until we can get everyone out. How do we decide who goes first? This wasn't a decision I could make alone.

There was a less desirable option, but it would work. Benson was looking for me; he doesn't know about Olivia and the others yet. I could use that in our favor.

"I know what I have to do, but it won't be easy."

I hadn't noticed Willow get up and walk to the door.

"What won't?" Ryan asked from the doorway.

I jumped, and he looked down at the floor. Tyla was in his arms with her head on his shoulder while Tyler clung to his leg. "Sorry, I knocked, but you didn't answer." His eyes were red, and he looked as tired as Willow and me. I suddenly understood the missing pieces and why my father became enraged.

Ryan saw my expression and whispered. "Olivia felt it this time, too, and so did the twins." I looked more closely at Tyla and Tyler; their eyes were red and puffy.

"It's all the same thing?"

He nodded and walked in. Tyla reached for me, and Ryan handed her to me. I cradled her, and Tyler jumped up on my bed. Ryan sat down at the end and rubbed Tyler's back. The little pups began crying.

Willow climbed up on my other side to whisper to Tyla and patted her head. "It's okay, we will get our pack back." The three pups sobbed quietly, and I looked up at Ryan.

"Our window to rescue them might be smaller than we thought," I whispered.

Ryan nodded and sniffed as he processed what that meant for our families. We let Tyler and Tyla settle down. Ryan's eyes glazed over for a minute, and he nodded.

Willow looked at Tyla and smiled. "I smell chocolate." Tyla sat up, and I looked up at Ryan; he shrugged as the pups left the room.

"Come on, Olivia has her inventory done," Ryan said. I grabbed the map, and we followed the pups out.

At the dining table, there were three mugs. Willow, Tyler, and Tyla sipped their hot chocolate and laughed at their mustaches. Ryan and I walked over to Olivia, and she handed us both cups of steaming hot cocoa, then she picked up her own and sat on the couch.

"Chocolate makes everything better," she whispered weakly. Chocolate couldn't fix this, but our little ritual felt more normal than anything.

"I wish it was French silk pie," I said as a tear ran down my face.

Olivia smiled and let out a weak laugh. "I miss Greta; her French silk was the best. Did you know that's what inspired my mom to become a food critic?"

Ryan smiled as we all remembered our pack cook.

"Greta's pie did that?" I asked.

"Yeah, I guess she created the recipe with a friend of hers, and my mom fell in love with it."

Ryan sipped his cocoa. "I liked how Greta would use a large chocolate cookie for the crust because she knew I didn't like flour crust."

Tears fell from our eyes as we talked about Greta Sloan. This was the most normal conversation we'd had in a long time, and for a small moment, it felt like we were back in my bedroom of the packhouse.

Ryan sniffed, and it brought me back to the cabin. I missed them all. This morning with Benson had been a frightening experience, but I couldn't let that stop me from doing what had to be done. We needed to rescue the pack.

Olivia held her mug and her notes on her lap. I sat down next to her and put my arm around her. Olivia's eyes were red, and she was still shaking.

"Are you okay?" It was a silly question, I know.

"I will be when we bring our pack home."

"I'm not sure home is the safest place for them," Ryan whispered as he sat on the floor by us. I needed a distraction from this topic.

"How do our rations look?" I asked, getting us back on task before my mind wandered.

Olivia reviewed her notes. "The good news is that we have enough food to last us a couple of months."

"The bad news?" Ryan asked.

"After what we experienced, I don't think our pack will last that long."

"What about diapers and formula for Alice?" I asked.

Olivia shook her head. "The formula canister we opened last week is almost empty, but we have two more canisters, and that should be enough formula to last two more weeks. The diapers are going too fast, and Alice is growing out of the extras we do have. One of us needs to make a grocery run to pick up more."

Two weeks should be plenty of time. Then again, a lot can happen in two weeks.

It was Ryan's turn. "I checked the truck, and everything is in working order. The truck has a full tank of gas, and the Kia has close to half. We have three one-gallon jugs filled with gas.

That should be enough if we only make one trip to Shadow Moon. Unless we use our emergency cash."

Olivia tapped her notebook. "I have a feeling that will all go to diapers."

Ryan nodded. "Unfortunately, if something happens to the Kia, I can't fix it. It's too high-tech."

I brought out the map and set it in front of us. "It's a good thing we won't be going farther than Shadow Moon."

"That's still 140 miles," Olivia said.

Ryan pointed to the shorter route. "The Kia will get us there as long as nothing happens to it before we leave."

"How are we on weapons?" I asked.

Ryan pulled a piece of paper from his pocket and handed it to me. "Everything is how Dad left it. We have three rifles and six boxes of ammo. There are two bows and at least 60 arrows in the basement."

I pointed to the routes on the map. "We have two options to Shadow Moon, I think we should take both."

"What do you mean 'both'?" Olivia asked.

"Someone has to throw Benson off." I traced the longer route up to Norwood with my finger. "I can get him to follow me on the longer route while you drive the pups up the 550 to Grand Junction. I'll be at least an hour behind you and that should give you enough time to get to Shadow Moon without Benson finding out its location."

"That sounds too risky," Ryan said. "What if you're caught?"

I swallowed the lump in my throat. "Then he will be too busy with me to follow you."

"I don't like the idea of us splitting up," Olivia said.

I sighed. "I don't see any other way."

"What about that FBI guy?" Ryan asked. "What if he distracts Benson long enough for us to get out of here?"

"How would he do that?" Olivia asked.

"Not only that, how would he know about it?"

Ryan looked me in the eye without blinking. "Meet with him again tomorrow."

"I am not going back there."

Olivia began playing with her hair again. "Amber, I agree with Ryan. We shouldn't split up. There has to be another way."

"Then what do you suggest?" I asked. Olivia and Ryan thought about it, but didn't speak.

I pointed to the longer route on the map. "This is our best option. I agree, it sucks, but what choice do we have?"

"Okay, but I'm not giving up on a better solution," Olivia said. I hoped she finds one because I didn't see any other options.

CHAPTER 13

Amber

That night after dinner, the pups all looked worn and anxious.

"Amber, can you tell us the story about the White Alpha?" Ellie asked.

"Again?"

"Yeah," Tyler said. The rest of the pups got excited, so Ryan and I gathered them around the fireplace while Olivia started a fire. Once it was going and the pups were settled, I sat down on the floor with them. It was weird. Now that I knew who I was, I was telling my story; it felt surreal.

"Is everyone comfortable?"

Willow sat in Olivia's lap while Ryan sat between Michael and Tyler. Everyone's eyes were on me.

"Long ago, the moon goddess stood among the royal wolves and their allies."

Tyla raised her hand. "What did she look like?"

Tyler leaned over to answer his sister. "How would Amber know?"

Olivia placed her finger on her lips, and the pups quieted down so that I could continue.

"The Moon Goddess is the most beautiful woman anyone has ever seen. Her skin is the color of cinnamon, with hair as dark as a moonless night, and her dress twinkles like the stars. She doesn't wear any shoes, and her eyes are as bright as a full moon on a clear night."

The kids all sat forward with their mouths open. "Whoa."

I continued before I could laugh at their reaction. "There is a threat coming to all shapeshifters. It will destroy the balance of nature, and all will suffer."

Ellie raised her hand before asking, "Is Balor the threat she was talking about?"

Her question caught me by surprise. I hadn't thought about what the threat was, but it made sense that it would be him.

"I'm not sure, Ellie. The goddess didn't say. Instead, she gave them hope. She chose champions to help defeat this threat. Leading them will be two wolves."

"The White Alpha!" Tyler excitedly jumped up, and Ryan nudged him to sit back down.

Ellie rolled her eyes and leaned back on her hands. "Why is it always the Alpha that gets the attention? The story should be about the White Luna."

I laughed. "Yes, the White Alpha and his Luna. They are meant to save us all." I looked at Ellie. "They are equals, and each has their own path. We hear more about the Alpha because there isn't a lot known about the Luna. That is how the Moon Goddess wanted it."

Ellie shrugged. Willow sat forward with tears in her eyes. "Do you think the White Alpha could find our parents?"

Olivia rubbed soothing circles on her back. "If he was here, he could find them for us."

I continued, hoping to give my sister hope. "The White Alpha is said to have many abilities, but he won't get any of them until he finds his mate."

"What are his powers?" Tyler asked.

"No one knows. People have guessed for centuries. Some say he will talk with the dead; others say he will read minds. One legend says that the White Alpha will even have wings."

Josh rolled his eyes. "That one's made up; there is no way a wolf would have wings."

Michael beamed with his fists close to his body, trying to contain his excitement. "But it would be so cool; if he could fly, he would be unstoppable."

"What about the Luna? What are her powers?" Ellie asked.

"I'm not sure; I do know that she will inspire peace." If I could help spread peace and kindness as quickly as hatred, maybe there would be more balance in this world. I wasn't so sure I could inspire anyone, but I didn't like seeing people suffer.

"When the Alpha and Luna come together, then it's only a matter of time before the threat is defeated, and shapeshifters will live in peace once more."

Josh slapped his hands on his knees. "That's it? You can't end the story like that. What happens to the human threat?"

"How would you end it?"

Michael and Tyler then began their own conversation about how the ending should go, making us all groan and laugh.

"They put Balor in a trash can," Michael laughed.

"Yeah, and he finds underwear in the trash can and puts it on his head." Tyler pumped his little fist in the air. "The White Alpha takes Balor to Mars, where he puts him in jail, and the only thing he has to eat is Martian boogers."

Michael pretended to pick his nose. "Martian boogers!"

Josh responded more seriously, "I would make them king and queen."

Ryan, Olivia, and I chuckled. The other boys were already in a silly mood.

Tyler jumped up again. "King of the boogers!"

He and Michael were in their own world now. Both of them were jumping around and laughing about Martian kings picking their noses.

I focused on Josh and his response. "That seems a bit much. I would think they would be too tired from saving the world to rule all the wolves."

"But they can't stop at that! They will be needed after the war is over," Ellie chimed in.

"They can still help people without being royalty," I said.

Ryan pulled the two rowdy boys back to the floor, then wrapped his arm around Tyler before he ran for his room to get what he called an 'underwear crown.'

"Yeah, that's what our Alpha did." Ryan added, "Alpha William helped other packs as an ambassador. The White Alpha could do the same."

"I guess," Josh said, then mumbled under his breath, "It sounds better than going to Mars."

"Hey!" the boys shouted before Ryan quieted them down.

Willow asked another question. "Is the Luna more powerful than the Alpha?"

Ellie answered her before the rest of us could. "Of course! Girls are tougher than boys."

"They are not," Michael shot back.

I didn't want this to become an argument. "That's enough; time for bed."

"But…."

Olivia pointed at him. "No arguing, Michael. We've all had a rough day; let's end it peacefully."

Michael hung his head. "Okay."

We gathered the pups and herded them to their rooms, but they still talked about the White Alpha and the White Luna.

Ryan, Olivia, and I were in the hallway as the pups got ready for bed.

Tyler tugged on my shirt to get my attention. "Who do you think the Alpha is?"

Michael poked his head out of his room. "I don't know, maybe it's Ryan."

Ryan chuckled. Then ruffled Michael's hair. "Trust me, I'm not the White Alpha."

"You could be," Michael chirped before going back into his room.

Josh approached Ryan after giving Alice to Olivia. "He's right; technically, you haven't merged with your wolf, so you could be."

Ryan folded his arms as if to shield himself. "I think my dad would have told me if I was."

Ryan's reaction to this was entertaining. I couldn't help but join the fun. "What if Dad doesn't know?"

I tried to sound playful, but my curiosity got the better of me. Did my parents know who I was before I did?

"He would know. Dad knows more about the White Alpha and White Luna story than anyone… except the king. Dad would have known what to look for long before anyone else figured it out." Then added, as if to end the conversation, "If they were real."

Olivia held Alice as she snored in her arms. She looked as annoyed by this as Ryan. "Exactly. The White Alpha and White Luna are just stories. They aren't real."

Ellie came out of my room and ignored Olivia. "Who is the White Luna?"

Willow was right behind her and didn't miss a beat as she spoke with her toothbrush in her mouth. "Ish Amber; who elsh woul it be?"

I was shocked that they thought of me so quickly.

Ryan looked at me playfully. "I don't know; Amber looks a little too scrawny to be a super wolf."

"Super wolf?"

The girls giggled and Ellie folded her arms with an air of superiority. "Amber is a future Luna. Why not her?"

Willow ran to the bathroom, and I heard her spit into the sink.

Olivia stared at Ellie. "The story doesn't specify her origin. For all we know, the White Luna could even be a rogue."

Willow came back with her hairbrush and a band. "Why would the goddess choose a rogue? Aren't they smelly?" Ellie took the brush and began working on Willow's hair.

I had to admit. I did feel like a rogue and it hadn't changed how the goddess saw me. "They are still her children. The goddess loves rogues too; you never know, the White Luna could be a rogue."

Ellie began braiding Willow's hair and Willow smiled at me as her head moved in different directions. "No, it's you."

Against my will, my cheeks turned red. "Well, either Ryan is the White Alpha, or I'm the White Luna. It can't be both."

"That would be gross," Olivia laughed.

Ellie finished the braid and tied it up. "Why?"

"The legend says the Alpha and Luna are a mated pair. Ryan is my brother, so there's no possible way for us to be both the Alpha and the Luna."

The kids all stopped what they were doing. "It's Amber," they all said.

Ryan and Olivia laughed.

"It's not real," Olivia stated.

"Right," Ryan agreed. "If it were real, then the Alpha would already be here."

This conversation was now making me uncomfortable. "Enough; everyone needs to go to bed."

Ryan, Olivia, and I got the pups into their beds and breathed for a minute.

"That was a good story tonight," Olivia said. She had a suspicious look in her eye, I knew she wanted to talk more about it with me.

"You used more details this time. I liked your version of the goddess," Ryan said. I wasn't sure how to respond since they already didn't believe any of it was real.

"Thank you." I backed into my room, making my escape from this conversation. "I'm exhausted, so I'm going to turn in for the night." I went into my room before they asked any questions. Now wasn't the time for me to tell them.

How was I supposed to tell them that I knew what the goddess looked like because I've met her? They think the legend of the White Alpha is nothing more than fiction. Ryan only said all those things because he was playing with the pups.

As I got myself ready for bed, I felt an immense weight on my shoulders. I wasn't sure how I could bear the heavy responsibility while stuck in this cabin. Not to mention that being confronted by Deputy Benson still scared me.

When Balor revealed our existence, he made things more dangerous for us. Human laws don't protect us, that's why we still live in hiding.

By human law, no matter how small the crime, a shape-shifter could be lawfully imprisoned as long as the officer had evidence supporting their claim. The government stated that it was for the protection of the human citizens.

Then there's what Josh said. The thought of being royalty on top of being a champion for the goddess was enough to make my palms sweat and my heart race. I wiped them on my pants and took a few cleansing breaths. After the war, I wanted to retire in a quiet, peaceful place with a small pack. Maybe somewhere remote, where civilization was scarce. Somewhere like Alaska or the Dakotas.

I climbed into bed, and the girls were still awake and chatting.

"Good night," I said.

"Good night, Luna," they said, then burst into giggles.

I lay there, letting the sound of their laughter comfort me. Today, there had been much pain; it was nice to end it with the sound of joy. I would love to tell them who I am. Maybe it would bring them hope. Moments like these would happen more often, but I couldn't, and I wouldn't deny it either; I'm not a liar. Since I couldn't say anything, I just listened to them and smiled as they talked. Their laughter and hopeful whispers were the last things I heard before I fell asleep.

Once again, I woke up in the Forest of the Gods. I was at the base of the Lunar tree, and the Moon Goddess was sitting on a low branch, petting a small squirrel curled up comfortably in her lap.

"Hello, my child," the goddess smiled.

"Why am I back?"

"I can feel your apprehension about what you have been asked to do."

I wasn't sure why, but all of my emotions poured out of my mouth. "I'm just a small country wolf; how can I be expected to live up to everyone's expectations? The White Luna is a legend expected to save the world."

The little squirrel jumped off her lap as the goddess came down from her branch and touched my lips. "Shhh. You are rambling, and I hear everything you are saying." The goddess removed her finger, and I tried to breathe, but the full extent of what was expected of me still crushed me. The goddess placed her hand gently on my shoulder.

"Amber, I know this all feels like a heavy burden, and you are wise to see it that way. Do you know why an Alpha has a Beta and a Gamma?"

I remembered my mom's wise words, but, the goddess continued. "It's to ease the burden of Alpha. The Beta has certain responsibilities separate from the Alpha, as does the Gamma. You've heard the phrase, 'it takes a village to raise a child'?"

"Yes, but what does that have to do with me?"

She smiled warmly at me and motioned for me to sit beside her in the grass at the tree's base. "A pack is like a family; the Alpha and the Luna are like parents. Their Betas and Gammas help them watch over and protect the pack."

"What does that have to do with me?" I asked again.

"Olivia is your Beta, isn't she?" The goddess asked and I nodded in response. "Then let her in, allow her the chance to share this burden with you."

"What if she doesn't believe me?"

"She will in time, but you won't have the answer to that question unless you take the risk and be honest with her."

"Why me? I'm not special."

The goddess smiled. "You only say that because you don't see yourself the way I see you. You are far more than a 'small country wolf,' as you put it. Be yourself; that is all that is required to be my champion."

"That's it?"

"Have faith in yourself, Amber. You're stronger than you think."

Caleb

The air in Telluride was cold for this late in the month. Lucas knocked on Jasper's hotel room door, and we entered after he opened it. Zane Ellis greeted us, and Lucas and I took a knee. As the Royal Beta to the king, he is the highest-ranking wolf here.

Zane placed his fist over his heart, letting us up. When I stood, Zane embraced me. "It's been too long, Caleb."

"Yes, it has. Forgive me." I pulled away and smiled at him before walking over to Jasper's open laptop. "What is the progress on the case?"

Zane hugged Lucas and then joined me at the desk. Jasper sat down in the chair and went over his findings.

"We discovered one deputy is definitely working for Balor." Jasper handed me a file. "His name is David Benson." He brought up a picture of a sun tattoo in gray ink. "Yesterday, he made a show of this tattoo on the inside of his wrist."

"A sun?" Lucas asked.

Zane pulled out another file and handed it to Lucas. "Not just any sun. When we were at the diner, he handed a waitress a pin that looked identical to his tattoo and welcomed her into the 'Silver Suns.' According to our research, it's a symbol for a hate group."

Lucas opened it and raised an eyebrow. "The Silver Suns? Sounds like something from a comic book."

I looked up at Zane. "Is Balor behind this group?"

"We believe so. Everything in their mission statement is made up of quotes from Charles Balor."

Lucas flipped to the page with the Silver Sun's mission statement.

Humanity First

Humans are the supreme being.

We deserve to live without competing for our place in this world.

We believe in the eradication of all non-humans for the safety and well-being of the human race.

"Live without competing for their place in the world? Does that include all animals, or just shapeshifters?" I rolled my eyes at the statement. These humans had no idea what they were talking about.

Lucas pointed to the file and scoffed. "They claim the 'safety and wellbeing of the human race,' but humans are responsible for most of the violence. They think they are superior to everything."

I shook my head in frustration. "It's that way of thinking that goes against the law of the forest and tips the balance of nature. This is why we exist, to keep the balance."

Jasper turned to the next page in the file. "It gets worse. Benson isn't the only one in town affiliated with the Silver Suns. We discovered that he's recruiting. The waitress wasn't the only one with a pin matching that symbol. The diner's owner also had the same pin on his shirt this morning when we had breakfast."

Lucas looked at me meaningfully. "It's like the Purple Lotus that Tyrell told us about."

"What is the Purple Lotus?" Jasper asked.

"They are a group of humans who have allied themselves with shapeshifters against Balor," I said.

Zane put his hands on his hips and sighed. "The humans are drawing lines in the sand. This won't be good for those not involved in either group."

"No one asked us how we feel about it either," Jasper grumbled.

"The Purple Lotus works mainly with the Cats. That's why we haven't heard of them before," Lucas said.

His face darkened. "When will King Damien get over what happened? His Pride isn't the only one in danger here."

I closed the file I was holding and studied his response. I knew he wasnt telling us everything. "Put yourself in his shoes. What would you have done if it was Claire?"

Lucas eyed Zane suspiciously. "I agree with the Tiger King. I would have killed Nolan for what he did, but Damien showed mercy, and I respect that."

Jasper scoffed and shook his head. "You have other reasons for wanting Nolan dead." Lucas shrugged; it's a subject we didn't talk about.

"What does any of that have to do with the Purple Lotus or the Silver Suns?" Zane asked.

"One of the four founders of the Purple Lotus, the one who started it all, was a man named Jarom Vickers. He's been a close friend of King Damien's since they were kids; but, you already knew that. Didn't you, Zane?"

Jasper looked at Zane in shock. Zane looked guilty as he realized how much I knew.

"Yes, I did, but I don't know as much as you think. Jarom only met with two members at a time. That was how he kept his identity secret. I was no longer included once the king brought Alpha William into the meetings with Jarom."

"Why were you pretending that you didn't?" Jasper asked.

I tossed the file on the bed and approached Zane. "Why hide it from me?"

"The Purple Lotus is more secretive than this other group. They don't want anyone to know who the members are for their safety and the safety of their families. We didn't tell you, Caleb, because you don't have your mate. Once you do, we will tell you everything, and you can join the meetings with Jarom."

I balled my hands into fists. "You can't use that against me. We've always had open communication. What else are you guys hiding from me?"

Zane's eyes flickered, but he didn't say anything.

"Don't make me order you," I said. Apollo's consciousness came forward, and my eyes began to glow their brilliant sapphire blue. Zane may outrank us, but Apollo is the only one who can force orders on a high-ranking royal wolf. I didn't like doing it, but I wouldn't put up with disrespect.

Zane put his arms up and backed away two steps. "All—all right, fine. Yes, there is more, but please trust me, Caleb. We are only keeping it from you because it's more important for you to discover on your own. It wouldn't be fair for us to tell you."

"How does that help me?"

"You will understand when the time comes," Zane said.

Lucas gave his file back to Jasper, "Why keep the Purple Lotus a secret then? Caleb doesn't need his mate to know about this group. That was just an excuse, and you know it."

"If you want to know, then ask the king yourself," Zane said, his brow beginning to sweat, and I realized he couldn't tell me.

"He ordered you to keep this secret from me."

I growled, and Apollo echoed my frustration. "You knew about my wolf! You know who I am! This should have never been kept from me."

Zane bowed his head and closed his eyes. "You're right, and you can take it up with the king when you see him again; but arguing like this isn't helping the Forest Moon Pack."

I felt Apollo's growl through my chest. I let it out and sucker-punched him, breaking his nose. Zane's head snapped back, and he groaned.

I shook my hand. "Now I'm ready to move on."

"Agreed." Zane's voice was muffled with his hand covering his face.

"I will let it go for now, but once we locate Alpha William and the rest of the pack, we will discuss everything you have been hiding from me," I said. Zane silently walked to the bathroom. My head was aching. It was mild but still painful.

"What else do you have?" Lucas asked Jasper while Zane cleaned up the blood and snapped his nose back into place. Jasper went to the closet and came back with a box.

"This is what Benson gave us when we joined the case."

"Do you have anything on him at all?" I asked.

"Benson has been careful; I don't have much."

Lucas folded his arms across his chest. "I remember that first meeting. He was nervous as if he wasn't expecting anyone else to get involved."

I tapped the box, "Are you sure the evidence here is credible?"

Jasper took the box over to the bed and opened it. "Yes. We are still looking into everything in here and more. I've started to question the deputies that work with Benson, but none of them are talking."

Zane came out of the bathroom, as I looked at my watch; it was getting late. "While the rest of you continue to investigate here, I'm going into the forest to guard the cabin."

"Wait until after the snowstorm; it looks like a big one, making it unsafe for anyone in the mountains right now," Zane said.

"That includes those who live in the cabin."

Zane put his hands on his hips as he relented. "I want you back by morning."

I shook my head. "No disrespect, Zane…" He gave me a skeptical look since I had just punched him. I ignored it and continued, "I won't be idle. Someone needs to keep watch and prevent Benson or his recruits from finding the cabin. And if they get snowed in, someone should be there to either get help or dig them out."

Zane shook his head and looked up at the ceiling. "Fine. How long will you be out there?"

"As long as I need to be."

"I won't stop you, but Lucas should go too."

"I wish I could, but we talked on the way up, and he made a point. With the red wolf there, we would create too many tracks and bring unwanted attention to the cabin."

Zane looked at me with eyes as wide as saucers. "Caleb, this is too dangerous! What if something happens?"

"Something already did."

"I mean to you!"

"It's a risk I'm willing to take. William fought alongside my father when he needed him. Now it's my turn to help William the only way I can until we locate him."

"Caleb…" Zane said, then stopped and sighed. "Be safe out there."

Jasper nodded as if he expected as much. "There's a cave about a mile and a half from the cabin; we will meet you there with our updates."

"Thank you."

Lucas placed his hand on my shoulder. "I agree you shouldn't be out there alone, but since you don't have a badge, you might be safer near the cabin."

"What about what you said a moment ago?"

Lucas just looked at me as if I shouldn't press my luck. "If you are that worried about me, then I suggest you locate Forest Moon." Lucas smiled and removed his hand.

"Eat a good dinner before you go; who knows when you'll have a decent meal again," Zane said.

I smiled at my old friend. "You sound like my mother."

Zane laughed. "I will take that as a compliment."

We left for the restaurant soon after Lucas settled into the hotel room. All I had was a bag that I placed in the closet, keeping my phone and wallet with me.

Zane took us for burgers and then drove us back to the hotel. An alert sounded on my phone. I turned it off and smiled stoically. "Time for me to go."

"Be safe out there, Caleb." Zane placed his fist over his heart and bowed his head. I nodded, and Lucas pulled me in for a hug.

"I will check on you as often as I can," he said.

"Find the pack. That's more important."

Lucas nodded. Jasper was next, and he hugged me, too, "Stay downwind from the cabin; they are still hostile to strangers."

"I will."

They walked me to the door, and I closed the door behind me. I walked down the stairs to the main floor and out to my jeep. The weather was colder than when we came back from dinner, and my nose burned from the dry air. Snow was coming.

I drove out of town and headed south. I smelled the decay once I got close enough to the territory. The scent of humans was strong enough that I knew they were close. I parked my Jeep on a side street and walked into the territory. Once I was inside the entrance, I hid behind houses and stayed out of sight of the humans.

The destruction was heartbreaking. I remembered the packhouse; now it's a pile of ash. Humans in gray uniforms, rubber gloves, and masks walked around trucks parked on the streets next to some houses. I watched as two humans loaded a body bag into a truck. One human in a deputy uniform walked up to the truck with a clipboard. He marked something on it and handed it to the man standing there.

The other man looked angrily at the deputy, then yanked the clipboard out of his hands, scribbled on it, and tapped the deputy's chest with it. He yelled something at him as he pointed to the back of the truck.

I was close enough to catch some of what they said. "Balor isn't happy with you, David. You were supposed to inspect this place weeks ago!"

The deputy shrugged. "I had complications."

The man shoved the clipboard at the deputy for him to take back. "By that, you mean an excuse. You took too long to inform us about the casualties. This was unacceptable. How can you be so careless? Three of these men were reported missing. Balor wants you to notify their families tonight." The deputy just nodded his head.

I waited for a long time before the humans cleared out of the pack lands. Once they were gone, I texted Jasper.

"Humans in the pack territory, I'm assuming they were cleaning up their dead."

Jasper's text returned quickly, *"It's about time. Have they found the cabin?"*

"Hope not, I'll check it out."

I inspected the houses where the humans had been. There were fresh footprints on the floor; they had collected their dead. Even without the dead bodies, the scene was horrific.

I returned to my jeep, then drove past the territory and found a secluded spot to park. I covered it with a lean-to made from branches and leaves. Satisfied that my jeep and everything inside was safe from intruders, I prepared to shift.

My bones cracked and reformed from my feet to the top of my head. I went from standing on two legs to four, and white fur sprouted from my limbs. As the fur grew down my back around my chest and shoulders, my nose and ears cracked and elongated as my head took the shape of my wolf. Fur sprouted simultaneously, and once the shift was complete, Apollo shook our fur and stretched our legs.

We ran through the forest near the cabin; then found a place close enough to keep an eye on the survivors and far enough away that they wouldn't see us as a threat. Thankfully, it looked as though the humans still hadn't discovered the survivors.

The wind blew, and snow began to fall sometime in the middle of the night. I was grateful that Apollo's fur coat was thick and warm enough that we wouldn't freeze.

CHAPTER 15

Amber

The light coming in from the window was brighter than usual. At first, I thought we had all slept in, but the clock on the wall read 6:30.

Like before, I still had the sense of peace and awe from being in the goddess's presence. Not even my parents had made me feel as loved as the goddess did when I was with her.

I was also weighed down by the other girls. Each girl clung to me somewhere. I didn't want to wake any of them. They deserved to have as much peace as I could provide. Who knew how long it would last?

I closed my eyes and relaxed. Eventually, I dozed off, only to be woken up by the smell of bacon. The girls all began their morning routine. They didn't fight, and it was tranquil as they cleaned themselves up. I stayed where I was, afraid to disturb the atmosphere in the room. No one seemed to mind that Tyler was in here; that was good because we needed to get him and Tyla out of the hall.

Once the kids left the room, I got myself dressed. The room was still peaceful when I walked out and into the kitchen. Ryan was at the stove, and Olivia handed Alice to me. "Your turn."

The stinky baby giggled in my arms. I carried Alice to the bathroom, where we had set up a changing station. I took care of Alice's dirty diaper and as I cleaned up the mess left behind, I realized that the baby wipe package was empty. I didn't remember Olivia mentioning wipes on our list of needs.

I got Alice dressed in clean clothes and then walked to the living area. "Add baby wipes to our shopping list."

Olivia went over to our grocery list and wrote it down. "I didn't think about it before, but now that you mention it, we had three packages of wipes in the basement."

Ryan came in and handed me a plate of bacon and eggs. "Three packs won't get us very far."

The dish smelled weird, but I took the plate anyway. "More powdered eggs and freezer-burned bacon."

My brother smiled and rubbed the back of of his neck. "I don't think I could ever be a picky eater again after being in hiding."

It made me chuckle as I remembered all the things he refused to eat when he was younger. "I remember when you would only eat peanut butter and jelly sandwiches."

Olivia smiled and pointed at Ryan. "Wasn't that last year?"

"Laugh all you want. I miss fresh home-cooked food," Ryan said.

Olivia smiled sympathetically. "Me too, I have an idea. Can you guys keep the pups occupied for a few hours?"

Willow had crept up behind me. "Can we go play in the snow?"

I jumped, making her and Alice laugh. "Willow!"

Josh walked in from the kitchen with a fresh baby bottle. "Can I feed Alice this time?" He'd done it once and was good with her, so I handed Alice to him and he took her to the couch.

I looked at Olivia. "Did it snow last night?" That would explain why the light from the window was so early.

Ryan gestured to the window. "How did you sleep through that storm? The wind kept me up last night. I measured six inches this morning."

"It would be a good way to keep the kids busy," I said, then looked at my sister. "After breakfast, Willow, we will all go out and play in the snow."

"We need to make sure they all have coats and boots," Olivia said.

"We can look through the boxes when everyone's done eating," Ryan said, then he walked over to Josh and helped him with Alice.

Olivia stepped into the kitchen, and Willow followed me to the table, where she sat in the chair next to mine. Across from us, Ellie poured herself a bowl of cereal.

"You don't want eggs?"

She shrugged. "I want something sweet." Then she looked down at her cookie cereal and poured the milk. None of us liked powdered milk but the more often we had it, the easier it was for us to drink.

Before I took a bite of my eggs, I noticed something odd on Ellie's spoon.

"Can I see that for a minute?" I asked.

She put down her spoon and looked at me, puzzled. I peered into her bowl, and strange-looking chocolate chips floated in the milk. They didn't look like the rest of the chocolate pieces. When I realized what it was, I gagged.

"Don't eat that." I took the bowl from her, gave her my plate, and then dumped the bowl into the trash.

Ellie got stood up with tears forming in her eyes. "Amber, what are you doing?"

I returned to the table and picked up the bag of cereal. Olivia looked up from what she was doing. "Amber, why are you wasting cereal?"

I threw the bag into the trashcan and signaled her to the pantry. Olivia gave me a worried look as she followed me down the stairs to the basement. Ellie was still crying after I left her without explaining why I threw her breakfast away. I would make it up to her later.

"Amber, what is going on?" Olivia asked.

When we got to the bottom of the stairs, I explained. "There were mouse droppings in Ellie's cereal bowl. We need to inspect the rest of the food."

"Ew, gross." Olivia gagged and then shuddered. "I do not want to come across a mouse or, worse, a rat."

I began looking on the shelves for our mouse traps. When I found them, I also saw bigger traps, so I grabbed those too.

"Help me with these." I handed Olivia a pack of mouse traps, then grabbed a jar of peanut butter. Most people think you need cheese to catch a mouse, but peanut butter works better. Rats, on the other hand, like meat, preferably fish.

"Are we out of tuna?" I asked as I searched the shelves for the cans. "Nope, I found them." I had just grabbed a small can when I heard Ryan coming down the stairs.

"What are you two doing? Ellie won't stop crying."

I looked at my brother on the stairs. "Bring me a can opener."

He stopped halfway down the steps, turned, and went back up. Olivia tapped my shoulder, and I looked over at her. She was staring wide-eyed as she pointed to one of the bags of rice. I noticed a good-sized hole in the bottom, and grains of rice on the surrounding floor.

"I heard something," Olivia said.

I walked over, but Olivia pulled me back before I got too far away.

I turned and looked at her. "You're a wolf."

She looked at me as if that shouldn't matter. "So?"

"You scared an entire hibernaculum of western rattlesnakes. Are you telling me you're afraid of a little mouse?"

"Don't judge me."

Smiling, I rolled my eyes and tried to walk away to investigate the bag of rice. Olivia pulled me back again, so I freed my arm, and she clung to my shirt. I walked towards the bag. Ryan was halfway down the stairs when I got to the rice. Slowly, I touched the edge of the bag. It flew open, and two giant rats jumped out.

Olivia screamed, so I screamed. It all surprised Ryan, who lost his footing and slid down the stairs to the floor. The rats went running in different directions. One of them scurried over to Ryan, who backed away.

"Stomp on it!" I shouted at him.

Ryan got up and lunged at the rat before it got too far from him. The other rat came at Olivia, who squealed and jumped out of the rat's way as it ran under the shelving unit.

The basement door was left open, so all the kids heard the chaos. Willow and Ellie were at the top of the stairs as Ryan and I cornered the rat under the shelf.

It ran at Ryan since he was closer. "Ah!" Ryan yelled and jumped away, making Olivia, Willow, and Ellie scream.

The rodent then ran away from Ryan, too fast for me to catch. He ran straight for Olivia, and climbed her leg. She shrieked and kicked it off. The rat flew across the room, and his little body twisted as he landed on his feet.

I was about to stomp on it when Willow shouted, "No, Amber!"

Instead I jumped and landed on my stomach as I trapped the rat in my hands. The little rodent bit me a few times as he tried to get away, but I picked it up by his tail and then held it by the ribs.

The rat bit me again, and it hurt. His little rat claws did damage, too. I began looking for a bucket or something to put him in. Ellie and Willow came running down the stairs.

Ellie's eyes were still red and puffy. "What are you going to do with it?"

"We can't keep it," I said, knowing what my sister was thinking.

Willow's eyes filled with tears. "What are you going to do?"

Ryan knelt beside her. "Willow, if we keep the rat, it will eat all of our food."

Willow shrugged. "I don't want to stay here anyway."

"It isn't safe to leave yet," Olivia said.

"And the snow needs to melt some more before we can leave," Ryan added.

Willow's eyes welled up with tears as she looked between us. "The rat was just hungry! He won't eat much, and we have enough to share!"

Olivia said, "Rats eat a lot."

Ellie looked around the room, and I wasn't sure what she was doing until she found one of the plastic totes with clothes in it. She dumped out the contents and brought it over to me. "Here."

My cousin pointed to the pile on the floor. "What are you going to do about that mess?"

Ellie shrugged. "They came from my house and don't fit."

Willow walked over to the clothes and began picking out some things. Ellie held the plastic box while Willow put in one sneaker, a T-shirt, and a fuzzy coat.

I knew what they were going to do. This wasn't the first time. "This rat is a wild animal, and rats carry diseases."

"That's not his fault," Willow said.

"Willow, look at how this guy is fighting me," I said as the rat continued trying to get out of my grip. My fingers were now bloody from all the scratches and bite marks.

"You would too if someone held you like that," Willow snapped.

Well, she had a point. I moved my hands to gain more control of the rat, and my fingers went around his neck.

"NO, don't kill it!"

Before I could do anything else, Willow ran up to me, took the rat, and ran up the stairs. Ellie followed her as the three of us realized we lost to a five year old.

Ryan pointed to the dead rat on the floor. "What do we do with that one?"

I sighed. "I guess we give it a funeral; Willow won't be happy any other way."

"A funeral for a rat?" Olivia asked.

I gestured up the stairs where my sister had gone. "Do you have any better ideas?"

"Put it in the trash."

Ryan looked at her and grinned. "You can explain to Willow what happened to it then."

Olivia groaned. "Fine."

I went up the stairs to wash my hands. The water stung and I hissed. After that, I put antibiotic ointment and bandages on my fingers and hands. I noticed that all the pups had gathered in the living room and were hovering over the plastic tote.

"What are we going to name it?" Tyler asked.

"Why are we keeping a wild rat?" Josh asked. He was still holding Alice, who was content in his arms.

Ellie wiped away a tear, "Because he doesn't have a home… Just like us."

CHAPTER 16

Amber

Olivia, Ryan, and I were cleaning the basement. Olivia looked in the bag of rice the rats had jumped out of; "Ew, this rice has droppings in it." She moved it away from her as she scrunched up her face.

Ryan held out his hand, and she gave him the bag. "I'll take it."

I looked at our growing pile of trash. "How much have we lost?"

Ryan added our cereal to the top and wiped his hand on his pants. "All three cereal bags had droppings, and I found a mouse in one. Don't tell Willow."

"Is that why you smacked the bag?" I asked. He nodded.

Olivia shook out a trash bag and began loading it up. "Three bags of cereal, a container of oats, and one bag of rice? It could have been worse."

I continued to look through our shelves. "Do we have enough eggs to last?"

Ryan moved cans around on the shelf next to him. "No."

Olivia tied off her bag and set it down by the stairs. "I guess my plan to make homemade bread is out."

"Is that why you wanted us to keep the kids occupied?" I asked.

"Yeah, I thought it would cheer everyone up."

I smiled reassuringly at her. "We'll find something else."

Ryan grabbed four cans of food off the shelf and added them to the new trash bag. "We will have to get creative with our meals now."

I picked up a jar of cherries and checked the expiration date. They had expired two months ago. "No," I sighed. "We need to leave as soon as possible." I added the jars to the extra bag.

Ryan went back to the shelf he was working on. "What about Benson?"

"We can get past him. If we let Benson scare us into staying here, things will only get worse for us."

Olivia examined the contents of one freezer. "I don't want to stay either, but I have a bad feeling about leaving."

"Did you have a dream about Benson?"

She closed the door and faced us. "No, but my dreams are changing. I don't know which one is accurate."

I stopped what I was doing when I heard the tremor in her voice. "What was your latest one?"

Olivia was quiet. A tear ran down her face, which she quickly wiped away.

I walked over to her and put my arm around her. "What happened?"

She shook her head and sobbed. I wrapped my arms around her, and Ryan came over and rubbed her back. I had a huge burden to carry, but I couldn't imagine reliving potential futures as often as Olivia does.

"We were too late; they all died," Olivia said. "That was two nights ago. Then, last night, it was the same as the first dream. Our parents lived, so I don't know what to believe now."

Ryan continued to rub her back. "Maybe we just have to make a decision."

I released my cousin, and she wiped her eyes. "Yeah, maybe your dreams are changing because we can't decide what to do."

Olivia nodded her head. "Sage said the same thing this morning."

"Does she have any suggestions?"

"She said we should plan for one thing and see what my dream is that night. We focus on that option and see if it leads down the path we want."

"I think we need to plan to leave now," Ryan said.

I nodded. "I agree."

Olivia shook her head. "Deputy Benson…."

I placed my finger on her lips. "Is one human I can handle."

"What about the last time you were around him?" Ryan asked.

"I admit, he was intimidating; I don't want to get arrested. What would happen to all of you if I was; but, once we leave, I will do whatever it takes to make sure you get to Alpha Cole safely."

Olivia's voice was stronger and her eyes were dry. "I don't like you risking your life, that needs to be our last option."

I sighed, wishing there were better options. A lump formed in my throat. "I've looked at every different scenario and haven't found one."

"What if we ask that FBI guy to keep Benson busy for a few hours?" Ryan suggested.

I smiled at my brother's term for Agent Hayes. "Benson is too careful, but maybe I can ask Jasper to get Benson to let his guard down."

"Who is Jasper?" Ryan asked me.

I held my fingers up and made air quotes. "That 'FBI guy.'"

He shrugged. "How would he do that?"

"I don't know, but I'll talk to him."

"When the snow melts, we will make arrangements to leave," Olivia said. We all agreed that we couldn't stay in the cabin much longer.

Ryan walked back to the trash and picked up the bag. He shook it, tied it off, and carried it upstairs.

Olivia and I finished what we were doing and left the basement with the bag by the stairs. This also included the clothes Ellie told us to get rid of. She didn't fit into any of it and didn't need them for the rat they were all still trying to name. I think he had nine different names in the last hour.

As I locked the basement door, I thought about the other things we hadn't checked yet. Using that tote for the rat had cleared some clutter. Olivia studied my face and waited for me to speak. "I think we should go through the rest of the clothes here and burn the ones that don't fit the pups."

She agreed. "We'll need to go through each tote with the pups."

"Any extra totes we can use to transport food and important items when we leave," I suggested. We agreed that after the funeral for the rat Ryan killed, we would come back and consolidate the clothes.

I let Olivia take the trash bag while I washed my hands and picked up the baby monitor from the kitchen counter. I clipped it to my back pocket, then checked on Alice, who was asleep in her makeshift bed.

The pups had gathered around the burn barrel on the north side of the cabin when I joined them. Olivia had placed our trash bag on top of the other bag, then joined the circle.

I stood between her and Willow with Ryan on the other side of our sister. The wind was cold and whipped my hair across my face.

Willow held a small tissue box. I recognized it and shook my head as I smiled. "Willow, did that box come from the living room?"

"Yeah," she looked down at the box, then up at me with glassy eyes, "but I stacked the tissues on the table nicely."

"I helped," Tyla added.

I had just opened that box three days ago. It was still full. Ryan leaned over and whispered, "It was our last box of tissues."

Willow scrunched her little face at him. "I wouldn't have had to use it if you hadn't killed Hatty in the first place!"

"Hatty?" Olivia asked.

"That's what Tyla named the rat in the box," Josh said.

"You mean the dead rat?"

"Shut up, Michael!" Willow yelled.

Michael lifted his hands and looked at Willow in disbelief. "What did I do?"

"All right, that's enough. The rat, Hatty, is gone, and this is all that's left for us to do. Willow, place Hatty on the pile." I instructed.

"Why are we putting her on the trash? She deserves better," Willow protested.

Ryan put his hand on her back. "With all of the snow, this is the best option for a fire."

Willow reluctantly walked forward and placed the box on top of the trash. I looked at my brother and nodded. "Ryan, light the fire." This was the best place to burn our spoiled food. Hopefully, the smoke wouldn't attract unwanted attention.

He stepped forward, struck a match, and lit the box on fire. Olivia looked around as if she was concerned about something. I gave her a curious look, and she shook her head.

I turned my attention back to my sister. "Willow, do you want to say anything?"

She took a big shaky breath. "Moon goddess, please accept Hatty into your realm and give her a place to make her happy."

I realized it wasn't the moon goddess who would receive Hatty, since she wasn't a shapeshifter.

I placed my hand on her shoulder. "Willow, start again." She looked at me, confused. "Hatty wasn't a shapeshifter, so Pan would be the one to receive her spirit."

Willow thought about it. Olivia gave me that same calculating look that she did last night.

Ryan looked as confused as Willow. "What does it matter?" Ryan asked.

Olivia narrowed her eyes. "Who's Pan?" My heart sped up; I knew she was testing me, but I stayed calm as I focused on my little sister.

Willow repeated her prayer and changed it as I had instructed. "Pan, please accept Hatty into your realm and give her a place to make her happy."

I felt the calm approval from somewhere deep within me. **_It is done, little one._**

Hearing Pan's small confirmation gave me goosebumps, and I felt tears sting my eyes. I blinked them away before anyone would notice.

"It is done," I whispered to Willow. She smiled before reaching for me to pick her up.

"Thank you, Amber," Willow said as she laid her head on my shoulder. The fire engulfed the box with Hatty inside. The wind changed directions, making the smoke come towards us. Willow and I coughed as I waved it away.

"Whoa! What was that?" Josh pointed behind me in the distance. All the kids looked up to where he was pointing. Olivia began to growl. I couldn't see anything.

"It's an intruder," Olivia said.

Ryan squinted his eyes, "It looks… like… it's hard to tell."

"What do you smell?" I asked Olivia.

"The smoke is confusing my senses; I don't know exactly. I want to say a wolf, but I can't be sure."

"I don't see anything; what is it, Josh?" I asked.

"It almost looked like a wolf, but all I saw were it's eyes. They were bright blue."

"What color was its fur?" Ryan asked.

"I couldn't tell; all I saw were the eyes and maybe a black nose." Josh squinted as he looked into the distance. I tried following his line of sight, but didn't see anything.

"I'll take care of it," Olivia said as she began to walk away. I held Willow with one arm and used the other to reach for Olivia.

"Not today," I whispered. Olivia glared at me, and I shook my head. She yanked her arm away and went into the cabin.

Ryan began herding the pups towards the cabin. "We should all go inside."

The fire had died down enough that we weren't worried about it spreading. I helped Ryan with the pups, but they were all excited about what Josh saw, even Willow. I put her down, and she ran over to Ellie and Tyla.

I heard a whistle and saw Olivia and Ryan by the pantry door. I was walking towards them when we heard Alice from the baby monitor.

"I got her," Josh said as he ran to Alice's bedroom.

"I told him to take care of Alice when she woke up so the three of us could talk." Olivia still looked upset. She nodded towards the basement, and I walked down with them.

As we sorted the clothes, Olivia would sigh or huff.

"You might as well get it out now," I said.

"Why did you stop me?"

"Because it wasn't a threat to us."

"How do you know?" Ryan asked. "None of us saw it."

I looked directly at my cousin. "You said it was a wolf?"

"I said it might be; the smoke made it hard to tell."

"It could have been Jasper or Zane. I know they're both here and doing all they can to help us."

Olivia gestured with her hand towards the hillside on the other side of the wall. "How can you be so sure?"

"I don't know, but we have to trust someone. We won't get anywhere if all we do is chase off anyone who tries to help. What if we run off the person who could help us find the pack before we lose them all?"

Olivia narrowed her eyes at me and then turned her head.

Ryan saw this as an excellent time to change the subject. "Who's Pan?"

I stopped sorting the shoes in Michael's bin and looked up at him. "He's the god of the wild and the keeper of the Forest of the Gods."

"Why haven't we heard of him before?"

I placed two baby shoes on the floor next to me. "I don't know."

"How did you hear about him?"

I took a deep breath, remembering the goddess advising me to open up to Ryan and Olivia.

I looked them both in the eye and my heart raced as I came clean. "I've met him."

Olivia dropped the shirt she was folding and looked over at me. Her eyes filled with tears, and her voice was soft. "You mean, three years ago? When you were in that human hospital?"

I shook my head, "No." I didn't want to talk about the time a human had tried to kill me. He was mad because I wouldn't give him what he wanted.

"You don't smell like you've merged; how could you have met Pan?" Olivia asked.

Ryan raised an eyebrow. Their sympathy from before returned to suspicion. My heart pounded in my chest; I could feel heat in my cheeks. They must be as red as tomatoes.

My voice shook as I continued to explain. "The first night here, I had a dream. At least, I think that's what it was. Pan welcomed me into the Sacred Forest. I also met the Moon Goddess."

Olivia's eyes were wide, and instead of folding the shirt in her hands, she wadded it up. "That's not possible… but it explains how you knew what the goddess looked like."

"You've met her too?" I asked.

"Everyone meets the Moon Goddess when they merge. I had forgotten what she looked like until you described her."

"Why, though? Why did you meet her?" Ryan asked. "It would have made sense three years ago when you were on life support, but not now."

This was the part that made my heart race; I was afraid they'd think I was crazy. I took a deep breath and confessed. "I'm the White Luna. I didn't want to talk about it before, because I was afraid you wouldn't believe me."

Ryan raised an eyebrow and then shared a look with Olivia before he responded. "You have to admit, Amber, it's a bit far-fetched."

He wasn't wrong. Olivia got up from the tote we were sorting and paced as she chewed on her thumbnail.

"I can't…." Olivia shook her head. "If what you are saying is true, then what does it mean for our pack?"

I could see the vein in her neck pulsating, and her response was exactly what I had been afraid of. My heart fell to my stomach, my throat burned, and my eyes stung. "What does Sage say?"

Olivia shook her head, but her eyes gave her away. They flickered from blue to green. She shook her head and refused to answer me. I wish I knew what Sage was telling her.

I set down the socks I was folding and stood up. "I know you're worried about the pack, so am I. But who I am has nothing to do with what happened."

Olivia spun around and faced me, her eyes wild and glassy as she spoke. "Doesn't it, though? You know the legend as well as I do. 'When tragedy strikes, the White Luna will begin her journey.' Amber, if you are the White Luna, then our pack is doomed!"

My stomach was in knots. It was one thing not to believe me, but it was another to make this accusation. "That's not what the story means."

Ryan's eyes were now welling with tears. "Then what does it mean? We lost our pack, and you have been talking nonsense."

Nonsense? It was as if his words stabbed me in the heart. Ryan has always had my back. He's never doubted me… until now.

I felt like my world was caving in. My body shook as I tried to reason with the only people I trusted in this world. "What about you, Olivia? You were home for a whole day, knew about the attack, and avoided me. We could have saved everyone if you hadn't been so stubborn!"

"That's not fair! You can't put that on me. Your parents ordered me not to say anything."

I glared at her as I balled my hands into fists. Tears streamed free from my face. "We have never kept secrets. You have always come to me first. You could have told me before you went to my dad. It wouldn't have been the first time."

Olivia took a step back. "I was still trying to understand the dream. I didn't know it was going to lead to an attack. Be reasonable, Amber. You're upset that we didn't believe your story about you being the White Luna, so now you're making accusations at me."

Ryan walked towards me and put his hand on my shoulder. "Come on, Amber. You don't have to pretend with us. Olivia's right; if Dad ordered her not to say anything to you, he had a reason for it. There's no need to act like this."

I couldn't stay down here. I couldn't look at either of them. I knew there was a chance they wouldn't believe me, but I wasn't expecting this. My chest tightened, and my eyes burned. I shook off Ryan's hand and ran up the stairs into my room, where I closed the door behind me. I didn't want to be around anyone.

CHAPTER 17

Amber

There was a soft knock on my door and Willow walked in. She came over to my bed and stroked my hair. "Are you okay, Amber?"

I sat up and smiled at her. "I will be."

It wasn't a lie. I may not be okay now, but when I'm ready, I will pull myself together and rescue my pack. I'm no help to anyone like this.

Willow climbed up and sat with me. "What happened?"

I put my arm around her and hugged her. "Nothing you need to worry about."

"Olivia says it's time for dinner."

"Have I been here that long?"

Willow nodded and laced her fingers with mine. "You missed lunch."

My stomach and chest still hurt. "I'm not hungry. Will you tell Olivia to start without me?"

Willow nodded, and went to the door, then returned to give me a hug. "Amber, thank you for helping me. I know it was your idea for Hatty's funeral. She didn't deserve to die."

I smiled and held my sister tight. She has always been tender about animals. This wasn't our first time having mice or rats in the basement. Even in the pack house, we had issues. My parents always caught the mice and disposed of them before Willow found out.

She was right about one thing, though. "You're welcome. I know she didn't deserve it, but it's better than starving to death in the snow. We couldn't have fed her, and if we had released her back into the wild where she belonged, she would have either died or come back, and we would have lost more food."

Willow's eyes filled with tears, and she sniffed. "It's not fair, and the other rat is hurt, too."

"It is?"

Willow left and came back with the tote. She took the lid off and placed her hand inside. The rat limped over and sniffed her hand before letting her pick him up. She cooed at him, and he squeaked at her as she brought him over to me. When I reached for him, he bit me, and I withdrew my hand.

"You deserved that," Willow said.

"He's never going to trust me, is he?"

"Would you trust you after what you did to him?"

I grinned. "I guess not."

I looked at the rodent's legs as Willow held him. Sure enough, the rat's left front leg was broken. "There's nothing we can do for his leg; it will heal on its own. All we can do is make him comfortable."

Something about this conversation made me think about my parents. Humans took our pack, are torturing, and probably killing them. I'm sure scaring the rats like Olivia and I did and then killing the one isn't much different. The rats just wanted to survive.

Then again, rats carry diseases. They also multiply quickly. They leave poop everywhere, and we have to throw away food and wash surfaces after the rats have touched it.

Shapeshifters live like humans. We want to survive this life just like humans do. We hold jobs and volunteer in our communities. We live in houses, cook, and clean the way humans do. We don't believe in waste, at least not in my pack. We always used the food we had.

"It isn't the same for the rats as it is for us," I said. Willow looked at me curiously. "You are right; Hatty didn't deserve to die, but we didn't kill her unnecessarily."

A tear ran down Willow's cheek. "An animal should only be killed if it's food for another animal."

"There's more to the law of the forest: Kill to eat or to defend oneself. Kill quickly and honor the web of life." Willow recited the last part with me. The law of the forest is something we are taught and live by from the time we are young.

Willow pouted. "You didn't do any of that when you told Ryan to stomp on Hatty."

I reach up and brushed a strand of hair off her face. "It was a quick death, and we were defending our livelihood in the cabin. Most animals will kill other animals when their homes are threatened. We saw Hatty as a threat to our food supply; if we had released her somewhere else, she would have ended up as prey for another animal."

"That's honoring the web of life; it would have been better for her to die in the forest than our basement." Willow had a better understanding of the law of the forest than anyone I knew, and she was only five.

"How about I make a deal with you? If we catch any more mice or rats, they will get released into the forest when the snow melts, and they have a better chance at survival," I said.

Willow held her pinky finger up for me. "Deal, but what about this guy? Can we help him?"

I linked my pinky with hers and we shook. "We can wait until his leg heals." Still holding the rat, Willow hugged me, then let go and tried to pull me off the bed.

"Where are you taking me?"

"You need to eat."

I got up and let Willow drag me to the dining room. Olivia didn't make eye contact, and Ryan looked uncomfortable with me in the room. Maybe I shouldn't have told them the truth.

"Willow, get that rat out of the kitchen," Olivia said.

At first, I wasn't sure who she was talking about, me or the rodent. Willow let go of my hand and took her rat to the tote.

"Squirt, we need to come up with a better name than 'The Rat,' I said as she left the room.

"Can we name it Bear?" Michael asked from the living room. He was sitting with the other children.

"You don't give a rat a name like Bear," Josh said. "Shu Nian is better; it fits his lineage."

"Lineage?" Ryan asked him.

"Yeah," Josh continued. "Rats are sacred in China; they're considered intelligent and hardworking."

Ellie was sitting on the floor, she rested her elbow on her leg then put her cheek on her fist. "Here he goes again," she sighed.

Michael rolled his eyes. "This isn't China. It's Colorado."

I walked into the living room to join the others. "What would you name the rat, Ellie?"

She lifted her head and smiled. "Brownie."

"Not bad; what about Mr. Rat?" Ryan suggested. "It's at least a little dignified."

"It's better than 'The Rat,'" I said.

Tyla began bouncing in place with excitement. "I like Patty."

Tyler rolled his eyes at his twin sister. "If you are going to name it Patty, you might as well go with Ratty."

"You could put them together," I suggested. "Or you could call him George."

Willow walked back in carrying the tote, but the rat was now on her shoulder. "What if we named him Miko?"

"Austin is a good name." asked Olivia.

I smiled at her suggestion, then at the rest of the pups. "Let's put it to a vote."

"You're just going to take charge now?" Olivia asked. She looked annoyed at me.

"Amber is a future Luna," Willow said quietly.

"You never know; I could be, too," Olivia said. Her statement cut deep. We had always talked about her being my Beta.

I realized that I was alone until I met my mate. Suddenly, I felt this voice, and I knew it was from my wolf, Emerald.

It doesn't have to be that way. In time, you will know what to do.

Ryan spoke up as he walked over from the table carrying Alice. "That may be true, Olivia, but since that hasn't happened, Amber is the highest-ranking wolf here." He still wouldn't make eye contact with me.

I threw my hands up, not wanting an argument. "Enough. After dinner, we will vote on the rat's name."

"Most of us have already eaten," Ellie said.

I walked out of the dining room and into the living room. "Oh, well then… everyone, get into a circle."

All the pups sat in a circle with Willow and the rat in the middle. I listed the suggested names, and we voted on Josh's name first. It wasn't surprising that no one wanted Shu Nian. Austin didn't any votes either.

"Who wants, Miko?"

Three hands went up.

"George?"

Seven hands went up.

"You can't vote twice," Michael complained to Willow.

"Why not?" she asked.

"It won't be fair," Michael said.

Ryan held up his hand to quiet them. "Tell you what? If we have a tie, we can re-vote the two names." Michael shrugged and nodded.

"Brownie?" I asked.

Five hands went up.

"Bear?"

Michael raised his hand, and so did Ellie.

"Ratty?" I asked. Willow, Tyla, Tyler, Ryan, Ellie, Olivia, and I all raised our hands. Josh and Michael eventually raised their hands, too. As I finished the tally, the other kids raised their hands, and Ryan raised Alice's little arm, making us laugh. It was unanimous.

"I guess the rat is now Ratty," I said.

Tyler puffed up with pride and moved closer to Willow, "Hi, Ratty, I named you."

Tyla put her hand over her mouth as she giggled. "What if we called him Ratty Patty?"

"I think that's cute," Ellie said, "Ratty Patty."

"That can be a nickname," Willow said very seriously.

The room filled with laughter as Ratty scampered on three legs between the kids. Even with his broken leg, he looked happy around the pups. They all enjoyed having him around. Who knew that a rat, of all things, could make the mood in the cabin lighter?

I noticed that he always returned to Willow; she didn't have to do much to get him to stay with her. He never tried to run away, not that he could. Hopefully, Willow could let him go when the time came.

I went to the kitchen and grabbed some chicken soup while the kids, Olivia and Ryan played with Ratty. As I ate my dinner at the table, I thought about how crazy this day had been. It had only been one day, but it felt like an entire week.

My destiny was like a heavy burden; but after seeing what I could do for Willow and the peace she gained from my gift, the responsibility felt worth it.

The pups' laughter and seeing them happy strengthened my resolve. Olivia and Ryan's denial still hurt, and I wasn't okay yet, but I would be. The burden of my fate felt more bearable. I wiped away a tear before anyone could see it.

I will fulfill my responsibility as the White Luna with or without Olivia as my beta, and I will begin by locating our pack. I will do whatever it takes to bring my pack home; but first, we have to leave this cabin.

CHAPTER 18

Caleb

The snow was deeper than I expected. It was unusual for us to get this much snow this late in the month. I was grateful to have it, though. When it was this cold out, snow could make things seem warmer. Keeping watch over the cabin was easier to bear with Apollo's thick fur coat as well.

Our first day in the forest was interesting. We heard yelling and crying coming from inside the cabin. At first, we thought someone had broken in. Apollo stayed downwind as we got closer, but we soon realized that there wasn't an intruder; it had something to do with breakfast.

When things calmed down, Apollo retreated to our spot on the small hill above the cabin. The trees and the snow kept us hidden, so no one saw us when they all came outside. At first, it was just a young man. He threw away full bags of cereal and a large bag of rice. Apollo and I weren't sure what was going on.

Why are they throwing away food?

I'm not sure, Apollo. Maybe they are preparing to leave.

We watched and an hour later, the kids trickled out. The young man from earlier came out with a little girl holding a tissue box. Then, the red-headed woman came out with Amber.

Amber whispered something to the little girl, who carefully placed the tissue box on top of the food and other trash. Everyone had gathered in a circle. Apollo crept closer to hear what was going on. We got as close as we dared without being seen. We heard the little girl's prayer and then Amber's correction.

How does she know about Pan? Most wolves don't.

From what I remember of Alpha William, he believed in the prophecy. I bet he told her.

She must have been the only one. Look at their expressions.

When we observed the older two with Amber, the young man looked doubtful, and the woman looked suspicious.

Then, one pup spotted Apollo, and we ducked down quickly into the bushes and watched. The redhead was ready to shift and look for us, but Amber stopped her. They all went inside, but we didn't want to move in case the red-haired woman came looking for Apollo. We didn't want to scare them any more than they already were.

The rest of the day was quiet, and we were safe from being discovered. But I had this overwhelming feeling that I should go to the cabin—to shift, knock on the door, and make my presence known. Someone in the cabin needed me; I didn't know who, and I didn't know why.

We can't risk it.

Why do I feel this way?

I feel it, too.

As we approached the cabin, I was ready to throw caution to the wind and just let them know we were there. Once again, Apollo advised against it.

If others learn of our existence before we have our mate, then we become a target.

I don't like this, Apollo. You know someone needs us right now; what if it's Amber? What if she's our mate?

There's no way to tell without a scent.

She was just out here; she's inside the cabin; how can you not catch her scent? Come on, Apollo, you are the most powerful wolf I know. Give me something.

Apollo stuck his nose in the air, then snorted.

We are too close to the smoke, and I'm not getting much of a scent around the cabin.

Apollo, that can't be right. We know Amber is here.

Caleb, you don't think clearly when it comes to Amber. We need to leave.

Apollo ran away from the cabin before we were discovered. I was so angry with my wolf that I wanted to shift and return to the cabin. When we reached the cave, Apollo refused to give me enough control to shift.

Apollo, you have never blocked me out like this.

You are too emotional at the moment. Caleb, your mind is always clouded when it comes to Amber. You are not ready to face her.

What are you talking about?

Caleb, you haven't even told Amber the truth. Are you ready for her reaction when she finds out you haven't been honest with her?

I thought about it, and he was right. I'd lied to Amber, and I knew her well enough to know that she would hate me when she learned I wasn't who she thought I was. I was a coward and I didn't know why I hadn't told her the truth. It was the only reason I hadn't returned to see her.

We stayed near the cabin until dark. Once the sun set, we retreated to our place on the hillside. We sat and watched the cabin as I thought of Amber.

I have to fix this, Apollo. Even if she isn't my mate, I have to fix this.

Then Amber needs to hear the truth. It would be better if you told her.

Do you think she will understand?

I think so, based on what I learned from your memories; but you must be the one to tell her.

Each day after that, as we continued to watch the cabin, the atmosphere became more tense. On the fourth day, we heard yelling as the red-haired woman and the young man came out of the cabin.

"Amber!"

"Amber, where are you?"

"Ryan, you check the shed; I'm going to the cave," the red-haired woman said. The young man, Ryan, ran to the shed while the woman went to some bushes nearby. Thankfully, they were on the other side of the cabin from me.

"Olivia!" Ryan ran over to the woman, Olivia, and kept his back to her as he told her what he found. "Amber took the truck. She's gone."

Amber's gone?

From what we have witnessed, she isn't one to abandon these pups. She will return.

Olivia came out of the bushes, and her eyes flickered as her wolf attempted to calm her down. "How could she just leave without telling us?"

"It's not like you guys have been on the best of terms," Ryan said.

"What about you? She still talks to you."

"Not that much; listen, Amber wouldn't just up and leave us. She's probably meeting with that FBI guy, Jasper."

Olivia pushed past Ryan. "I'm going back in; I can hear Alice crying. You stay here and wait for Amber." Ryan sighed as he sat on the steps of the cabin.

Should we look for Amber?

If she left in the truck, she would be difficult to track, and we would also have to leave the cabin just for her. If something happens while we are gone, we will have failed this mission.

If something happens to Amber when we are supposed to be keeping watch, that is also a failure.

If she is with Jasper, she is safe.

I needed to walk off my frustration. I hated not knowing where Amber was. Apollo understood my need and ran circles around the cabin and then down to the territory to see if she was close. There was no sign of her, so we went back to our usual watch point. We arrived just as Olivia came out with a baby on her hip.

"Did Willow come out here?" Olivia asked Ryan.

"I heard the back door, but I didn't see her," Ryan said. Just then, we heard a giggle next to us. Surprised, Apollo looked to our right, where we found a little brown-haired girl holding a rat. Apollo's stomach growled.

The rat isn't food. Look how she's holding it.

"Who are you?" Apollo asked the little girl through a mind link, as that was the only way he could communicate.

"I'm Willow," she said and walked closer to us.

"It's dangerous to approach wolves you don't know."

"But I know who you are, and you're here to help us."

"How do you know that?"

"My sister told me. She's the smartest person I know."

"Who is your sister?"

"Her name is Amber. She's gone, but she promised to come back."

"Do you know where your sister went? Everyone seems to be worried about her."

"Yeah, she went to ask Agent Hayes for help; Amber says it's time to go."

"Go where?"

"Shadow Moon with Alpha Cole." Willow sat beside me, and Apollo kept eyeing the rat in her hands. Willow furrowed her eyebrows at him and shook her little finger, turned her body, and scrunched her little face. "No! Bad wolf. Ratty isn't food for you."

I laughed, even though the only one who could hear me was Apollo.

I told you.

Willow's a cute kid. Apollo whined, and our stomach growled again. He lay in the snow and watched the rat climb on Willow's shoulder. It chittered nervously at him, and Apollo responded by licking his lips.

"No," Willow scolded again. Apollo whined.

"I'm sorry, little one, I have had little to eat since I arrived. The cold has many animals still in hibernation."

Willow petted Apollo's fur. "I'm sorry it's been so hard for you. I can bring you a snack."

Apollo looked up at Ratty, who was still squeaking at him. He sighed and nuzzled Willow, making her giggle.

"Willow!" Ryan yelled from the cabin.

"I don't want my brother to find me," she said.

"Why not?"

"He and Olivia got into a fight with Amber."

"I'm sorry to hear that."

Willow sat with Apollo as Ryan searched for her. I felt terrible that she was sitting here while her brother searched. He seemed increasingly worried. Eventually, we lost track of him. The last time we saw Ryan, he was coming this way.

"Willow, what are you doing—" Ryan approached us and stopped mid-sentence as he looked closely at Apollo, then paused as he recognized my wolf's authority as a high-ranking alpha.

Ryan surprised us as he immediately took a knee for Apollo. "I'm sorry for intruding, Alpha. I was looking for my sister."

"You are not intruding, and your sister is safe."

Apollo bowed his head to Ryan. ***"You may rise."***

The young man looked nervous as he raised his head, but stayed on his knee.

"See Ryan? Amber was telling the truth," Willow said.

"I see that." he swallowed as his heartbeat increased, and tears filled his eyes.

"What is the matter, young alpha?"

The look on Ryan's face was something like regret. "My older sister told us a story; we thought that's all the White Alpha was, but… here you are."

We heard tires crunching the snow by the cabin. "We need to head back. Olivia is really upset with Amber for leaving. I need to stop them from fighting." Ryan placed his fist over his heart and bowed his head again. "Thank you, Alpha, for caring for my little sister and watching over us."

"Rise. I will continue to watch over you until you leave for Shadow Moon." Apollo said, bowing his head and letting Ryan up again.

Willow did not take a knee for us or bow her head. We didn't mind. She was cute. It wasn't out of disloyalty. She's an innocent child.

Willow left with Ryan, and Ratty chittered and squeaked at Apollo the whole way down the hill.

CHAPTER 19

Amber

The cabin no longer felt like a refuge. I felt more suffocated than anything. Olivia wouldn't talk to me unless it was about the pups, and Ryan spent most of his time with Josh outside, trying to clear the snow.

It had melted some, but not much, worsening my feeling of being trapped. But that wasn't as bad as when we felt the pain of our families. When we noticed the pups rubbing their chests and looking distressed, Olivia, Ryan, or I would take them into a separate room and sit with them until the pain passed.

I needed to find the pack. As often as we felt their suffering, I was worried about those who hadn't made it. Luckily, none of the pups had lost their parents, but the anticipation had everyone on edge because it was only a matter of time.

I wished I didn't feel so alone; we need to leave this cabin before it's too late to save anyone. Our parents, or us. The only one I have been able to talk to lately is Willow.

It was still early morning, and since the truck was a four-wheel drive, I knew it could get me down the road. I snuck out of the cabin before Olivia or Ryan could protest. The only one who saw me was Willow, but her only protest was that I wasn't taking her with me. I pulled out and drove down to the territory. Like before, my chest hurt, and I wanted to vomit at the sight of the burned homes.

I drove out of the gate and down the road, up the highway and through town, to the Court Yard Diner where I knew Jasper would be.

I was right; he got out of a car near the door when I arrived. I pulled into the spot next to him. When he saw my truck, he walked over to me. Zane seemed nervous as he looked around.

"What brought you back?" Jasper asked. "I was sure you would stay up at the cabin, and I wouldn't see you again."

"I changed my mind."

Jasper gave me a slight grin. "Good."

Zane smiled and nodded. "I see the spark of the person you were before this all started. It's good to see the old you coming back, Amber."

A cold wind hit my face and I shivered. "It's cold out here. Can we go inside?"

"Yes," Jasper said as he made room for me to walk past him. I met up with Zane, and Jasper walked behind us. I knew enough about security formations to know that Jasper and Zane were on high alert.

Placing my hand on Zane's shoulder, I whispered, "What is going on?"

"This place isn't safe," he whispered back.

"Then why are we still here?" I asked. We approached the door, and Zane opened it for me.

"We were hoping you would come back."

Jasper walked in after me, then stood in front of me. "What happened last time? You ran out so fast; I wasn't sure what I did to scare you."

A waitress approached us. "Three?"

Jasper smiled pleasantly at her. "Yes; thank you, Tina." She walked us to a familiar spot in the restaurant.

I followed her to the same booth as before and slid into the seat facing the door. Like last time, Zane sat next to me and Jasper sat across from me. "Do you sit here every time?"

"Sure, it makes it easier to find our table this way," Zane said, then he leaned in an whispered. "Eat breakfast with us, then we can go somewhere safe to talk."

I took a menu from Tina and asked her what the special was.

She smirked at me and said, "A large stack of pancakes with two scrambled eggs and your choice of bacon or sausage."

I returned the menu without looking at it. "I'll have a Denver omelet."

"What to drink?" she asked.

"Water is fine."

She took Jasper and Zane's orders and then walked away. I smiled as I noticed that neither of them ordered pancakes.

Jasper leaned forward with his hands clasped together on the table. "What brought you back?"

"I need help."

"We know. We've been waiting for you to ask."

Zane cleared his throat and whispered. "Not here."

I looked up, and saw Jim watching us from his place at the counter.

I tried to find another way to ask my question. "Have you made any progress on your case?"

Jasper didn't answer. Tina brought over our drinks. The men were pleasant, but they remained cautious until she left.

I folded my hands in my lap. "You guys don't have to put yourselves through this for me."

Zane turned his body to face mine, which was a feat in the small booth. "Yes, we do, Amber. I've known you for years. As far as I'm concerned, you're my family. I would never forgive myself if anything happened to you."

"I won't be the reason you get injured or worse."

Jasper snorted as he raised his water glass to his lips. "I knew you had a feisty side."

"The arrow wasn't enough of an indication?" Zane teased. Jasper blushed and looked away as he cleared his throat.

"The case has made some progress. We know Rose went north; we don't know how far," Jasper said, going back to my question and ignoring Zane. I made a show of placing a straw into my water as I sent a mind link.

"And my pack?"

Zane grabbed the sugar on my other side and sent a mind link of his own.

"We found footage indicating they were taken south." He poured the sugar into his coffee, and Jasper handed him the creamer.

I sat there thinking. Why would Rose be separated from the pack?

"None of this makes sense," I whispered. Jasper nodded his head once in agreement.

Tina brought us our breakfast, and I couldn't help but devour mine. It was much better than the freezer-burnt food we'd been eating lately. When Tina brought us our tickets, I sat there with mine. I hated depending on people, but I had no money for this meal.

"I don't mean to be presumptuous," I whispered.

Zane took the ticket out of my hand and smiled. "No need, I understand."

He paid for my omelet with his eggs and bacon. As we waited for Jasper to pay for his mushroom and swiss omelet, I noticed a new flag on the wall beside the register.

"What does the gray sun mean, Jim?" I asked. He handed Jasper his receipt and then gave me an arrogant smirk.

"It's for the Silver Suns, a group David Benson told me about. We believe in protecting humanity," Jim said as Zane paid for our meals.

I smiled genuinely. "That's a good thing to believe in; too many people are suffering out there." Jim didn't know what to think about my response. "All who suffer should be helped, don't you agree?"

"I do. About humans…" Jim began.

I stopped him mid sentence with a knowing look. "All people are important; no one should be left out just because they are different. You know that better than anyone, Jim." I remembered what my father had told me about Jim's past.

Jim didn't know what else to say, so he just nodded and gave me a regretful smile. Zane then walked me out, with Jasper at the front. The door opened, and Benson stood there acting friendly as he held the door for us.

"Soon," Benson whispered under his breath. Unlike last time, I wasn't afraid. I knew what I had to do, and I wouldn't let this bully keep me from rescuing my family. I walked past him as if he didn't matter.

Zane walked me to my truck and got in the passenger side. "Follow Jasper." We pulled out of the parking lot, and I followed Agent Hayes two blocks from the diner. Then, we turned into a motel parking lot.

Zane smiled as we got out of the truck. "There's someone who will be happy to see you." We walked into the room, but no one was there.

Jasper picked peeled a sticky note off of the mirror. "Lucas is following a lead; he'll be back tonight."

"What is the lead?" I asked.

Zane looked at a notebook on the table. "It looks like the license plate for the van Rose was in."

Jasper turned to me. "What do you need from us?"

I didn't want too stay long, so I settled by the wall. "I need help getting everyone out of the cabin."

Zane pulled out a chair at the table for me, as he sat down. "What kind of help?"

"I need someone to keep Benson busy while I lead them out of town. I don't want him to follow us north to Shadow Moon."

"Does Alpha Cole know you're coming?" Zane asked.

"I don't have a way to inform him," I reminded him.

"Right, I forgot. Sorry."

"When are you leaving?"

"As soon as possible, especially now that our food supply is in danger." That wasn't the whole truth, but I didn't want to worry them.

"What happened?" Jasper asked.

"We found rodents in our basement. They ate through our cereal and one of our bags of rice. Thankfully, that was all we lost."

"Rats?" Zane asked.

"After the snowstorm, we found two rats and a mouse in our basement. Two of them died, but Willow rescued one of the rats."

"You said you want out as soon as possible? Are you leaving now?" Zane asked.

"Not until I report to Olivia and Ryan."

Zane looked at me as if something was off but he didn't push it. Instead he asked. "You don't have a phone. How are we going to know when to distract Benson?"

"I will meet you at the diner on the morning I plan to leave."

Jasper folded his arms across his chest. "When?"

"Tomorrow, but wait for me to come to you first. That will give Olivia and Ryan time to get the kids ready."

"Then we will wait for you."

"If you don't show up, then we will hold off until the next day. Is there anything else you need from us?" Jasper asked.

"Our biggest obstacle is having enough room for everyone. Between our two vehicles, we can only fit eight, and we have fifteen," I responded. Jasper thought for a minute.

Zane nodded his approval. "I wish I could do more; King Varrick has me on strict orders to locate your father and the pack."

I nodded; there wasn't anyone else I wanted looking for them. "Thank you."

"I know that doesn't help you."

"It helps, and we are resourceful."

"I know you are," Zane smiled.

"I will try and have something ready for you by morning. Amber, what did you mean when you told Jim that he 'would know better than anyone'?" Jasper asked.

"Thank you. As for Jim, six years ago, doctors diagnosed him with liver disease. He needed a transplant. No one in town would help, and he didn't have any family."

"Why wouldn't anyone help him?"

"Jim was an alcoholic. He almost lost the diner, but it survived, unlike his marriage. Jim's wife couldn't take it anymore and left. People didn't want to risk giving up part of an organ to someone who was at risk of ruining it. He got the transplant from an anonymous donor… from someone in my pack."

"He got an organ from a shapeshifter?" Zane asked.

I nodded. "Jim's been sober ever since."

Jasper looked at him and said, "Once the organ leaves the body, it's as good as a human's. Better, since it's healthier thanks to our wolves."

"It seems ironic that Jim would join an organization as divisive as the Silver Suns," Zane said.

I shrugged. "Benson isn't someone to be trusted, but he is popular with most of the older generation in this town, like Jim and Tina. He does a lot for the community and he volunteers at the senior center on Wednesdays."

Jasper lifted an eyebrow at me. Obviously, they didn't know any of this, yet. "How do you know that?"

"My dad didn't trust him, so he had him followed. Two of our retired warriors kept tabs on him until we realized how predictable he was."

"Then I bet we can still find him there," Zane said.

I felt an overwhelming sense of anxiety. I had to focus when I realized that it was coming from Olivia.

I wrapped my arms around myself. "I've been gone too long."

"Don't the others know where you are?" Zane asked.

My face heated up as I tried to think about what to say. I didn't want to tell him too much. "Not this time. Olivia and I aren't speaking at the moment."

"Why not?" Zane asked; he looked worried.

"I don't have time to go into the details. I can explain another time." I left for the cabin before Zane could ask anything else.

Amber

I had never seen Olivia so angry. When I pulled up to the cabin, she was returning from the forest looking for Willow.

"Where have you been?" Olivia demanded.

I got out of the truck and closed the door. "I went for help; as soon as possible, we leave for Grand Junction."

"We haven't discussed this. You can't just make executive decisions like that, Amber!"

"I can when you refuse to talk to me. You know we can't stay here."

"When I refuse to talk to you? When have you tried to talk to me?"

She had a point there.

I placed my hands on my hips. "Would you have listened to me if I had?"

Olivia thought it over, then shrugged her shoulders and folded her arms. "I guess we'll never know, now, will we?"

"We leave Friday, latest; this isn't up for discussion."

I tried to walk past her, but she stopped me. She grabbed my arm, and her eyes flickered. "Where were you? I smell three wolves on you."

I picked up her hand gently and removed it from my arm. "I was with Jasper Hayes. Royal Beta Zane Ellis was also at the diner; he's here on orders from the king to locate our pack."

Olivia shook her head, her eyes still flickering from blue to green. "There's someone else, and Sage is going nuts; who was he?"

"There was no one, only those two."

Olivia's nostrils flared, it was like she had just snapped. "You're lying; I can smell him." I'd never seen her face this red. Her eyes were narrow, and her body rigid. She needed to calm down, but I didn't know if I could help her. I was still upset about being accused of lying, which made me angry.

"Who was it, Amber?" Olivia demanded.

"There was no one else!" I repeated for the last time. Olivia had tears in her eyes, and she went from rigid to defeated. I had nothing else to say to her. I hadn't been with any other wolves.

A tear ran down her face. "Why won't you tell me?"

I took a deep breath and tried to hold her, hoping it would calm her down, but she backed away and shook her head angrily at me. Then she swung out to slap me, but I caught her hand and held on to her.

I tried to focus on being calm, but she yanked her hand out of my grip and stormed off. Ryan came running down the hill with Willow right behind him and Ratty perched on her shoulder.

Ryan called out, "Olivia. Stop!"

She glared at him as she closed the door to the cabin.

"Where were you two?" I asked.

"I went looking for Willow, who ran off," Ryan said. He looked like he wanted to say more, but Willow interrupted with a big grin.

"We saw the White Alpha!"

Her statement caught me off guard; I hadn't thought he would be here. How would he even know about us? "Oh, I forgot, he's really hungry; I need to make him a snack." Willow scampered into the cabin before Ryan and I could stop her.

"What does she mean?" I asked. Ryan looked at the ground. Just like before, he was avoiding eye contact. "Ryan."

"I should go talk to Olivia," he mumbled, shoving his hands into his pockets.

Fine. If I had to get us out of here on my own, then that was what I would do. I needed to go down to the territory, but the thought of going in and out of those houses again made my stomach turn.

I gripped the keys tighter and turned back to the truck, but driving through the territory had been hard enough. The thought of walking through the destruction again made me nauseous. My head hurt, and I felt dizzy. I couldn't go. I needed to think of something else.

I walked slowly into the cabin. The kids were excited about something, and I could hear them in the kitchen. When I walked in, they were all making sandwiches, and peanut butter was everywhere.

"What are you guys doing in here?" I asked.

Willow had peanut butter on her nose and cheeks as she grinned at me. "The White Alpha is out there, and he's so hungry he almost ate Ratty."

Ellie was just as excited as she dipped the knife into the jam jar. "So we're making sandwiches for him to eat instead."

The White Alpha, as in my mate. He was close, and I wasn't ready to meet him. I couldn't help my curiosity, but these pups came first.

"Do not go out there alone," I told them.

"Will you go with us?" Willow asked. I had to stay focused. I worried that if I went I would get distracted from my responsibility of getting the pups to safety and locating my pack.

"It's my turn to take care of Alice. Talk to Ryan."

"Okay," Willow said happily. I found Josh with Alice on the floor playing with the bunny I'd grabbed when we left the packhouse.

"Thank you, Josh. You can take a break now," I picked Alice up, and she smiled at me.

She was getting better at holding her head up. She must be four months old now. Her head came forward, and she mouthed my nose. I giggled at her, and she pulled her head away from me and cooed. I turned her over and checked her diaper; it was clean, but she had drooled all over her clothes.

"I'm going to change her," I said. Josh nodded and went to the couch while I walked into the hall. As I came close to the bedrooms, I overheard Ryan and Olivia talking.

"I'm telling you, Livy. Amber was telling the truth. I saw the White Alpha with my own eyes," Ryan whispered. I was frozen in place. Alice looked at me curiously, and I smiled at her.

Olivia sobbed and I peeked in to see her head on Ryan's shoulder. "I always knew Amber wasn't lying. Sage told me she was telling the truth. I'm scared of what it means. I don't want to be at war. I don't want to lose our pack. Why did this have to happen to us?"

"What does that have to do with Amber being the White Luna?" Ryan asked.

I knew I shouldn't eavesdrop, but I also wanted to hear her answer.

"If Amber is who she says she is, then this war is so much closer to us. I don't know if I have it in me to fight. I always thought we would lead a small pack somewhere away from all the violence. Why do we have to lead our kind into battle?"

Now I realized that she feared the war and losing our family more than anything. I should have known fear fueled her doubt. I won't ask her to fight if she wants to avoid the battle.

I walked into my room and the bathroom that had Alice's clothes in it. I changed her out of her onesie and put on a dry one. Ryan knocked on the door.

"Uh…." Ryan shoved his hands into his pockets and looked down.

I picked Alice up and walked over to him. "What do you need, Ryan?" Again, he looked like he didn't know what to say. I was getting tired of this.

He stared at the floor as if it would save him. "Do you have the keys to the truck?"

That wasn't what he was going to ask and we both knew it. I rolled my eyes, pulled the keys out of my pocket, and put them into his hand, then, walked past him.

"Amber…." he said. I turned, not knowing what to expect, but he clammed up again and shook his head.

I shifted Alice on my hip as I held up my other hand. "Let me know when you finally get the guts to tell me what you want to say." Then I walked into the kitchen where Josh was cleaning up.

"Where are the rest of the pups?"

He shrugged. "They went outside."

"I told them not to go alone," I said.

"That's why they all went together."

My heart rate picked up, and I was afraid something would happen to them. "Ryan! Olivia!" I shouted, making Alice cry. I rubbed gentle circles on her back to calm her down as the other two ran into the kitchen.

"The kids are gone."

"Why weren't you watching them?" Olivia shouted.

Ryan punched her shoulder. I was sick of their secrets. I'd told them mine; I no longer had anything to hide, so I wished they would give me the same respect.

"I think I know where they went." Ryan ran out the door, leaving me with Olivia, Alice, and Josh.

Josh looked between us and threw down the sponge he used to clean the counter. "You two need to kiss and make up; your fighting has gone on long enough."

Coming from a fourteen-year-old, that said a lot. I was sure our argument had made things harder for everyone.

"I'm sorry, Josh," I said.

"I should go help Ryan." Olivia walked past me and out the door without a glance.

Even though I understood she was just scared, her behavior stung. I took a breath and smiled at Josh.

"We should start lunch; everyone will be hungry when they return."

"You don't have to pretend with me, Amber. What Olivia just did was cold."

"She's scared."

"We all are, but that doesn't make it okay," Josh said. He was only fourteen, but he sounded so much older.

"I know. We'll work it out. Olivia and I always do."

An hour later, Josh and I had eaten lunch and fed Alice. I was putting her down for her nap when I heard the door.

Ryan brought the pups in, and they were all excited about something. Ryan was still having a hard time looking at me, so he distracted himself with the kids, getting them food and cleaning up.

"Where's Olivia?"

Ryan shrugged. "Haven't seen her, isn't she here?"

"She said she was going to help you."

"Maybe she shifted and went for a run. Olivia was pretty shaken up after you got back."

"I still don't know why."

"She didn't tell you?" Ryan asked. He got up and pulled me over to the pantry. "Olivia told you she smelled three wolves on you. Right?"

"That's what this is about?"

"Humor me."

I sighed and shook my head, "Yeah, but I was only with two."

"Is there any other way she could have smelled the third wolf on you?"

"I guess. The diner wasn't a safe place to talk, so I went back to Jasper and Zane's motel room." I remembered what they had said. "Lucas was there. Actually, he wasn't because he was out following a lead up north. They expected him back tonight."

"Olivia is going to kill me for telling you this, but… Sage was going nuts over that third scent because she thinks he's her mate."

Everything made sense now. Olivia wasn't in her right mind. Now that she had the scent of her mate, it was the only thing that would calm her down, but Olivia's sense of duty would keep her here, and she wouldn't seek him out. It would only get worse for her.

CHAPTER 21

Amber

After my revelation about Olivia, I needed time to think, so I walked out to the shed. The sooner we left, the better, especially for my cousin; she deserves to be with her mate. I refocused my thoughts on getting us out of here.

The truck still had a full tank of gas and can hold three passengers in the cab. The Kia will hold five. I haven't seen how much gas is in the tank, and I didn't look when I brought it up here. We can still fit all the pups in the Kia if we squished them together. I didn't want anyone with me in the truck in case Benson arrested me.

I started thinking of ways to get all fifteen of us out of here when I heard the door, and Ryan joined me.

He was tentative before he said anything. "I know you're upset with me."

"Do you blame me?"

He played with the snow on the ground with his boot. "No, I doubted you, and I'm sorry, it's just a lot to process."

"Why doubt me now when I've always been truthful?"

"I don't know, I'm sorry," Ryan said. I didn't want to say anything yet, so I kept myself busy with the truck. "I get why you don't believe me; I'll prove it to you."

Ryan made eye contact with me before standing up straight, bowing his head, placing his fist over his heart, and taking a knee for me. My cheeks felt hot as I looked around, hoping no one was looking.

This was weird. "Get up," I said.

Ryan stayed on his knee and declared, "Amber, I'm sorry, and just as the White Alpha is doing his part in searching for our pack, I know you will, too. I, Ryan Cahill, pledge my loyalty, promise to trust you, and always follow you whether we are in the same pack or allied by blood."

I placed my fist over my heart, accepting his promise. "That's great; now get up before someone sees you." Ryan stood up and hugged me. As much as I disliked the attention, his pledge meant the world to me.

When we parted, he cleared his throat and shoved his hands into his pockets. "I heard you want to leave before Friday."

"Yep."

"That doesn't give us much time."

"We can't stay here, Ryan. The cabin feels like a prison."

"Especially now for Olivia. She's back, by the way."

"Where was she?"

"She never left the cabin; she was sitting in the Kia the whole time," Ryan said.

"Did she try to go after her mate?" I asked. Ryan shook his head. The pain she must be feeling right now had to be unbearable. At least for me, I wouldn't be as affected without my wolf.

"How are we getting to Shadow Moon?" Ryan asked as he walked over and rested his arms on the truck bed.

"I'm still working on that; between the truck and the Kia, there is enough room for eight to sit comfortably."

"That leaves seven without a seat."

"Not if you hold Alice, and we double up the twins."

"That still leaves four without a place to sit." Ryan tapped the bed as he thought. "What will you do if Benson pulls you over while you have pups with you?"

"I don't know yet," I admitted.

"Will Agent Hayes help?"

"Yes, we can expect an hour before Benson realizes we're gone. I will meet him and Zane at the diner, and as soon as they see Benson, they will distract him while I get away," I explained.

"So we need to be ready to leave by the time you return," Ryan said.

"Yes, as many in the Kia as possible, plus everything else we need."

"Do you still plan to take another route?" he asked.

I nodded. "If we're late and Benson comes looking for me, then I want him to follow me instead of you."

"We'll keep the younger pups, and you can take Josh, Michael, and the older ones," Ryan said.

"If we do that, then we can use the truck bed."

"You'll get pulled over."

"We need a camper shell," Olivia suggested.

I looked over to find her on the edge of the porch. She still looked shaken up. I couldn't imagine her pain right now, which was probably why Alice was crying in her arms. I walked over and took the infant from her. Alice calmed down as soon as she rested her head against my shoulder.

Now that I had more information, I was more determined than ever to get us out of here.

"How do you do that?" Olivia asked. I shrugged, then placed my hand on her shoulder. She took a deep breath and relaxed. Tears came to her eyes, and she smiled at me. Then Olivia turned and glared at Ryan.

"You told her!"

"I had to. You disappeared, and before that, you were acting like a Harpy with caffeine withdrawals." I laughed at his random statement, and Olivia punched his shoulder.

"Ow," Ryan said as he rubbed the sore spot. For a moment, it was like things were almost normal. I looked back at the truck and thought about Olivia's suggestion.

"A camper shell would be suitable cover, but…." I couldn't admit that I didn't want to go back and see the destruction of our home.

"Ryan and I will go," Olivia said. I handed Alice to Ryan as I hugged Olivia.

She cried on my shoulder, "I'm sorry, Amber."

"Shh, I know," I said. "We'll get out of this cabin, and then you can find your mate."

Olivia sobbed harder and squeezed me tighter. Tears filled my eyes as I held my best friend. I wished I could take away her pain.

"I'll take Alice and let you two talk," Ryan said, then walked back into the cabin.

"How can you be so forgiving after everything I said to you?" Olivia cried.

"You're my cousin and my best friend. How can I stay mad when I know you are suffering like this?"

"It still wasn't right of me. I've had headaches from Sage since we first met Agent Hayes. She wouldn't tell me what was going on until this morning."

"You will have your chance to be with your mate, I promise."

Olivia began playing with a strand of hair. "You're my Luna; I can't leave you."

"I overheard you talking with Ryan. If you don't want to fight, I won't make you. You know that. You should be happy with your mate."

Olivia laughed through her tears, then put her hands on each side of my face. "You dummy, I'm afraid of fighting, but not as much as I am of losing you. If you died in a fight that I couldn't help you in, I would never forgive myself. I'm your beta. I will always have your back."

Tears fell from my eyes as I hugged my cousin again. "I've missed you."

"I missed you too."

We laughed and cried for a long time. My throat was sore, and my eyes hurt. Eventually, we climbed into the bed of the truck to talk. It was nice to have my best friend back. Even after everything, there wasn't anyone else I trusted more than Olivia.

"How are you so calm about being the White Luna?" she asked. "I freaked out at the thought of just being your beta."

"I think I'm still in shock. I don't know what to think about it, but I focus on what's needed of me: getting out of this cabin and rescuing our pack."

"We will. I know it," Olivia said. Then she looked nervous and deep in thought.

"Just ask."

She began playing with her hair again. "I know you said there were only two wolves with you, but do you have any hints as to who the other wolf was?"

"Yes, and I've met him before. A long time ago."

"Who?"

"Lucas, I didn't get a last name, but I'm pretty sure it was Lucas Barnes."

"Lucas Barnes, as in the beta of the wolf you have been obsessed with since you were fifteen?!"

"Yeah, I think I remember Caleb telling me that his beta is now a cop or something like that."

"No way. How can we trust anyone who doesn't have the decency to show their face to our pack after everything we did for them?" Olivia had never thought much of Caleb or Lucas since they broke their promise to return.

"Give him a chance. You deserve to be happy," I said.

"Who said he would make me happy? Carl Gallo was Lillian's mate, and he was terrible to her. She was miserable."

"True, but you won't know anything about Lucas if you don't give him a chance."

Olivia panicked. "I guess. Wait, if Lucas is my mate, what about you and Caleb? What if this means I'm not your beta after all?"

"Do you not remember that your dad became my dad's beta because of your mom?" I asked.

Olivia shrugged. "I guess."

"I still have a say over who my beta is, no matter what."

Olivia smiled and seemed more at ease. We continued to talk until Ryan came out.

"We need to leave now before we lose sunlight," he said.

I hugged Olivia, and then we got out of the truck bed. Olivia went to the bushes and shifted, then she and Ryan left to search for a truck shell. For a moment, things seemed normal again, but I knew it wouldn't last.

CHAPTER 22

Caleb

We weren't expecting Willow to return, let alone bring nine other pups with her. They were too precious to turn away. They all had food for Apollo to eat, and their generosity was touching.

We felt sleepy after Apollo ate the sandwiches made of freezer-burnt bread and old peanut butter, but the children were so excited to see us, that they began to play. The boys wrestled and sometimes would fall on top of Apollo. A peaceful contentment filled us as we shared that moment.

The girls wanted to sit and talk; some played with Apollo's fur, and we enjoyed the attention. Eventually, the girls joined the wrestling, and watching them all laugh and play was fun. We would never forget this moment. We didn't get any rest until Ryan came back and found them all wrestling around us.

When Ryan left with the pups, we walked back to the cave and napped. It felt good to have a full stomach. Movement by the cave startled us awake.

I don't recognize this scent.

Whoever they are, they're human.

This is what we were afraid of; humans finding the cabin and threatening the wolves. We thought of the pups, their innocence and joy. We won't let these humans near them.

Apollo growled. The movement stopped, and we followed the scent as it approached the cabin. We circled and found another unfamiliar scent. Apollo snarled, his fur raised and then we heard voices.

"Who's there?" the man said.

They were close enough that I could hear their hearts pounding in their chests and smell their sweat. Apollo is a powerful wolf. His commanding aura radiated around us, making the humans tremble, even though they couldn't see us.

One human fired a gun, and it was so loud our ears rang. Apollo let out a loud howl.

"I'll shoot again," the human said. His voice shook with fear, and Apollo snarled.

The second human broke twigs under his feet as his voice quivered. "Benny was right. Those magic wolves are out here."

A growl from somewhere behind me alerted me to Atlas's arrival. I hadn't heard Jasper's wolf approach, but I knew why he was here. It was the humans who were intruding. A gun went off in the distance, followed by wolf cry. The whine from the other wolf was enough to get my blood boiling.

How many, Apollo?

I only smell the two humans and Atlas.

Atlas was now injured, and I wanted these humans to know they were not welcome here. Apollo began to growl and gnash his teeth at the human in front of him. He still couldn't see us because we blended in with the snow and used a bush for cover.

"Leave, human," Apollo warned.

The human was so shocked from hearing Apollo's voice that he dropped his gun, and it went off again. This time, a bullet nicked our side. We weren't badly injured. Apollo growled and snarled as we pursued the human.

Atlas growled just as fiercely from behind us.

"How are we supposed to get close to the cabin with these two here?" one human asked, his voice shaking. The other human was a little more confident.

"Come on, I have an idea," the other human said, then the two men ran off.

Atlas ran up to us. *"Should we pursue them, Alpha?"*

Apollo snorted as we watched their retreat. *"No, and the first one left his gun."*

"I'll take it with me when I go."

"We have a problem."

"I heard. They're after the cabin. I think I know who Benny is. If I'm right, it's good that you're out here."

"I'm glad you were here to back me up."

Apollo sat down, and Atlas walked over and looked at our wound. It was already healing. The bullets weren't silver.

"Me too, but I wasn't expecting to encounter humans when I came to give you my update."

"What do you have for me?"

"Amber is planning to leave the Cabin as soon as she can," Atlas shook his fur, and I heard metal hitting the ground.

"Then we will be ready to follow them out," I said.

"What do you think that human meant when he said he had an idea? Hopefully, they get out before those humans attack the cabin."

"We will keep a closer eye on the cabin until they leave."

"Zane and I have to stay and finish the investigation."

"I'll take Lucas with me."

Atlas was silent and wouldn't look at me.

"What aren't you telling me?"

"We had to take Amber to the hotel room this morning so we could talk privately. Lucas was gone, but Amber's scent was in the room when he returned… I don't know how to tell you this." Atlas laid his ears back, looking away with his head down.

"Spit it out." Apollo barked to get Jasper's attention.

"Lucas thinks Amber might be his mate," Jasper said quickly. His words were like knives to my chest. The knives would have been better. I haven't had a headache at all since I shifted, until now.

"That can't be true. No, how could Amber be Lucas's mate?"

"He said there was a faint smell of apple blossoms."

"Amber isn't his mate." I wouldn't accept Amber was anyone else's mate but mine.

"How do you know?" Jasper asked.

"I just do."

"Caleb."

"Jasper, tell me, what do you smell when Amber is around?"

"It's hard to find her scent. She always has a mixture. She has been living with fourteen other people for the last few weeks. I'm sorry, Caleb." Jasper said.

"Do better," I growled.

Jasper was quiet as he thought it over. *"Berries, Amber's scent is berries."* Then Atlas huffed, and Jasper added, *"I never said she was Lucas's mate. Only that he believed she was because that was the scent he picked up the most."*

I admit it made me feel a little better, but not much. *"Exactly. Amber doesn't smell like apple blossoms. That scent could have come from any of the others in the cabin."*

I was surprised at how quiet Apollo was. Then again, he wanted me to stay away from Amber. Maybe he already knew she wasn't our mate. I didn't think getting a headache while confined to my wolf's body was possible, but my head began to throb, and Apollo wasn't reacting.

Atlas sat down next to Apollo with his ears lowered. *"Are you going to be okay?"*

"I wish the bullet that hit me was silver. Go set Lucas straight. I want to be left alone."

Atlas whined, and I retreated deep into Apollo's consciousness. I didn't want to talk to anyone, not even my wolf.

CHAPTER 23

Amber

Iwoke up feeling just as tired as I had been when I'd gone to bed the night before. After Olivia and I made up, things became a little better. I don't think I will have a good night's sleep until we leave this cabin.

I went through my morning routine as the girls got dressed, then walked into the hall. It was nice not to be tripping over Tyla and Tyler. Thankfully, the girls haven't said anything about Tyler sleeping in our room. He hasn't complained about being in a room with girls either.

When I walked into the kitchen, Olivia was holding Alice and getting her bottle ready. Ryan entered from outside, it was surprising to see him already awake.

"I checked the shell we found yesterday. It'll fit, but we have nothing to secure it to the truck's bed," Ryan said.

"I'll go shopping and get what we need," Olivia responded.

"Pick up baby formula, too. It looks like that was our last container," I said as I looked through the cupboard.

"It was," Olivia agreed. "The last one I opened smelled rancid, so I threw it out."

"Take the Kia; Benson won't be looking for it." I opened the drawer and pulled out the keys to the Kia, then traded them for Alice. Olivia wrote down the things we needed.

Ryan handed Olivia a bolt and a screw. "We need three more that look just like this."

"Got it." Olivia grabbed a slice of toast and walked out the door. I took Alice over to the couch and began to feed her.

"Can we go outside and play?" Ellie asked.

"Not this morning," Ryan said. "We found footprints near the trail late last night."

I echoed his statement. "Everyone stays inside until we know the cabin is still hidden."

If the humans had found us already, we may not get out in time.

Michael gestured to the door. "But Olivia left."

"She left to get supplies," I said.

"Aw, man," Michael said and walked away.

I finished feeding Alice her bottle and sat her on my lap. She burped, and then I felt my leg get warm. Alice just looked up at me and smiled. My leg was dry, so at least this mess was contained. I stood up and looked at Ryan. "I'll walk the perimeter as soon as I finish up with Alice." He nodded, and I took her into the bathroom to clean her up.

Once I got Alice changed, I handed her to Ryan. Then I went to my closet, grabbed my bow, and put the quiver over my shoulder. When the kids saw me with my bow, they ran to the window. "Bring back a buck!" Tyler said.

"She's not going hunting," Josh told him.

"In a way, I am. But I'm only going to chase it away," I said as I walked out the door.

About a hundred yards from the cabin, I found the footprints Sage discovered last night. She was right. These didn't belong to anyone we knew.

I followed them to the cave, where I found two other sets of footprints and large paw prints. The paw prints were large enough to be wolves. There were too many prints to have been just one wolf. It looked like the paw prints and the footprints were facing off against each other.

I also found shell casings and what looked like a flattened bullet. It had blood on it. Someone must have injured a wolf.

I pocketed the bullet and continued to walk along the footprints. I was now looking at three distinct sets. I followed them to the trail, where I found tire tracks.

I walked back to the cabin, feeling more worried than ever. If we've been discovered, then we need to leave now.

I walked in the door and Ryan looked up, concerned. "Olivia isn't back yet."

"It will take her longer to get what we need."

"It's been an hour."

"It will probably be another hour before she gets back."

Ryan studied my face. "What did you find?"

"Three sets of human tracks and paw prints from at least two wolves."

"We already know one of them was the White Alpha; who do the other prints belong to?"

"I don't know; I also found this." I handed him the metal from my pocket.

"A bullet?" Ryan's eyes widened, and his Adam's apple bobbed. "Have they found us?"

"It's possible. The tracks Sage found last night were close enough for the cabin to be seen. The wolves by the cave stopped the other two, but whoever the other set belonged to could have found us."

Ryan closed his eyes, and his brow brow knit together, as his shoulders sagged. Then his face hardened and he wrapped the bullet in his fist. "We need to leave as soon as Olivia returns."

"I agree, but leaving like this will make it impossible to contact Agent Hayes for help."

"We don't need it. If we drive carefully and avoid town altogether, then we should be able to stay out of Benson's way. He stays close to town, anyway."

"All right, but we will have to split up if he follows me. We can't risk him seeing the pups in the Kia."

"We can't risk him catching you, Amber."

"Better me than you," I said. "I will be fine."

The muscles in his neck and shoulders tensed. I placed my hand on his shoulder. "Ryan, it will be all right. As you said, if we are careful and stay out of town, we can avoid Benson."

Ryan nodded, and we worked for the next hour to prepare the cabin for departure. We had nearly finished storing clothes and sleeping bags in the basement when I felt Olivia's anxiety, followed by hatred and disgust. Something was happening to her. I wanted to go to her, but I couldn't leave the pups.

The feeling of being trapped and scared lasted for more than an hour. I paced the cabin, inside and out, while waiting for Olivia to return.

I wrapped a blanket around myself as I tried to calm down. That didn't seem to help; I still felt trapped. I walked outside and threw the blanket onto the bench. I couldn't stay still. Why was I so anxious?

I stopped pacing at the front of the cabin when I saw red fur running up the path. Sage was running fast, and her eyes were wild and unblinking. I grabbed the blanket off the bench and held it up while Olivia shifted, then wrapped her up. She was frantic and shaking uncontrollably. I could see her pulse beating rapidly in her neck.

We walked inside and into her room, where she collapsed on her bed. Olivia continued to sob, and I held her, hoping to give her the same peace I provided the other girls when I visited the Sacred Forest.

Olivia was practically choking on her sobs as I held her tight. My anger bubbled up, and I was ready to beat the snot out of the person who had done this to my cousin.

I silently prayed to the Moon Goddess, *Please help me ease Olivia's pain.*

As I held Olivia, I felt the calming peace of the Sacred Forest fill me. She took a deep breath and then another, and I felt the peaceful aura flow from me to her. Eventually, she fell asleep. I went to her bathroom and found her pajamas. She didn't sleep long and woke up panting. Her skin was still pale, and tears threatened to fall from her eyes.

"It's okay, Livy, you're safe," I said, handing her the t-shirt. Olivia put it on and shook her head.

"No, it's not. We're not safe, Amber, and there's nothing we can do about it. I failed."

"Olivia, you didn't fail anything. What happened?"

Olivia took the shorts from me and put them on. "Lindsey Larsen… I'm so sorry. Sage kept telling me to leave her alone and not to provoke her. I didn't think I was. I was only reacting to her. It was stupid, and now we are stuck here, and it's all my fault."

Olivia began sobbing again, and I wrapped the blanket around her. I had no idea what she was talking about. Nothing she said made sense.

"Stop saying that," I told her, but Olivia kept shaking her head.

"You don't understand," Olivia began. "Benson…. He…." Olivia's heart raced, and her anxiety was so strong I could feel it as if it were my own. My whole body felt itchy, like something was crawling on me.

"What did Benson do?" I asked.

"It was stupid, and I should have listened to Sage…" Olivia was speaking so fast I couldn't understand her. I held her hand, and she took a deep breath before beginning her story.

"When I entered the market, I saw a missing person's flyer on the bulletin board next to the cart stall. It was the same flyer about Rose that Agent Hayes gave you. I grabbed a basket and turned to walk into the store, but I wasn't watching where I was going. I bumped into a man in a brown police uniform; he smelled like he'd taken a bath in cheap cologne. Sage growled in my head, and I had to duck so Deputy Benson wouldn't see my eyes flicker.

"There was something about him, Amber. I've never trusted Benson. Sage could feel my anxiety, and it agitated her. She didn't want me near him. At first, she told me to leave. Circle the block until he left the store, but I knew if I did that, I would have looked suspicious. Instead, I went into the store and went in the opposite direction of him. On my way to the baby aisle, I had to pass Lindsey in the liquor section. She was holding a bottle of wine. When she saw me, she began to taunt me. She even called me wolf girl. How did Lindsey know about us?"

I wiped the tears from my eyes. "Lindsey found out after what happened in the locker room."

Olivia's eyes reflected the memory. "I remember that; it's a good thing I wasn't there. I wouldn't have used the restraint you did."

"What else happened at the market?" I asked.

Olivia's eyes dropped a few more tears before she went on. I never let go of her, allowing the calming aura of the Sacred

Forest to seep into her so she could tell her story and hopefully begin to let go and heal.

"After my encounter with Lindsey, I got what we needed and went to the checkout. I was so angry, Amber. I wasn't paying attention to my surroundings. It was stupid. Lindsey was right behind me, but I should have looked to see who was behind her. We have been so careful. Lindsey howled at me. It was a quiet howl meant to annoy me, but it was loud enough for Benson to hear, too." Olivia began to sob, and her breathing became more erratic.

After hearing about Lindsey's wine bottle, I understood why she was at the market instead of the grocery store. At the market, they don't check your ID, and Lindsey is still nineteen.

"Amber, I should have been more cautious with Benson there or said something to throw her off, but my mind went blank.

"I paid for the diapers and wipes and saw the cashier put the receipt in the bag. It was in the bag! I know it was!" Olivia was sobbing. Her breathing came harder and faster.

I rubbed her shoulder. "Olivia, if it's too much, you don't have to say any more."

She shook her head. "No, I need to get this out so you know where to look."

My eyebrows pulled together. "Look for what?"

"I walked out to the Kia, and Benson followed me. He accused me of stealing the groceries, which was stupid because I had the receipt. He saw me pay for it, but that wasn't the point. Benson made his point when he accused me of having a weapon and frisked me, claiming it was for his own safety. His hands…." Olivia sobbed and hiccupped. She had snot and tears running down her face as she described what Benson did to her before putting on the silver cuffs.

We have all known what a pig he is. The older residents liked him, but the women he'd arrested, justifiably or not, would all tell you the same thing. He does it to excuse where he places his hands; not everything he does is legal. But no one has charged him with anything, and complaints fall on deaf ears.

"Whe—when he shoved me into the back of his car, Amber." Olivia had to control her breathing before she continued, "Benson told me he was going to send me to be with the other mutts, to be locked in a cage where I belonged."

"Benson said that?" I asked, horrified.

She nodded as she looked down at her lap. "It was Agent Hayes who released me. He threatened Benson about the arrest, and once Benson was gone, Agent Hayes released me from the cell. He and Carrie got me out of the police station, and I ran. But…" Olivia sobbed and heaved again as she tried to tell me what happened. "Amber, I'm so sorry. It's all my fault."

"You didn't do anything wrong," I said.

"I did. If I hadn't let Lindsey get to me, then…."

"Then what?"

"When I went back for the Kia… Benson was there with Hooker Towing. They were pulling the Kia onto a trailer." Olivia's voice became high-pitched, and her words ran together. "I watched as they drove away with the Kia, Amber. The Kia is gone. Our way out of here is gone, Amber. How are we going to get the pups to safety now?"

I held her close and increased the connection with the Sacred Forest. Olivia began to breathe a little better, and I cried with my cousin. She wasn't just upset about what happened to her. She also felt guilty over losing our way of escape, but this wasn't her fault. Benson made an illegal arrest.

I let Olivia cry until she fell asleep, and using that much power made me sleepy. I lay down with her and closed my eyes until a knock on the door woke me up. Ryan poked his head through, and I looked down at Olivia, still crying in her sleep. I wiped her eyes and let go of her as I approached Ryan.

He tried to come into the room, but I pushed him out. "What happened to her?"

"Benson happened," I told him. It wasn't my place to say anything else, but I didn't have to.

"Did he…"

I nodded, and Ryan balled his hands into fists.

"I'll tell Josh and the others to keep their distance until Olivia is ready. What are we going to do about the Kia?"

"I don't think there's anything we can do. Benson had it towed. And with it, the supplies we needed," I explained. Ryan looked like he was going to punch something. Then he looked at me seriously.

"What about that FBI guy?"

"Jasper?"

"Yeah, ask him for help; when will you see them again?"

"I'm supposed to meet them at the diner in the morning."

Ryan pushed me out of the hall. "We need that Kia. You have to go now."

CHAPTER 24

Amber

I knocked on the motel room door, and Zane opened it. He looked at me with a mixture of sympathy and anger.

"Amber."

"I need to know what happened to the vehicle Olivia drove to the Market."

"Come in," Zane said. I walked past him, hoping to find Lucas and convince him to return with me; Olivia needed her mate.

"Where is Lucas?" I asked.

"He's out for a run," Jasper said from his desk. He had two computers open in front of him. I saw grocery bags on the bed behind him.

"I thought you were here because of what happened to Olivia?" Zane asked as he closed the door.

"I am… I hoped Jasper could help me get our Kia back," I said. Jasper and Zane shared a look. Then, Jasper walked over and invited me to sit. I sat down on a nearby chair.

Jasper sighed and backed away, his hands in his pockets. "I followed Olivia after she left the station. When I saw the Kia being towed away, I knew where it was going. Olivia ran down a side street, and I followed her until I saw her shift. I met up with the tow truck, but when I got to the junkyard, the Kia went straight to the crusher. I'm so sorry."

If I wasn't sitting down, I would have fallen over. It was as if time stopped. How were we supposed to get to safety now?

"We waited too long," I whispered. My hands shook, and I felt cold. "It's too late."

Zane walked over and sat at the edge of the bed across from me. "No, it isn't."

I shook my head. "We've already been discovered. Now, we have no way of getting anyone to safety. The truck will only hold so many," I explained.

The anguish on Zane's face was apparent. "Let me make a call," he said, then stood up, took his phone off the desk, and walked away.

Jasper went over to the bed, picked up the bags of groceries, and brought them over to me. "I paid off the tow truck driver for these. The receipt was still in there." I looked into the bag of groceries. Everything was there, even the hardware bag of nuts and bolts for the truck bed. "How do you know you were discovered?" he asked.

"I found footprints close to the cabin. I followed them to the path just north of the cave; then followed the prints to where they met up with tire tracks," I said. Jasper shook his head.

"That can't be right; we intercepted the two humans before they could get close."

"Thank you, but… there was a third."

Jasper breathed out in frustration. "Crap."

"Amber," Zane said from across the room. "What are your plans now?"

I looked over at him. "Our only option is for me to go alone, then bring back help. But I don't want to just up and leave Olivia and the pups."

Zane nodded and replied to the person on the other end. It must have been the king. King Verrick is one of the most honorable men I have ever met.

"You will need to act fast; the humans we encountered plan to go after the cabin. You don't have much time," Jasper said. I nodded my agreement. That was our assumption when we discovered the footprints.

"Yes, Alpha," Zane said, then hung up his phone and addressed me. "We will watch the cabin while you are gone. Once everyone has left the cabin and is safe at Shadow Moon, we will continue our search for your pack."

I tucked a strand of my hair behind my ear and licked my lips. "I have an idea, but locating them will be tricky and I will need your help."

"What do you have in mind?" Jasper asked. I watched as Zane's eyes flickered, his brow furrowed, and his knuckle rested on his lip as I explained my idea. Jasper looked just as serious as he shook his head.

"If you think it will work, but you're right, it is risky," Zane said.

"I don't like this. I won't go along with it," Jasper said.

"Then I will find someone else," I told him, and he glared at me.

"I think we should trust her, Jasper. Stay close to Benson. I don't want him sneezing without you knowing about it. If we are going to get everyone out of the cabin safely and locate the Forest Moon pack, then we need to know where Benson is at all times."

"What about his recruits?"

I looked between them. "Recruits?"

"Benson is part of an organization called the Silver Suns," Jasper said.

"That sounds like something from a comic book," I said, making Jasper shrug.

"Benson has been recruiting. Do you remember his tattoo?" Zane asked. I nodded. "Anyone with a matching tattoo, pin, or patch is a member of that group. So far, we have counted twenty-seven others in this town with pins matching his tattoo."

"What's important about this group?"

"They are prejudiced against shapeshifters," Jasper explained.

"So they work for Balor?"

Zane nodded. "We think so."

I shuddered. "Twenty-seven people is a lot to keep track of."

"If we do this right, we won't have to worry about them. Benson is our only concern," Zane said.

"I still don't like this idea." Jasper looked directly at Zane, "Neither will he."

"He who?"

Jasper ignored me, and Zane only shrugged. "He's not here to object. This is a solid plan, and we're going with it. Just stay close to Benson," Zane said, with the authority of his title.

Jasper bowed his head. "Yes, Beta."

They didn't tell me who they were talking about. I wasn't sure what the big deal was, and I never asked; I had more important things on my mind than someone I didn't know.

I agreed to check in with them at the diner in the morning before I left for Shadow Moon. I wished I could go now, drive to Shadow Moon, and return with Alpha Cole and his warriors, but I couldn't leave Olivia in her current state.

I picked up the grocery bags. "Thank you for these, I need to get going." I nodded to them and started for the door.

"Amber, wait," Jasper said. He had this look on his face as if he wanted to say something else. Jasper bowed his head and placed his fist over his heart. I thought I saw him start to bend one knee, but he didn't. I was probably seeing things. "Be safe."

I raised my right fist over my chest and bowed my head to Jasper. "Thank you. I will."

I walked out the door and drove the truck back to the cabin. This time, I took a different route. I thought I saw lights behind me, so I changed directions. It took me twice as long to return to the cabin.

When I walked in, I smelled soup. Ryan was in the kitchen, and Josh had Alice on the couch with Ellie and Willow. Ratty was perched on Willow's shoulder. That seemed to be his favorite spot when he wasn't in the tote.

"What did Agent Hayes say?" Ryan asked. I walked over to him as he placed a bowl of chicken soup on the counter for me and poured more soup into a second bowl.

"He was able to get our groceries, and we came up with a plan for us to leave." I didn't know how to tell him my idea; maybe it would be better if I didn't.

"Good… why are you looking at me like that?"

"Ryan, there's only one option, and I don't like it either, but Zane and Jasper will look after the cabin while I'm gone."

Ryan dropped the spoon into the pot. "What do you mean, while you're gone?"

"We only have the truck now; that's not enough to get everyone to Shadow Moon. Our only option is for me to leave and bring Alpha Cole here."

Tears formed in Ryan's eyes. "What if you get caught?"

"That's why I'm going alone. If Benson arrests me, then the pups will still be safe. You will be safe. Ryan, you're the future of this pack. You are our future Alpha. We need you as far from Benson and his Silver Suns as possible."

"What are the Silver Suns? Are they supervillains or something?"

"I don't think so. They're a hate group against our kind, and Benson has been recruiting for them in Telluride. He has twenty-seven members."

"That's a lot for this small town."

"That's why two extra wolves will watch the cabin while I'm gone."

"When are you leaving?"

"When Olivia is back on her feet."

"Our supplies may not hold out."

I showed him the bags of groceries Jasper had given me. "We'll make do."

"Agent Hayes gave these to you?"

"Yeah, Jasper paid off the tow truck driver."

Ryan placed the hardware bag on the counter and the baby formula in the cupboard. I kept the bag with the diapers. "Here, take this to Olivia." He handed me a bowl of soup. I took it and then walked to her room.

I knocked on her door, but she didn't answer. I walked in and set the diapers down by the bathroom door. Olivia looked up at me and shook her head. Her eyes were still red and puffy.

"I'm not hungry," she said.

"You need to eat," I told her as I set the bowl on the bedside table. Olivia just looked at it and rolled over. "Agent Hayes was able to get our groceries for us."

Olivia sat up, more alert and curious now. "The Kia?"

"Crushed. I'm sorry, Olivia."

Her eyes welled up with tears, and she looked even more defeated. Olivia became more closed off, and I couldn't get her to respond.

I placed my hand on her side. "Please eat something. It will help." All I heard from her were soft sobs. Losing the Kia wasn't her fault; I wished she would stop blaming herself.

CHAPTER 25

Amber

That night, while most of the girls slept in my room with me. I lay awake as my mind raced with the hundreds of ways my plan could go wrong. Then I thought, what if it worked? How do I take care of my pack and fulfill my destiny?

I rolled over as I tried to fall asleep. Instead, I felt a searing pain in my side. It felt like I was being stabbed; I could hardly breathe. I looked down, but nothing was there. Before the pain eased, I felt electricity shock my entire body. I covered my mouth to keep my screams from waking the girls.

When the pain subsided, I sat up and examined my side. I thought back and focused on the pain that had been shared with me. I wasn't the one being electrocuted. It was my dad. I often felt his suffering more than the other pups felt pain from their parents.

I looked around the room, and all the girls looked like they were still sleeping. Good, I was afraid I'd woken them up. Willow was whimpering, but she remained asleep.

I couldn't stay in the room, so I left to get some water from the kitchen. When I reached for a glass in the cupboard, something caught my eye through the window.

There were small beams of light outside, close to where I had seen the footprints this morning. Remembering Jasper's warning, I was afraid they would get closer. I ran back to my room and grabbed my coat, boots, and hat. It was still frigidly cold at night, so I also grabbed a scarf out of my drawer and a pair of old gloves. Then I went to my crisis pack and found my hunting knife.

Once I was dressed, I left the cabin. The frosty night air shocked my lungs and stung my face. I pulled my hat down around my ears and put the scarf up over my nose. As I got closer, I felt like I was being watched. I spun to see if anyone was following me. I didn't see anyone, but the feeling never left.

Being in the open and outnumbered, I knew the best place to hide was up a tree where the human's flashlights were less likely to reveal my presence. I found a spruce tree and climbed as high as I could. I was only up to branches when their conversation's stopped. I paused my climbing and waited. Beams of light aimed my direction and my heart raced. I made myself as small as I could, which wasn't easy. They got back to what they were doing and I climbed higher. I had to stop a few more times. But I was well hidden by the branches.

The higher I climbed, the colder it got. Over the sound of my heart, I heard deep voices but couldn't make out what they were saying. I recognized one voice as Benson's. The beams from their flashlights were the only things I could see. The beams were spread out and stopped now and then.

I was in the tree for what felt like an hour before the men left. I was so cold that I couldn't feel my fingers. I climbed down the tree, but stopped when I saw a large white mound just under the tree. I was freezing, and the wind was making my eyes water. I couldn't make out what it was. It hadn't been there when I climbed up, so I waited.

When I was sure the white thing was gone, I jumped from my branch and walked over to where I last saw a flashlight beam. In its place was a steel leg-hold trap. Judging by the size, they were looking for shapeshifters. This must have been the Silver Suns Jasper was talking about. I grabbed a large stick and used it to trigger the trap. The force of the pressure from the metal snapped the stick in two pieces. The snap of the trap echoed in the quiet night. I looked up to see if I had attracted unwanted attention, then used my hunting knife to dig up the trap. If I had been human, this wouldn't have been possible, but it wasn't the first time I had removed a trap. It took some effort, but I got the anchor out of the ground, then I grabbed it with my gloved hands took it to the cabin.

Once I was inside, I sank to the floor. Suddenly, the light switched on. I squinted at the sudden brightness as my eyes adjusted to the light.

"Where were you?" Olivia asked; she had a blanket wrapped around herself.

My lungs still hurt from the cold. When I unwrapped my scarf, the air in the room was cold.

"I thought you would still be asleep," I said.

Olivia wrapped the blanket tighter. "It's hard to sleep after what happened. Also… I felt my dad."

I nodded my understanding. "I saw flashlight beams outside. They're gone now, but I found traps in the snow about two hundred meters northeast of here." I pointed to the trap, and the color drained from Olivia's face.

Her voice shook with fear. "Who were they?"

"I don't know; I only recognized a few voices. Principal Reed, Jim from the diner, and…"

"Benson?" Olivia asked. I nodded as I placed my hat and gloves next to me. Removing my knife was more difficult because my hands were cold. I got it off and then placed it on top of my gloves.

"I didn't say this before, but when I found the footprints last night, I caught the scent of cheap cologne. When Benson…." Olivia cleared her throat and looked away. "I recognized the scent on him today."

"I was afraid of that."

My brother came in, rubbing his eyes. "What's going on out here?"

"Ryan, what are you doing awake?" I asked.

He yawned. "I felt cold, then heard you guys talking." I looked at his chest; it was red where he had been rubbing it. The cold wasn't the only thing that woke him up; he just didn't leave his room. He saw my doubt and looked at his feet. "I couldn't go back to sleep after I felt it."

I looked at my still freezing hands, not knowing what else to say. They still didn't know that my experiences were different. They don't need to know yet.

I stood up and removed my coat. "One thing is for sure: Benson and those other men will be back."

"Who's coming back?" Ryan asked. I hung up my coat, picked up my hat and knife, and carried them over to the couch.

"There were intruders in the forest," Olivia said.

"Again?" Ryan asked. I removed my boots and socks and placed them next to the couch, then, grabbed a blanket off of the back and wrapped myself in it.

"Olivia, will you be alright if I leave for Shadow Moon?" I asked. I pointed to the trap. "We can't wait any longer to go for help."

"Amber, what's stopping them from coming to the cabin?" Olivia asked.

"I don't know. There aren't that many laws protecting us since we aren't human, but there might be enough to keep Benson from approaching without a warrant. He wouldn't risk losing his badge."

"Didn't you say Agent Hayes and Zane will watch out for us while you're gone?" Ryan asked.

I fidgeted with the blanket. "Yes."

"What else did you see out there?" he asked.

"It was too dark much; but this white thing was on the ground below the tree I was hiding in."

Ryan grinned. "That's three wolves who will watch over us while you're gone. That should be more than enough."

I hadn't thought of the white heap as the White Alpha. My cheeks felt hot, but they were already red from the icy wind so Ryan and Olivia didn't notice.

"Did it look like a wolf?" Olivia asked me.

I shrugged. "Maybe. Like I said, it was dark, and all I saw was a white heap."

"We should get some rest." Ryan looked at me closely. "As much as we can."

"Are you going to leave in the morning?" Olivia asked.

I nodded. "We will stick to the plan; nothing has changed except that I'm going alone."

"You should have just left today," Ryan said.

"Not without telling you where I was going."

"I would have known; I trust you, Amber," Ryan said.

"Thank you, but that's not what worried me; if Sage wasn't able to protect you all, I wouldn't be able to go for help."

CHAPTER 26

Amber

In the morning, I pulled into the diner's parking lot just as Deputy Benson walked in the door. I turned off the ignition and got out. Then, as I locked the door, I noticed a white convertible parked next to mine. The license plate read 'Lindsey,' as if she couldn't be more obvious.

I walked into the diner and up to Jasper and Zane's booth. Jasper moved over for me as I sat next to him.

"We weren't expecting you until tomorrow," he whispered.

"Change of plans; the sooner I leave, the better."

"I agree," Zane said. "We'll do our part. Eat a good breakfast before you go."

I didn't have an appetite. From where I was sitting, I could see Lindsey, and she kept looking at me. It was almost as if she had something to say, but was too nervous to say it.

Deputy Benson walked out of the hallway by the front door. He must have come from the restroom. He sat down at his table in the middle of the diner, facing me, and gave me a smug look, almost as if he knew something I didn't.

Tina brought Zane and Jasper their meals and me a glass of water. When she left, Lindsey looked like she had finally gained the courage to approach me, but she never got the chance. Benson called her over to him, and she looked uncomfortable.

"Who is that girl?" Jasper asked. "You keep staring at her."

"Lindsey Larsen. She and I have never liked each other."

"Then ignore her."

"Larsen, that name sounds familiar," Zane said.

I nodded. "My dad took her family to court three years ago with the king's help. It was the first time I had met the king and queen."

"I remember now. That contract is still in effect for another seven years."

"What contract?" I asked. My dad had sued Lindsey's family, but I never knew the specifics.

"If Lindsey does anything to you, or harms you in any way, her father will have to forfeit the resort to King Verrick," Zane said.

"That doesn't make sense. Why?"

"It was the price of the lawsuit. The damages caused to you by Lindsey and that boy added up to the value of the resort. Verrick now holds the lien to it," Zane explained.

"That still doesn't seem right," Jasper said. "Why would her father do that?"

"Remember a few years back? We had you look into a resort owner and his dubious accounts," Zane asked.

Jasper thought it over, then looked at Lindsey. When he looked back at us, he nodded. "I remember a resort owner who sold alcohol to minors. On numerous occasions, he allowed drugs and other illegal activities on the property."

"It wasn't just to pay for damages," Zane said.

Jasper smirked. "That's why I was asked to hold on to that report."

"I never knew the specifics. Why just a lien, though? My dad would have taken possession of the resort," I asked as Zane nodded.

"William tried, but the king didn't see that stopping anything and even thought that would make things worse. Instead, Bradly Larsen agreed to the lien on his resort in exchange for continuing to operate it as long as he kept his business clean and Lindsey stayed away from you. It's a ten-year contract, and so far, only a few minor discrepancies have come up." Zane said.

"Let go!" Lindsey yelled from across the room. Everyone was now looking at her and Benson. Lindsey seemed upset that he had pulled her onto his lap. "I mean it. Let go of me!"

A family was sitting two tables over, and the mom tried to use her body to block the view of the scene. An older couple shook their heads at the commotion but made no move to stop anything. A couple of men were sitting at a table next to them, and they looked conflicted about helping. No one wanted to go against Deputy Benson.

I didn't care what my history with Lindsey was; no one should be treated like that. I got up, and Zane reached for my wrist. "If you aggravate Benson, it will be harder for us to protect you."

I pulled my hand away and walked over to Lindsey with Jasper behind me. As we got closer, Lindsey was still trying to fight off Benson.

Placing my hands on my hips I summoned the courage to confront the deputy. "She told you to let her go." He just grinned at me and held her tighter.

"Go away, Amber, I can handle this," Lindsey grunted as she tried to get up again. Her face was red with embarrassment.

"It looks like you're doing a good job," Jasper said. "Benson, the girl said to let go. I suggest you listen to her."

The deputy sneered. "Or what?"

Jasper moved his coat to reveal his badge. "I will arrest you for sexual harassment. Now let her go."

Benson released his grip on Lindsey. She got up, and Benson grabbed her hand.

"I'll see you at dinner," he winked at her. Lindsey looked sick and yanked her hand out of his grip. Jasper escorted her to a nearby table and checked for injuries.

"Who do you think you are?" I asked the deputy. Benson stood up and got in my face. Jim looked upset at the commotion we were making in his diner. "Do you think that just because you have a badge, you can treat women like playthings?"

I heard someone choke on their food. The elderly couple in the corner looked at me with scorn.

Jim walked over to us. "Is there a problem here?"

Benson ignored him and grinned at me. "Your time is up; I'm coming for you." He leaned over to whisper in my ear, "You and all of those runts in that cabin of yours."

I shoved him away, and Jim got between us. Jasper turned away from Lindsey while Zane walked over from their booth.

I pointed around Jim at the Deputy. "David Benson, you are nothing more than a bully."

Jim faced me. "Get out." Zane was ready to intervene if he had to. I stood my ground. There was so much I wanted to say to Benson, and I finally had the courage to say it.

"Benson, you think that just because you have a badge, you can touch women in places your hands don't belong. You cover it up with excuses. You single out the young women and make them feel helpless because you wear a badge. A badge you don't deserve. Your abuse of power is a disgrace, and if you ever come near my cousin again, that badge won't save you!"

My heart was pounding, but Benson just stood there with that smug smile. "That would be so much more convincing if you didn't remind me of a mouse in a trap."

Jim pointed at me and then at the door. "Amber, get out of my diner. That was the last time you harassed one of my customers."

"Yet you let this man physically harass another young woman?" Zane asked. "I didn't know my breakfast came with a side of misogyny."

Jim stepped aside and faced Zane. "You too, get out of my diner and don't come back."

Benson got in my face and tried to grab the back of my neck, but I used my left hand to push his arm away and force his body to rotate just enough for me to use my right hand on his shoulder pushing him down farther as I twisted the arm I was holding, effectively pinning Benson to the table.

Other patrons stood up and cried out in shock at the scene. The mother took her kids out of the restaurant when her little girl began crying.

"Keep your hands off me," I said before I let go of him and walked over to Lindsey. Benson looked angry with me, and I didn't care. I was tired of letting this dirty cop win. I would do whatever it took to rescue my pack, starting with the pups in the cabin.

Benson tried to come at me with his cuffs, but Jasper stood in his way. "Don't you walk away from me!"

I took Lindsey's arm and headed for the door. "Jim told me to leave, so that's what I'm doing." The ring of the bell announced our departure.

Lindsey stopped me by the window. "Why did you do that?"

I faced her not knowing what to expect. "I didn't do it for you, if that's what you're asking."

"Yeah, right."

"I'm tired of the way Benson treats women in this town. No one seems to care either."

She folded her arms around herself. "So what? My dad says he's a good man." Though her eyes told a different story. This was the first decent conversation I had ever had with Lindsey Larsen. She looked behind me and stiffened.

Zane and Jasper came out, followed by Benson. "I need to go," I said as I turned to get into my truck.

"Amber," Lindsey said, and I looked back at her. "Thank you."

Benson tried to come for me, but Jasper got in his way. The deputy pointed at me over his shoulder. "I'm going to arrest you for assaulting an officer."

"That's not what I witnessed," Zane said.

Jasper pushed Benson off of him. "Me neither."

"Tell your cousin I'm sorry about yesterday," Lindsey said. I nodded once to her before getting into the truck so I could drive back to the cabin.

Caleb

After receiving Jasper's report on Olivia's arrest and finding the humans in the forest in the middle of the night, I had questions. I didn't understand why the humans hadn't made a move on the cabin.

Benson has twenty-seven recruits, and he knows the location of the wolves. What was he waiting for? Unless, someone had ordered him to wait. That would mean Benson wasn't the one in charge. If not him, then who?

Apollo paced as we ran through scenarios of how our efforts could all fall apart. As our legs gave out, Apollo began to pant. We laid in the snow and closed our eyes. I didn't realize we had fallen asleep until we heard yelling in the distance.

"Willow!"

"Willow, get back here!"

Apollo sat up and yawned, shook his fur, and went on full alert. Then we heard sniffling and the breaking of branches. Soft footsteps were coming this way quickly. Then, the little girl approached us with her rat in her hands. Apollo laid down so she would be at eye level.

"Willow, your family is looking for you."

She sat beside us. "I don't want to talk to them right now."

"What is the matter, little one?"

"Amber is leaving and won't take me with her," Willow said. "I hate this cabin."

"I'm sure Amber has her reasons for leaving you here. Did she say when she would return?"

"Probably in the morning." Willow sniffled and used her arm to wipe her eyes and nose. She was still holding the rat with both hands, and it didn't seem to mind.

More branches broke, and soon we saw Ryan again. He took a knee for us. After Apollo let him up, Ryan spoke to his sister. His eyes were red, and he looked relieved to find her unharmed.

"Willow, we told all of you that the forest isn't safe right now. You shouldn't be out here."

Ryan hugged his sister tightly, and she cried in his arms. "I want to go with Amber."

"I know you do, but if something happens, and you were with her, she wouldn't forgive herself for putting you in danger."

"I already am. You showed us the trap."

"Trap?"

Ryan looked over Willow's shoulder at Apollo. "My sister found a trap lined with silver in the forest early this morning."

Apollo stood up. *"Are there more?"*

"We don't know; that's why we want to keep the pups in the cabin for as long as possible. But they're restless. It will be hard to keep them inside once Amber leaves," Ryan said.

We looked at the little girl. *"Willow."* She made eye contact with Apollo. *"You are needed here. Amber will need you to be an example to others and stay inside the cabin. Be the leader I know you are."*

Willow's eyes glistened with tears. "But I can help Amber."

Apollo licked her cheek. ***"Sometimes doing what's right is about doing what's needed, and right now, you are needed here."***

"I guess," Willow said. She wrapped her arms around our neck, and her rat jumped onto Apollo's head. His little rat claws made our skin crawl. Apollo let out a whiny growl, and Willow giggled as she let go of Apollo and held out her hands.

"Ratty, get down from there." Ratty jumped off of Apollo's head into Willow's waiting hands and crawled up to her shoulder.

Willow and Ryan then took a knee for Apollo again, and we let them up before they left. Apollo watched as they walked carefully down the hill.

Traps. So that's what the humans were doing in the middle of the night.

The ones we encountered were most likely scouts.

I bet that's what they were talking about, too.

That means those traps are set for us.

We can't just leave them out there. No matter who those traps are for, innocent people could be seriously injured.

Apollo put our nose to the ground as we searched for more traps. It was hard to find, but soon we smelled something metallic. The closer we got, the stronger it was, but we couldn't see it.

The sound of a door slamming and more shouting from the cabin distracted us from the trap we were locating. Apollo looked up, his ears focused on the cabin.

"I wanna go too!"

"Michael, get back here!"

That sounded like Amber.

She sounds worried.

Apollo took one step forward and to the right, ready to run after the pup, who might be in danger. When we didn't hear anything else, Apollo put our head back down to the ground, and our back leg went backward as we continued our search.

SNAP, CRACK.

Pain shot up Apollo's leg as the trap closed around it, instantly breaking the bones. The searing pain radiated through our leg and into our hip. We let out a loud yelp and began to cry and pull instinctively away from the trap, but the more we did, the more it hurt, and blood poured from the wound.

Apollo tried to dig around the trap, but we couldn't get a good angle, and all we got was snow. The more Apollo tried to escape the trap, the worse the pain was.

Apollo, stop; we can't get out of this on our own.

Apollo laid down as he whined. Our leg burned. Ryan was right; the trap was lined with silver. The pain was so intense that Apollo couldn't get comfortable.

Soon, we smelled sun-ripened blueberries. Something about it put us at ease, but we couldn't think clearly through the pain.

Then she came into view. She was like an angel, with dark brown hair and eyes like shining emeralds. She had a wool coat over a jean jacket, and I recognized her.

Amber knelt next to Apollo and carefully reached for the trap. Apollo didn't want her to get hurt by the silver or mess with the trap because of the pain. He nipped at her, and Amber pulled her hand back.

"It's okay. I won't hurt you," she said. Amber let Apollo see her hand before she touched the top of his head. Her touch was soft and soothing. Apollo let out another whine.

"Don't move. I'm going to release you." Amber pushed down on both sides of the trap and released Apollo's leg. He pulled our paw out, but it still hurt too much to move, and Apollo continued to whine as he lay on the ground.

"Hang on, can I see your paw?" she asked gently. Amber reached for our paw and examined it. She pulled something out of her bag. I smelled the peroxide; this is going to sting. Apollo whined and growled, and our leg jerked reflexively as she cleaned the wound.

"I'm sorry; I know it stings, but we don't want it to get infected." Apollo just looked at her. We couldn't think beyond the sting.

"Here, this helps with the pain," Amber gently rubbed something on our leg. It felt good as the coolness numbed the cuts and sores left by the trap. It still burned from the silver, and the bones needed to be reset. There's nothing that could be done until it healed completely. Amber wrapped Apollo's paw and leg in gauze and gently placed it back on the ground.

"Your leg is broken, so try not to use it. The cream should help numb the pain for a little while."

"Where is Michael? Did you find him?"

Amber looked up and smiled. "He didn't go far. When we heard you, he came back to the porch. I told him to stay put while I helped you."

"I'm glad he's okay."

"All the pups are worried about you right now. They heard you from inside the cabin. I've never seen them run so fast."

"I will heal. Tell them I will be okay."

"Well, at the moment, you can't even stand," Amber said as she sat down on the cold ground. She was correct; Apollo was so worn out from the pain that we couldn't get up, so we put our head in her lap.

"I'm sorry you are in so much pain. When I found one of the traps out here last night, my only concern was for the pups. I'm sorry; I should have known that you would be in danger, too." Her voice was soothing, and I wanted her to keep talking.

"I knew I could get injured as I watched over the cabin. It was a risk I was willing to take, and I would do it again. As long as it meant keeping you and the children safe."

Amber's face turned red, and she looked away.

"Tell me about your cousin; how is Olivia?"

"You heard about that?" Amber stroked Apollo's head absent-mindedly. "She isn't well; I'm worried about her. I don't want to leave her, but I don't see any other option. I could have Zane or Jasper send for Alpha Cole, but when I heard about Benson recruiting members into the Silver Suns, I couldn't risk them finding Shadow Moon. Or ambushing Cole on his way to rescue us."

"Are you scared?"

"A little, but I don't know what scares me more the possibility of getting arrested or not being here for everyone."

"They will be in good hands with Zane and Jasper watching over them."

"And you?"

"I won't be much good until my leg fully heals. I'm sorry; I didn't mean to be more of a burden to you."

"You are not a burden," Amber said.

As Apollo kept our head in Amber's lap and she stroked the fur between our ears, the pain began to fade, allowing Apollo to feel sleepy.

"If you need to rest, I will stay here."

We didn't mean to actually fall asleep, I wanted to hear more; but now that the pain had eased, sleep was unavoidable. I last remember Amber humming and gently stroking Apollo's head.

We woke up, and Amber was still stroking our fur. The trap was now out of the ground and next to her. Apollo lifted his head and licked her cheek.

"Thank you."

"You're welcome; how is your leg?"

Apollo turned his head and lifted it. *"It will do for now. Thank you. It may break again when I shift, but that's unavoidable."*

"You were the one following me last night, weren't you?" Amber asked.

Apollo nuzzled her. *"I saw you leave the cabin, and I wanted to make sure you were safe."*

Amber smiled. "Thank you." It was cute how her face got red before she took a deep breath before saying, "Would you like to come back to the cabin? I have some medical training, and I can help you after your shift."

"If I did, I would have to reveal my identity. I can't do that until I have my mate."

She blushed a deeper shade of red, and Apollo licked her cheek again. I have never seen him act like this. Before Amber could say anything more. We heard a scream in the distance, taking us out of our little world and back into reality. Amber looked up with worry.

"That sounded like Michael; I thought he was still on the porch."

"Go; I will follow."

"You are in no shape to move."

"Go help the boy. He needs you more than I do."

Amber got up, and Apollo licked her cheek one last time.

Amber took off her coat and put the numbing cream into the pocket. Then she wrapped the coat around our neck, tied it in a knot, and kissed Apollo's muzzle. It was the first time I'd felt jealous of my wolf.

Amber got up and ran off toward the scream. I couldn't tell what hurt worse, the pain in our leg or watching her leave. The burn was gone, but we could still feel the pain of the broken bones.

Why did the pain come back?

Because Amber left.

Does that mean—

I wish I knew for certain. I am in too much pain to tell whether or not she's our mate.

You certainly act like she is. I never thought I could be jealous of you.

Apollo chuckled before we tried to get up. It wasn't easy to stand on three legs. After a minute passed, we tried to put some weight on our injured leg. Amber had forgotten the trap, and Apollo sniffed around it. There wasn't any silver on the chain, so we picked it up in our jaws and limped slowly back to the jeep.

Once we got there, we shifted, and I screamed from the intense pain in my leg. I tried to stand, but I couldn't put any weight on it yet. Apollo was right; it broke again when I shifted and was now healing in all the wrong places. I used the side of the lean-to and the jeep to brace myself before opening the door. Once it opened, I set the trap inside and grabbed my clothes. By the time I got mostly dressed, I was sweating, and all I could feel was pain.

I looked down and saw how swollen my ankle was. I got out and found a spot in the snow, then sat down and leaned against my jeep. The snow eased some of the pain in my ankle.

Thankfully, I didn't have to wait long before help arrived. My bond with my beta is strong. I knew Lucas would feel my distress and come for me.

"Caleb!" Lucas yelled as he and Zane ran over to me.

"How did you know I was here?" I asked knowingly.

I'd never seen Lucas quake, but his body shook as he moved the lean-to away from me. "Are you kidding? I have been worried sick about you for the last hour. I knew you were in pain, but there was no call from you. Zane and I came to search for you."

"Caleb, we thought something had happened to you. Do you know how many calls from your parents I've dodged?" Zane asked. "Not to mention I had to leave Jasper to tail Benson alone. The deputy is on the warpath; now isn't the time for us to be alone around him."

That piqued my curiosity. "What got Benson so riled up?"

"Amber publicly humiliated him. Everything she said was true, but it could cost us all our safety," Zane said. I smiled, wishing I could have seen her fight back.

I chuckled and then pointed to the trap on the passenger seat. "Apollo stepped in a trap. The chain is the only thing not lined with silver."

Lucas examined the trap and growled. "This type of trap is illegal in Colorado. Where did you find this?"

"Just east of the cabin. Last night, I spotted humans in the forest. I didn't know what they were doing until Ryan told Apollo what Amber had discovered in the middle of the night. When Apollo got distracted by activity at the cabin, he stepped on the trap."

"The cabin? What about the children?" Lucas asked.

"Before Amber left, we heard one of them scream."

"We need to report this," Zane said. "How many more traps are there?"

"I don't know. This was the only one I saw, and Amber has one, so that's at least two."

"Sounds like you also found Amber," Lucas said.

"She found me; I would still be in that trap if it weren't for her."

"How long have you been working with her? She hasn't said anything to me," Zane said.

I looked away. "I haven't been. Today was the first time Amber spoke to Apollo, and he's the only one she saw."

Lucas shook his head, and Zane didn't respond. I could see the conflict on his face, though. He handed me a stick before ripping my pants to examine my leg.

"How did you even get dressed? Your ankle looks like a bowling ball," Lucas said. I glared at him, but he had a point.

"It wasn't this swollen," I said. "Besides, would you want to be caught right after a shift?" Lucas shrugged, and I shook my head. "You have no shame."

Zane finished examining my leg and looked up at me. "Enough talking. Put the stick in your mouth. Caleb, this is going to hurt. I have to break it in two places to reset this properly."

Lucas came over to help hold me down. He wrapped his arms around my shoulders and held me firmly against him as I bit down on the stick.

Zane then snapped my leg a couple of times to break it again. I screamed as my jaw clamped on the stick and my hands clawed at the snow beneath me. Then Zane snapped my ankle several times to get it back in place. When he was done, I panted and sagged against Lucas as Zane left to get a splint and gauze. He came back and wrapped my leg, but he cursed when he got to my foot.

"I can feel at least three broken bones here," he said. Lucas held the stick in front of me again, and I bit down on it. Then Zane proceeded to reset the bones in my foot, too.

Pain shot up my leg as Zane worked. It was as if every nerve in my leg was on fire. Once he was done, I stayed there and panted as tears ran down my face. Lucas took the stick out of my mouth, and I tried to breathe through the pain, but it wasn't helping.

The two of them helped me into the jeep, and Lucas shut my door for me. I grabbed Amber's coat and used it as a pillow; her scent was soothing, and I fell asleep.

I woke up to Lucas's loud knock on my window. "Stay here."

I picked my head up and looked around. "Where's here? And why?"

Luas opened my door. "We're at the forestry service. We came here to report the traps."

"What about Jasper and Benson?" I asked, taking off my seatbelt.

"That's why you are staying here," Lucas said. "Jasper followed Benson to a tent about two and a half miles southeast of the cabin; he was with his recruits. Jasper is asking for backup."

"You can't go alone; let me help."

"You can't put weight on your leg yet, Caleb. We'll be fine as long as you stay here with Joleen."

"Who's Joleen?"

"I am. Now get inside so these men can arrest those Silver Suns and get them out of our forest." A short, gray-haired woman approached us. The sun had weathered her wrinkled skin. She had a kindness about her even though she had a tough, no-nonsense exterior. She was a human I didn't want to cross.

Joleen helped me out of the truck, and Lucas bowed his head, raising his fist to his heart. I bowed my head to him in return.

"Come back in one piece," I told him. Lucas grinned, got into the car with Zane, and drove off.

CHAPTER 28

Amber

I ran towards the cabin as Ryan came running around the other side.

"Did you see Michael?" he asked.

"No, I thought he was here. I told him to stay on the porch."

"Help!" Michael's voice came from somewhere northwest of the cabin. Ryan and I ran toward him, and my blood ran cold when I heard a voice I didn't recognize.

"Hey, kid, do you want your mommy? I can take you to her," the stranger said. Ryan and I were almost there when we found a human towering over the scared little boy.

"No!" Michael screamed as tears ran down his face.

"Step away from the boy!" I ordered.

The man looked up towards me. "What are you doing out here?"

I made eye contact with him. "I should ask you the same thing." I held my hand out to Michael, who shook his head.

The stranger sneered. "I guess he doesn't want to go with you. We're out here looking for wolves. It's open season." I looked closer at him and noticed a gray sun on his neck. It was small, but I knew what it meant.

"You're lying." I stepped between him and Michael, whose face was red and tear-stained.

Ryan stood behind me, keeping Michael between us. "Wolves are endangered in this state; it's illegal to hunt them any time of the year."

"Not the magic ones. It's open season on those year-round."

I narrowed my eyes at the human. "Leave before I lose my temper."

The man laughed and then pointed at me. "What is a little thing like you gonna do to me?"

This guy was twice my size, and he probably thought he had the upper hand. However, I didn't need to take him down; I needed him to leave.

I kept my eyes trained on the human. "Don't make me repeat myself. Leave!"

"Not without my property," the man said.

I planted my feet and stared him down. His statement confirmed my worst fears. The Silver Suns were behind the traps and were looking for us. I needed to get him out of here.

The human got frustrated and swung his fist at me. I dodged to the right and caught his arm, twisting it with my left hand, then rammed my right palm up his nose, hearing it crack. I turned him around and push-kicked him away from Michael. The man lost his balance and fell to his knees. He got up and looked at me as he cradled his arm.

"You little—"

"Don't cuss in front of the kid," I said. The man gave up as he realized he wouldn't win a fight against me. He glared at me and pointed angrily. "This isn't over!"

I followed him to the road to make sure he drove off. I didn't get far.

"Amber!" Ryan yelled. When I got back to them, Michael looked pale, and he was shivering.

"What happened?"

Ryan uncovered Michael's leg, revealing the leg-hold trap he was stuck in. My heart sank, and my hands shook. That trap was identical to the one I'd found last night, and the one that caught the White Alpha. This is what we wanted to avoid. The stranger must have been one of the humans from last night.

I sent a mind link to Ryan to keep Michael from panicking. *"Ryan, we don't have everything to help him."*

"We can at least get his foot out."

"Michael, I want you to hold on to Ryan, okay?" I said as calmly as I could, but my voice was as shaky as my hands.

"No!" Michael cried as he pushed my hand aside and continued to scream. "I want to go home!"

"Michael, listen to me."

He looked at me with tear-stained cheeks, and my heart broke. "Michael, we have to get you out of this trap. Then we will get you back to the cabin."

"I don't want to go back to the cabin! I want to go home!" he cried.

I looked up at Ryan, and he nodded. He had tears running down his face, too. Ryan pulled Michael against him so I could release the trap.

"No! It hurts. Stop!" Michael cried. I tried unsuccessfully to keep my eyes from leaking as I focused on this scared little pup.

"I'm going to count to three."

"No."

"One."

"It hurts!"

"Two… three." I quickly pushed down on the sides to release the trap, and Ryan lifted Michael out. Michael's dangling leg filled me with dread, and my stomach dropped. The break was just below his knee. Had the trap closed any higher, it might have completely severed his leg.

"Ryan, take off your coat," I said. I no longer had a coat, but I still had a jean jacket. I removed it as Ryan set Michael on the ground and removed his coat. I took it from him, and when he saw me lining it up with mine, he ran for a couple of large branches.

This forest is no longer safe. I was afraid my brother would get caught in a trap, too.

Ryan returned and handed me one branch, which I threaded through the sleeves of the two coats as Ryan did the same on the other side. After we zipped up the coat and buttoned the jean jacket, making them tight around the sticks, we carefully placed Michael on the small makeshift stretcher. Michael was wailing, and his pants were now red. He'd lost a lot of blood.

I tried to stay focused, but the back of my throat ached, and my hands and arms shook as much as I wanted to hide it. We should have left last week; I should have gone for help days ago. My mind continued to race with everything I had done wrong. I'd failed Michael, and now he was severely injured.

We carried him back to the cabin, and everyone crowded around us. They were all worried about Michael.

"Move so we can treat him," I ordered.

The pups cleared a path for us, and Josh distracted them in the living room. Ryan and I set the stretcher on the table, and I got a good look at Michael's leg.

Olivia walked in and gasped at Michael's condition. Tears filled her eyes, and the color drained from her face.

I needed her to come out of her shock. "Olivia, go downstairs and get one of the large military first-aid kits." Her head snapped up to look at me then she ran downstairs.

My dad's Gamma, Jordan Clark, and her mate, Morgan, were both in the army. Morgan was a medic and provided us with medical supplies that we wouldn't have had without her connections.

I grabbed the scissors from a kitchen drawer and helped Ryan cut Michael's boot off. The blades of the scissors were red with blood. Michael continued to wail and tried to squirm away. The other children would look at us, and some covered their ears. Josh moved them to the bedroom. We cut away Michael's sock and his jeans up just past his knee, where it was soaked with blood. The wet fabric made it harder for the scissors to cut through.

"His leg is obviously broken; I just don't know how bad yet," I said.

Olivia ran in with the first-aid kit. I pulled out a QuikClot gauze and wrapped it around his wound. Michael whimpered, but at least we'd slowed the bleeding down. He still looked pale.

Ryan held Michael as Olivia and I worked to immobilize his knee and leg. I gave Michael some medicine for the pain, but I knew it would be useless.

"This isn't enough. The bone is shattered. Michael needs a doctor," I said.

"I know, but what if something happens?" Olivia asked.

"Something already has happened!"

"How are you going to get him to Shadow Moon?" Ryan asked as he carried Michael to the couch.

"I'll have to use the truck."

"He won't be able to sit in the seats," Ryan said. I thought about it and had an idea. I went to my bedroom and tossed all my blankets on the floor, then picked up my mattress and dragged it out of the room.

"I see what you're doing," Ryan said once I entered the living room. "Olivia, stay with Michael."

"Ryan," Olivia said, but he had already grabbed the other end of the mattress and helped me move it to the truck.

"What are we going to do about the shell?" Ryan asked.

"I thought you bolted it down already."

"I haven't had time and you were going to leave by yourself," Ryan said.

The stress of being discovered and now Michael's injury was getting to all of us. My stomach was in knots from the guilt over not leaving sooner. I was with Michael last; he was placed in my care. It was my job to keep him safe. I failed Michael; now I must leave the others and pray they would be safe in my absence.

A wave of peace filled my heart as I heard the words of my wolf from deep inside my soul.

We are all watching over them. Take care of the boy.

I sighed and focused on our task. "Let's get the mattress in the bed, and then we can figure out what to do with the shell."

Ryan held the mattress while I let down the tailgate. Then Ryan lifted the mattress, and I guided it into place as he shoved it into the truck bed.

"How are you going to secure Michael?" Ryan asked.

"I'm taking Ellie with me. She will help keep him stable."

Ryan and I walked over to the camper shell that he and Olivia had retrieved and carried to the truck. "What about Josh?"

"You might need him here; he's older, and the other pups respect him."

We lifted the shell and positioned it, then Ryan climbed into the truck bed while I searched for the bolts that Olivia had bought.

"The bolts are still in the cabin," Ryan said. I ran inside, grabbed them off the counter, and returned to the truck.

I handed Ryan a screw with a bolt and washer, and he gave me an extra wrench. I heard him sigh, but he didn't say anything. I secured the shell to the bed in one corner and then moved to the other. Ryan was still quiet.

"Are you worried about Michael?" I asked.

Ryan stopped what he was doing. "Yes, but that wasn't what I was thinking about."

"Say it."

"Earlier, when Willow ran off… she found him again, the White Alpha."

I stopped the wrench on my bolt. "Oh."

"I never told you this, but… I've seen him before."

I sighed. "I know. I overheard you and Olivia the other day."

Ryan nodded as if he should have known. Tears filled his eyes. "Amber, I'm sorry I doubted you."

"We've already been through this, Ry. I forgave you already."

"I know, but seeing him took me by surprise. Last time and even this time. I thought…. I was so sure that it was only a myth, and when you told me you were the White Luna… I wasn't sure what to think. I'm still ashamed that I didn't believe you sooner. You have never given me a reason to doubt you. I'm sorry, Amber."

I smiled sadly, "It's okay, Ry. I know it's a lot to take in."

Ryan furrowed his brows. "One thing that was weird, he didn't seem to react to your scent on me or Willow."

"What do you mean?"

"If you are the White Luna, that makes you his mate. He would have smelled you on us and gone completely nuts. But he didn't."

"I don't have my wolf yet, so maybe—"

"No, that wouldn't have mattered."

"How close were you?" I asked.

"We were pretty close both times."

"Maybe he was too focused on you and Willow."

"Maybe, but it was strange. I have never seen a wolf with that much self-control."

"He didn't react to me when I helped him." I smiled. "I guess he would have been in too much pain to realize who I was."

"What, just now?" Ryan asked.

I nodded. "I found him caught in the same kind of trap Michael was in." A tear ran down my face as I thought about both of them. How many more traps were still out there? That's three so far.

"Well, I don't care who the White Alpha is," Ryan said, returning to our conversation. "If he hurts you, I will kick his furry white tail."

I smiled at his protective tone as we finished securing the shell and returned to the cabin. Olivia was ready for us at the door. She had an odd look on her face.

"What is it?" I asked. Olivia just stood there by the couch. "The truck is ready, let's get Michael loaded up…." Olivia was making me nervous. She still hadn't answered me, and now her eyes were flickering. "Olivia? What's going on?"

"Intruders," she whispered.

My pulse quickened. "How many?"

Olivia's voice shook, and she went pale. "Too many."

My heart raced as I grabbed her face so that she made eye contact with me. "Shift. Let Sage hold them off." I turned to Ryan, "Get the pups in the basement. Keep them quiet."

Ryan nodded and ran for the bedroom to get Alice. I ran over to Michael and moved the couch away from the window.

I hoped this was enough to shield him from the violence about to take place. He had passed out on the couch and was too exposed but I couldn't relocate him to another room.

I didn't have a lot of time, so I ran for my weapons in the bedroom. I grabbed my bow and quiver, then returned to the living room, where, thankfully, no one had entered yet.

The kids were in the kitchen when I saw the first shadow. A window broke, and the kids all screamed as I dropped my bow and covered Michael with my body. When a flaming jar came through the back window, I ran for the fire extinguisher and put out the fire before it could spread. Ryan and the kids were in the basement, and now I had to keep the intruders from entering the cabin.

As I waited, I knelt under the window with an arrow nocked in my bow. Banging at the front door indicated where the first intruder was coming from. I saw the gun barrel first, and I raised my bow and pulled back the string, letting the arrow fly. It hit its mark deep in the intruder's arm. The human dropped his gun, and I ran for it. I grabbed the gun and slammed the weapon into his face, knocking him out. I shoved him out of the doorway and closed the door.

Everything sounded muffled compared to the rushing sound in my ears. I saw someone trying to sneak in through the back door. I took the gun and aimed it at him.

"Don't move, Mr. Reed."

The principal aimed his weapon at me. "Lower your gun." His voice was quivering, and I could tell he wasn't sure about what he was doing. His gun was more likely to go off by accident.

My hand was steady. I knew what was at stake. I kept my voice calm and firm, "You first. I know you don't want to do this."

"Humanity first." he said, but the look on his face was full of doubt. Sweat was forming on his brow, and his eyes began darting around the room.

"We have never been a threat to you or anyone else." I cocked the gun. "But I will defend my family. Get off my land!"

"I will once you put that gun down!"

"You invade my home and tell me to put down my gun? That isn't what you taught us in my history class. Where is the man who taught his students about freedom and justice?"

"I shouldn't have to fight for my right to live," Principal Reed said.

"You're not. *I am.* You came into a house full of kids, intending to take us prisoner! I won't tell you again; drop your gun and get out!"

He didn't move. "I don't want to hurt you, Amber."

"Then you never should have come. I have a right to defend my home."

Something hard hit me on the back of my head. I went blind for a second, and my gun went off, putting a hole in the ceiling as I fell to the ground. I heard the kids screaming from the basement.

The voice behind me was louder than I expected. "Go, I got this one." His hands restrained me behind my back. I didn't know what happened to my gun.

"Marty Perkins?" I groaned. The hands-on my wrists disappeared, and I rolled over to find an old friend. He was kneeling close to me, now shaking.

"Amber Cahill?" Marty was a year younger than me, and he had a huge crush on me in high school. He was always so kind and respectful. That's why I accepted his invitation to prom during my senior year. That seemed so long ago, now. How did it come to this?

I couldn't waste time; my hands were still free, so I moved one out and landed a solid blow to his jaw.

"Get out of my house!"

Marty groaned from the floor. Principal Reed looked at the boy on the couch. "Is that Michael Romans?"

The boy was too out of it to react to the surrounding violence. Principal Reed dropped his gun as the basement door opened, and Josh ran out with a rifle aimed at his school administrator.

The human backed away. "Josh Morrison?"

I found my gun and stood up, placing my foot on Marty's chest. I couldn't risk him harming Josh or Michael.

"I told you we were never a threat to you," I said as tears fell from the principal's face. Josh closed in on him, and I raised my gun again. "We will defend what's left of our home."

"I'll leave." Principal Reed trembled with shame as he raised his hands in the air. We walked him out, and when I looked back, Marty was gone, too. The front door was wide open.

I turned to the thirteen-year-old. "Josh, what are you doing up here?"

He put on the safety and lowered his gun. "Someone had to help you."

"Where's Ryan?"

"He's downstairs with the rest of the kids."

"Josh," I held his head against me as I cried. "You need to get down there too. I refuse to rescue your parents just so that I can tell them you died."

"Be safe, Amber." Josh handed me his rifle, and I ran outside with it. The fight was almost over. Sage was snarling at a human that was backing away in fear.

Another gunshot rang out. "This is the FBI and US Marshals! You have two seconds to vacate the premises before we arrest trespassers." I had never been so thankful to hear Lucas's voice.

Most of the humans ran down the path away from the cabin. Some weren't afraid. One ran towards me with a silver knife raised. I dropped to one knee, placing the handgun on the ground, and aimed my rifle at him.

"Don't move, or I'll shoot."

The man didn't listen, so I shot him in the leg. He went down and dropped the blade.

I stood up as another man ran up to me, and I used the gun to hit him in the stomach, making him double over as I rotated my body and raised my leg to kick the side of his head.

Lucas came out from the trees with Jasper and Zane right behind him. The forest rangers followed them. Everyone was shouting, and I felt dizzy, but I couldn't stop.

I recognized Benson as he fled the scene with the help of one of his recruits. The coward couldn't even face his punishment. Lucas ran after them, but Jasper was about to be ambushed.

I dropped the rifle, shook off my headache, and ran to help. I jumped on the back of the human who was sneaking up on Jasper and clasped my arms in place around his neck until he passed out. When he fell to the ground, I could barely stand.

I was sitting on the ground when Sage, snarling, came running from the back of the house. Her muzzle and hind legs were covered in blood. She also had blood on her side. She was too far away to talk to, but I could send her a mind link.

"Sage… What happened?"

"They were ready for me. I'm sorry I didn't get here sooner."

"You didn't kill anyone, did you?"

"No, but they will need a hospital."

"Amber, look at me." Jasper was frantic as he patted my cheeks. I tried to look at him, but everything was spinning.

"It's okay, no one died." I smiled at him as my eyesight blurred.

"Don't close your eyes," Jasper cried as everything darkened. "No!"

A purple glow filled my vision before I closed my eyes. When I opened them again, I was lying on the ground, and Jasper hovered over me. He relaxed when I sat up.

"Is it over?" I asked.

"For now. You need to get everyone out of here."

"I was leaving for Shadow Moon."

"I know, but the rangers here can help you transport the pups to Grand Junction."

"No," Olivia said, limping from the house in shorts and one of my T-shirts. "Michael needs a doctor, and we will slow them down."

Jasper didn't want to argue, but he clearly disagreed. I would love nothing more than to bring them all with me, but Olivia was right. They would slow down my drive north.

"I will make sure Benson leaves you alone." Jasper helped me stand. "You should be good to drive; I will make sure no one comes near the cabin while you're gone."

"I need Ellie to keep Michael stable in the back," I told Olivia.

"Josh would be better."

"Josh can help defend the cabin. He's already proved himself."

"Okay, Ellie, it is."

Jasper pointed to the cabin. "How can I help?"

"We need the window boarded up and the doors back on their hinges."

"How many got into the house?" Jasper asked.

"Two… well, three, but the first one didn't come past the door."

"Where are they now?"

Olivia pointed to the front door, "One of them is still lying there."

"I don't know where the others went."

"They just left?"

I looked at the cabin. "I don't know."

"You need to get Michael out of here."

"Jasper, do you know why they attacked? Everything has been quiet up until now."

"It could be what you said to Benson at the diner, but there were too many here for that. I guess they finally got past the one thing in their way."

I suddenly felt cold. "The traps were for the white wolf."

"He's fine. Don't worry about him. Go for help."

I ran up to Jasper and gave him a big hug. "Thank you."

He wrapped his arms around me. "Be safe."

CHAPTER 29

Caleb

The forestry office had a large emerald-green pennant hanging above the front desk. It had a gold lotus flower in the middle and a gold bead with a green lotus at the bottom and a green tassel.

"That pennant means something, doesn't it?" I asked.

"It does, and your friend already confirmed that you know what the Purple Lotus is. I want to know why you didn't come to us sooner." Joleen said.

I sat down in the nearest chair I could find. My ankle was throbbing. "We didn't know you were in Telluride."

Joleen left and came back with a first-aid kit. She pulled out an ice pack and placed it on my ankle, which was propped up on a nearby table. "I received a call from Carole Cawthra a week ago; you were supposed to check in with us."

I pulled my phone out of my jacket pocket and saw at least fifty missed calls and text messages. "I've been without my phone."

"What about your friend? When I asked him, he just dodged the question."

I smiled ruefully. "Lucas has no excuse; he's always been terrible at checking his messages."

"Well, we already have everything in place to rescue William's pack. Our first team will meet you here when you give the word."

"That was quick; how did you know who to send or what to do?"

"It wasn't too hard. I've been friends with William Cahill for years. He's the reason our pennant is green and gold instead of purple. When I heard from Carole that a pack had been taken from this area, I prayed it wasn't Forest Moon. But I hadn't seen William or Jessica, and they didn't respond to my call for aid."

"What do you mean?" "That same night, we were called to search for some lost hikers. I took my rangers out there to search for them, but we couldn't find anyone. I called William to see if he could help track them down, but there was no answer. That isn't like him. William has always helped us. I figured he would call me back, but the longer we were out there, the more the search seemed wrong. You know that feeling when you know something isn't what it appears to be?"

I nodded. "Do you think it was a prank?"

"I think we were kept busy that night. Someone didn't want us near Forest Moon."

"When did you first suspect they were connected?"

"When I drove to the pack and saw the devastation. I fell to my knees and prayed that everyone got out safely. There was no sign of William or anyone near the territory. I tried to investigate their cabin, but there was a red wolf I didn't recognize. She made it clear that she didn't want us there. Poor thing, I could tell she was afraid."

"Olivia, she's been the most hesitant one. She's also the most territorial," I said.

Joleen smiled. "I remember her. Feisty young woman, Colin and Vikki's girl. Anyway, I called it in, and Carole made sure Jarom made this pack a priority. Sometime in there, you called her and gave the same report. That's when Jarom sent his best team."

"What is your plan?" I asked.

"They will meet here, and then we were hoping to work with you on any leads you had," Joleen said.

"No, Grand Junction is a better location. Amber has already left to get help. The others won't trust humans," I said.

Joleen looked at me disapprovingly. "That is hours from here; we have a safe house that is closer. The team is already on their way; you should have organized this with us days ago."

I wouldn't argue, but I wasn't budging on this, either. Joleen grumbled, then walked out to the phone on the desk. Thanks to my sensitive hearing, I heard her conversation.

"Change of plans, Evan. He wants to meet in Grand Junction."

"It's too late, Jo. Landon is already in place. We can't move him now," said a man's voice on the other end.

Joleen sighed heavily. "Where are you?"

"The rest of the team is with me in Montrose," Evan said. As they talked, my mind drifted to Amber.

I shouted so she could hear me, "Have him look for a red pickup. A young woman with brown hair and green eyes will be driving. Find her, and Lucas and I will meet up with them."

"Who was that?" Evan asked.

"A man who couldn't care less about answering his phone; Carole says his name is Caleb something-or-other," Joleen said.

"He can't give me anything else? I will not follow every red truck I see."

"It's an old nineties pickup with a dark gray camper shell that looks like it doesn't fit."

"Did you get that, Evan?"

"I did. Tell whoever that is that I will look for the truck. Who is it I'm pulling over?"

"Her name is Amber Cahill. Tell her Caleb sent you," I replied.

"Fine, but this is my operation; I will be the one to decide what we do after that," Evan said, and then I heard a click.

Joleen hung up the phone and turned to me. "It's going to be awhile before we get an update. Do you want a sandwich?" Joleen asked. The thought of food took my mind off my predicament.

"Who's watching over the cabin?" I asked.

"What do you mean?"

"Benson has twenty-seven followers. They found the cabin the other day. With Jasper, Zane, and Lucas preoccupied with Benson. I'm injured here with you, so who is watching over the cabin?"

"You're a bossy one, aren't ya? Don't worry; we have five forest rangers downwind of the cabin, ensuring no one harms the children." Joleen said.

"Were they there the night the traps were set? What about this morning when a young boy stepped in one?"

Joleen disappeared into a small room. I heard the clanking of dishes and the opening and closing of doors, and soon she walked out with two plates of food. Joleen handed me a peanut butter and honey sandwich. I took the plate, and my hunger got the best of me. The bread was soft, and the peanut butter was creamy. It was the most delicious thing I had eaten in days.

"We knew about some of the traps, but we couldn't get close enough to the cabin to warn anyone." Joleen eyed me carefully, "You must have been the wolf that was injured. We heard your cry, but my scouts said that a white wolf was being cared for."

I took another bite of my sandwich. "I will neither confirm nor deny it. The presence of a white wolf is classified information."

Joleen waved her hand. "I won't tell anyone. I don't know much about it, anyway."

"Who's Landon?" I asked as I took another bite.

Joleen gave me a knowing look. "Landon Cook is Jarom's most trusted member of the Purple Lotus. Landon is married to Evan Cook, who happens to be a fox. Both of them were cops and good at what they did. That's why Jarom always sends Landon and Evan on missions like these."

I was worried that we had missed something big. "Like these? Has this happened before?"

"The closest I can think of was a report of a small pack in New York. I don't think it's related, though."

"What did Evan mean when he said, Landon was already in place?"

Joleen handed me a cup of water. "Landon is good at blending in."

That didn't explain much, but Joleen didn't say anything else.

I took a sip of the water, and before I knew it, I had drained the cup. Joleen smiled and got me more.

"You said you are friends with William Cahill; how well did you know the pack?"

Joleen didn't seem to mind all my questions. "We knew some better than others, like Rose; we've known her since she arrived."

"You know Rose Baxter?"

"I do, and I will never forget when she arrived, either." Joleen sat down and laced her fingers over her stomach as she told me about how she met Rose.

The story filled in some gaps in Lucas's investigation. I had forgotten how she had arrived at Forest Moon. I didn't know why Lucas didn't think of coming here first. Then again, we have also been a little preoccupied.

"Do you remember the man who came in looking for her?" I asked.

"He was older, which I thought was odd. The man was old enough to be her father but claimed she was his wife. I didn't believe it, especially when Rose shook her head when he walked in. She was so scared of that man, the poor thing. My rangers couldn't get him to leave. I had to call William to get him out of my office. He showed up with his beta, Colin Scott, and the two dragged that awful man out of here, kicking and screaming. Jessica and Vikki took Rose with them back to the pack, and last I heard, Rose was happily married with a little girl on the way." Joleen said.

"Can you tell me the name of this man?" I asked.

"Jules? Monte… Mont… mon-something," Joleen scratched her head.

"Julius Montgomery," I growled. I will never forget that name.

"Yes, that's it. Do you know him?" Joleen asked. I nodded. All this time, we had been looking for human captors. I would have launched a search days ago if I had known she was with a wolf pack.

"Julius helped another alpha try to take over my pack. They would have succeeded if it weren't for William and Cole."

"Cole Shepherd? I haven't heard that name in a long time. I went to school with his dad; how is he doing?" Joleen asked.

"Cole is doing well, and his pack is growing," I said. Joleen smiled.

I shook my head. "All this time, you held the missing pieces to Rose's case."

"Do you think she's with that Montague?" Joleen asked. I didn't see the need of correcting her.

"I know she is, and we are running out of time," I said, "for her and Forest Moon."

Joleen and I continued to talk about the Purple Lotus and our memories of Forest Moon. When Lucas returned, he was in a foul mood, with a bandage on his arm.

"What happened?" I asked him.

He just growled at me. "How's your leg?"

"I still can't put weight on it," I said. "Lucas, answer my question."

"We found and arrested the trappers. Jasper was right; those traps were meant for you and anyone else protecting the cabin."

"How do you know they were meant for me?" I had a feeling that I didn't want to hear his answer.

"They attacked the cabin." Lucas's eyes were red. My heart stopped, and the color drained from my face. My only thought was whether Amber had gotten out in time. I knew worrying about her more than the others was selfish, but I couldn't help it.

"Amber?"

"As far as I know, she's fine. I chased Benson and some other guy who was helping him. After that, I returned to the cabin; Amber had already left."

I knew there was more he wasn't telling me.

Lucas's eyes suddenly unfocused, and I heard his voice in my head. *"Not here, Alpha."*

I nodded my understanding.

"What about that sorry excuse of a deputy?" Joleen asked. Lucas's eyes narrowed, and he shook his head in frustration.

"Benson got away."

"How?" I shouted.

"He had help; one minute, I had him; the next, I was getting attacked from behind. The man with him hit me on the back of the head and sliced my arm with a silver blade. While I was recovering, the other man dragged Benson away from the cabin. I chased after them, but before I could catch up, they were getting into Benson's police car."

"What did the human look like?" Joleen asked. Lucas thought for a minute, then shook his head.

"He had blondish-red hair, light skin, and wore a gray CB uniform, unlike the other humans. I guess Balor sent him."

"Could be," Joleen said.

"Lucas, I know where Rose is," I told him.

"How? Her trail went cold," Lucas said.

"She's in Wyoming with Julius Montgomery."

Lucas's eyes flashed from green to yellow, then back again. "What does Rose have to do with that traitor?"

"I'll explain on the way, but we have to leave." I turned to Joleen and said, "Thank you for your hospitality and the information." I placed my fist over my heart and bowed my head. Joleen nodded.

Between Amber and Rose, we no longer had time to waste here in Telluride. Lucas looked like he didn't want to leave. I could guess why.

We got into my jeep, and he slumped forward as soon as he was in the driver's seat.

"Are you okay to drive?"

"I'm better than you. Jasper helped me a little, but I can't leave. Ajax is whining in my head."

"You saw your mate."

Lucas nodded. "She turned me away. She told me it wasn't the right time for us. Then she left and refused to come out of the cabin."

"Well, that's not a rejection."

Lucas smiled sadly. "There's hope, but I feel like I'm going to lose my mind. Is this what it's been like for you?"

"What do you mean?"

Lucas looked at me and started to say something but shook his head.

"What else happened?" I asked.

"Two of the recruits turned themselves in."

"What?"

"Yeah, one kept shaking his head saying, 'No one told me we were after children.' This experience traumatized him. I don't think he will recover."

"What caused such a dramatic turnaround?"

"Apparently, he's the principal of the middle school. Before that, he taught high school history."

"Ray Reed. Amber used to talk about him; he's a good man, I doubt he knew what he was getting into when Benson recruited him."

Lucas shifted in his seat. "That's what it sounded like."

"Have Zane or Jasper monitor him. What about the other one?"

"It was the guy who took Amber to prom. My guess is he recognized her and gave up."

"I hope he was bleeding."

"Yeah, I think she broke his jaw."

"Good. Where is Amber now? You said she was on the road."

"On her way to Shadow Moon. Jasper and Zane are going to watch over the cabin."

"Why can't they drive the others up there?"

"Jasper promised Amber he'd watch over the cabin; I guess her cousin didn't want to slow down her drive. He also wants another chance to arrest Benson. Zane doesn't want him staying here alone."

"Then it's time for us to go. If we leave now, we might catch up to Amber."

Lucas reluctantly started the jeep and drove us north, farther from his mate and closer to the woman I hoped was mine.

CHAPTER 30

Amber

As I headed west on the 145, it was clear. Thankfully, I didn't have to worry about Deputy Benson. He must have been somewhere, tending to his wounds.

When I got close to Montrose, a guy flagged me down, and when I wouldn't stop, he hopped on a motorcycle and chased me.

"I don't have time for this." I couldn't lead him to Shadow Moon, so I pulled over.

I opened the little door in the back window of the pickup. "Ellie, I'll be right back."

I got out, ready for a fight. The man got off his bike and approached me. When he got close, he pulled a red lollipop out of his mouth and asked, "Are you Amber Cahill?" He wasn't wearing a helmet, so his shaggy dark hair was windblown.

"Who wants to know?" I said as I approached.

"My name is Evan…" I tried to punch him in the jaw, but he caught my fist and spun me toward the truck. It would have been easy for me to get out of the hold, but what he said next surprised me. "My name is Evan Cook, and someone named Caleb sent me. He told me to watch for you."

"Caleb Dawson?" I asked. I hadn't spoken to Caleb in weeks. How would he know where I was? Unless Lucas told him, but then why didn't anyone mention him?

"I don't know; I didn't get a last name," Evan said. He let me go, and I turned back to face him. He put the lollipop back in his mouth, and his green eyes glowed a bright yellow.

"You're…"

"I'm a fox, and I'm here to help," Evan said.

"Is it just you?" I asked.

"No, I work with the Purple Lotus; I have a team of twenty men and women with me," he said. I remembered being told these guys were on our side.

"At the moment, I need to be on my way. You can help me once we locate my pack," I said.

"What do you have in mind?" Evan asked. He looked more like the guy who gave orders instead of taking them, but he listened carefully to my plan.

Evan pulled the lollipop out of his mouth and smirked. "I like you. You've got guts. We'll be ready for you."

"Evan, how did Caleb know I would be here?"

"I don't know; he was with a friend of mine, Joleen Roberts."

"Why would you help us?"

"My orders come from the top, so I'm here. I will see you soon, young Luna."

Evan placed his fist over his heart and bowed his head before returning to his motorcycle and driving back the way he came.

My interaction with Evan had been odd, and I still didn't understand why a fox would help a pack of wolves. Either way, I was grateful.

"Who was that, Amber?" Ellie asked when I got back into the truck.

"A fox, he says he's going to help us find our pack," I said. She didn't respond, and I heard Michael moaning. I looked back and saw Ellie trying to comfort him. He was pale, and he looked like he was sweating. I quickly put the truck back in gear and continued down the highway.

The rest of the drive to Grand Junction was slow because every bump in the road, every twist and turn I had to make, was painful for Michael. Ellie held him down to keep him from moving, but that seemed to hurt him as much as the truck's movement.

As I drove, my mind raced with thoughts of Michael and his injury, the kids back at the cabin, and now Caleb Dawson.

I met Caleb when I was fifteen, and he was almost twenty-one. I'd felt drawn to him, even though he was six years older than me. My dad helped his dad when another pack challenged him. On the day he left, Caleb admitted feeling the same attraction but also being conflicted. He made it clear that we would be nothing more than friends. That didn't stop us from emailing, calling, or texting almost every month until last year, when it became weekly.

My thoughts about Caleb were the only positive ones going through my head. I still didn't know how he knew where I would be; the last I knew, Caleb was working at a veterinary clinic in Utah.

My gas light came on just outside Grand Junction, interrupting my thoughts of Caleb, and the truck started to slow down.

"No, come on, just a few more miles."

"What's wrong?" Ellie asked.

"It's out of gas." The truck sputtered to a complete stop.

Ellie got panicked. She began holding her stomach and rubbing her chest. At first, I thought she was just scared because we were stranded.

"Ellie, are you okay?"

She didn't answer. The look in her eyes told me something was very wrong. Ellie sobbed, and Michael weakly reached over for her. Ellie lay on the mattress beside him, and Michael held her hand.

I felt an immense rage; why was this happening to us? I was grief-stricken. What if something happened to Michael? Now Ellie was suffering; when will this all end?

My truck wouldn't move, and I now had two kids who needed a doctor. Not knowing what else to do, I turned on my hazard lights, put the truck in neutral, and got out. With one hand on the steering wheel and the other on the door, I pushed it to the stop sign just ahead. I focused all of my anger, anxiety, and worry on pushing this truck as far as I could go.

Once I reached the stop sign, I needed more leverage on the steering wheel. I got in and turned it as far as the wheels could go. I got out to push the truck to the right toward Shadow Moon. The door closed on me, and when I caught it, I looked up and saw a gas station.

I turned the steering wheel in the opposite direction and pushed the truck to the left. This route required more work because the gas station was on a shallow hill. I tried as hard as I could, hoping I would get there without losing the truck.

"Please, Moon Goddess, help us get where we need to go; Michael and Ellie both need doctors."

I pushed the truck as far as I could, focusing on putting one foot in front of the other. I tuned everything out, so I was surprised when the truck became easier to push.

I looked behind me, and a man was pushing the truck from behind. He was a tall, burly man with dark hair and brown eyes. I thanked him after he helped me get the truck to the gas station.

"That's it?" he asked with what looked like a smirk. I was still feeling enraged. I struggled to keep my temper from flaring.

"Yep," I said. He put his hand on my shoulder, making me even more uncomfortable.

"You don't look so good."

I gritted my teeth. "Get your hand off me, please." If he didn't listen, he was going to wish he had. He never removed his hand, so I removed it for him. I spun out, twisting his arm in the process.

He grunted in pain. "I think there's been a misunderstanding. Is that any way to treat someone who helped you?"

"I thanked you. You should have left it at that," I said. I let go of his hand and turned to take care of my truck, but this guy was asking for a beating.

He grabbed my wrist. "Hey! Don't walk away from me; I just wanted to make sure you were okay."

"Hey, Monty! What's going on?" another man asked. He got out of a brown suburban that was parked next to the gas station.

"He was just leaving," I snapped. Then I stomped on Monty's foot, yanked my arm from his grip, and walked back to the truck. Instead of letting me go, the other man got out, ran up to me, grabbed my other wrist, and turned me toward them. I didn't have time for this; Michael was getting worse.

"You can't treat him like that," he said. I landed a left hook to his gut making him let go of my wrist.

The one named Monty grabbed me from behind, pinning my arms to my sides. "Are you crazy?"

I kicked my right leg behind me to fake a kick to his groin. He fell for it, and brought his legs close enough together for me to make my move. I widened my stance, moved my left leg behind Monty, grabbed him behind the knees, and used my hip and arms as I stood up, throwing him onto his right shoulder. I heard a crack, and when I turned to look at him, his face was contorted in pain. He tried to get up, but I stepped on his chest and leaned close to his face.

"I do not have time for this nonsense, so I suggest you get lost before I make time."

CHAPTER 31

Caleb

We came to the intersection for Shadow Moon.

Go left.

But Shadow Moon is the other way.

Trust me. Go left.

I looked at my beta. "Apollo says we need to turn left at the stop sign."

"Why?"

"I don't know."

Lucas changed his blinkers, and we turned left. Two blocks up the road, I saw a familiar red pickup in a gas station stall and a woman fending off two men. She punched one in the gut, and the other man grabbed her from behind, but she flipped him onto his shoulder and then got in his face.

I didn't have to say anything to Lucas. He pulled in right behind them. The woman walked away, and the two men got up and faced us when Lucas and I got out of the jeep.

"Leave her alone," I ordered. The two men smelled like wolves. The woman's scent gave her away; when Amber looked at me, fireworks went off in my head.

Caleb, you were right. Amber is our mate.

Hearing Apollo confirm my greatest hope was like a dream come true. No wonder Apollo wanted us to go this way.

"I helped her, and she disrespected me," the biggest one said.

"That looked like self-defense," Lucas said.

He held up his hands. "This is a misunderstanding."

"I'm going to give you a choice: leave now, or I'll arrest you," I told him.

"On what authority?" the tall one asked.

Apollo was a powerful wolf, and his authority spoke for itself. My eyes glowed, and I growled low and deep. The wolves wisely left the gas station.

"Caleb?" The tears in Amber's eyes were at odds with the smile on her face. She was still beautiful. Her sun-ripened blueberry scent filled my nose, and it was the most fantastic thing I had ever smelled. I wanted to hold her in my arms to ease her pain, but I wasn't sure she would like that. I shoved my hands into my pockets to avoid doing something impulsive.

"I thought you were going straight to Shadow Moon," Lucas said.

"The truck ran out of gas; how did you know I was here?"

I wasn't waiting for it to fill up, and now that I was with her, I didn't want Amber out of my sight.

"We'll take you there," I said.

"No, I can't leave the pickup here."

Look in the bed of the truck.

I did as Apollo advised and lifted the door to the shell, revealing two frightened and sick children. I was so absorbed with Amber that I had forgotten about Michael. The girl looked ill now, too.

"I can't move them," Amber said.

I shouted over to my Beta. "Lucas, get my kit."

He ran back to the jeep as I opened the tailgate. I could smell the blood, and the pale color of the boy worried me. I hopped into the back. The little girl looked scared and used her body to cover the boy.

"Wh… who are you?" she cried.

"My name is Caleb. What's yours?"

Lucas handed me medical kit. "I'll get this truck running."

"Don't come any closer," the girl whimpered.

"It's all right. I'm a doctor and want to help."

Amber's voice was soothing as she spoke to the little girl. "You can trust him, Ellie."

I reached into my kit, pulled out my thermometer, and put it under the boy's arm. It quickly went up to 102.4.

"He has a fever; his leg is probably infected," I said. There was a knocking sound on the side of the truck.

"Tank is full," Lucas shouted.

"Amber, I'm staying back here; Lucas will drive the jeep to Shadow Moon. Follow behind him," I instructed.

Amber nodded, but the little girl reached for her. "No, don't leave us."

"I'm not going far."

I reached into my kit for an ice pack as Amber closed us in the truck bed. My eyes began to glow a vibrant blue. Ellie gasped and then relaxed as she watched me break up the ice pack, activating the ammonium nitrate and water. When I felt the package get cold, I placed it on the boy's forehead. He groaned but didn't react much.

"You…." Ellie said. I placed my finger on my smile and winked at her. The truck moved as Ellie pinched her finger and thumb together and motioned as if to zip her lips. She was more comfortable with me.

"How is Michael?" Amber asked from the driver's seat.

"I have an ice pack on his forehead, but it's not enough; how close are we to Shadow Moon?"

"I can see the gate from here," Amber said. I rechecked the boy's temperature. The truck stopped at the same time the thermometer beeped.

"Identify…" Davis, the gate guard, stopped mid-sentence when he recognized the driver. "… Amber, we've—"

"Let us through, Davis!" I shouted. He looked in the back of the truck. "This kid needs Dr. Parks."

Davis signaled to the other guard. "Open the gate!"

Once the gate opened Amber drove through. "How bad is it?"

"His temperature is down, but not by much. It's only a 102," I said. The bumps in the road and my position aggravated my injured ankle.

The truck stopped; someone lowered the tailgate, and Amber was there with Alpha Cole and Lucas. Lucas's eyes were red, and he was breathing deeply as he struggled to keep himself under control. I realized that he smelled Olivia's scent on Amber.

My eyes stopped glowing, and Alpha Cole started to get in, but Ellie was just as scared of him as she had been of me.

Alpha Cole backed off, and Amber took the backboard from him and got in. "Michael, this might hurt, but we have to get you on the board so we don't injure your leg more." Michael just nodded slightly.

I placed my hands on the back of his neck and the small of his back, then, rolled Michael towards me as Amber put the backboard in place. She helped me roll him onto the board, and we strapped him in.

Cole reached for the board and pulled him out of the truck. Lucas was ready to take the other end. They carried Michael to a waiting gurney, and Amber held onto Ellie, who was clinging to her.

I got out and nearly stumbled as I temporarily lost feeling in my injured leg. Thankfully, Amber didn't notice; that would have been embarrassing. I held my hand out as she tried to move with Ellie hanging onto her. Once Amber was out, she reached for Ellie and held her in her arms.

Amber paused at the steps of the packhouse, and tears filled her eyes. I put my arm around her shoulders and let her lean against me, even though my ankle felt like it would give out at any moment.

"It looks just like my home," she whispered, then tears fell from her emerald eyes. "Or like the one I used to have. Now it's gone."

I nuzzled her hair. "Come on, let's get you inside."

Caleb...

Not now, Apollo.

He whined as I walked up the steps with Amber and opened the door for her. Once I let go of her, she noticed my injury.

"You're hurt."

I shrugged. "My foot fell asleep," I said, as if the ripped jeans didn't give it away.

Your secrets are going to get us in trouble. You need to tell Amber the truth.

I will when the time is right.

Tell her now before it's too late.

Amber

We stood in the pack hospital as Dr. Parks cut the bandages from Michael's leg. Blood was still caked on Michael's dressing. It looked worse than when we had treated it back at the cabin.

Dr. Parks was an older wolf in his fifties. He had gray hair and was on the shorter side for a shapeshifter.

The doctor dropped the scissors into ametal dish on the table next to him. "Amber, you did a decent job getting the bleeding stopped, but it didn't prevent infection from starting."

"I'm sorry." I wasn't sure who the apology was for. Michael, for not getting him here sooner. Or the Moon goddess for failing one of her precious children. Maybe I was apologizing to Dr. Parks for giving him more work.

"Amber, you did all you could," Caleb said. He was leaning on me. It felt as though I was holding him up. His injury was worse than he let on.

"Don't be too hard on yourself, young Luna," Dr. Parks said, then shouted to his nurses, "He's ready for surgery; let's go."

They wheeled Michael through the double doors at the end of the hall. I wanted to follow, but Caleb's weight on my shoulders held me back.

Alpha Cole approached the doorway from another hospital room. "Amber, can you come talk to us for a minute?"

I looked back at Caleb, and he nodded for me to go. He was trying to hide the pain he was in. Lauren Dawson, walked in and supported Caleb so I could join Alpha Cole. I walked with him to meet his wife, Luna Faye.

We found Ellie sitting on a bed as Faye tried to get her to speak. But Ellie had her knees up to her chest, her body trembling as she looked from the alpha to the luna.

Alpha Cole placed a gentle hand on my back as he led me into the room. "I don't think Ellie trusts us yet. Can you tell us what happened to her?"

"I'm not sure, but maybe I can get her to open up," I said.

Ellie relaxed as I sat down with her. Faye moved her chair closer to the bed. "Ellie, I noticed you were in pain on the way here. Did something happen?" I asked. Ellie began to cry and nodded her head. I put my arm around her. "I'm sorry, I didn't mean to go so fast. Does it hurt anywhere?"

Ellie shook her head. "It wasn't you," Ellie began to sob harder. "I… I wasn't the one who was hurt."

I thought back to when she started rubbing her chest; I was worried about her and Michael.

"Ellie, can you tell us what you felt?" Luna Faye asked. Tears continued to flow freely from Ellie's eyes.

"It was like something snapped inside my chest. It still hurts."

"Ellie," I said, taking her hand and using my connection to the forest to help her. She took a deep breath and sobbed harder. Ellie buried her face in my shoulder, and I moved her to my lap.

"M—mm—my mommy and d—d—daddy are gone, I can't feel them anymore," Ellie wailed. I realized the rage I'd felt earlier, the grief — it wasn't mine. It was my parents.

I held Ellie close as she continued to sob, and Faye got up from her seat and came over to calm her down.

My gift allowed Ellie to cry and release in the way she needed to begin healing. It might take a while, and this may not be the only time Ellie cries like this. But she would heal and become a woman her parents would be proud of.

This was what I told myself because, truthfully... I was devastated that I failed to reunite this family. I was supposed to bring Ellie's parents back to her, but I was too late. I was scared that I would fail everyone else the way I failed this little pup.

Ellie's sobs were loud and brought the attention of others. I never let go of her. With every deep breath that led to more crying, my heart broke. My chest tightened, and my head felt fuzzy. Like when you stand up too fast. Only I was sitting down, and for a moment, I wanted to believe it wasn't real, but Eillie's screams and sobs reminded me that this tragedy was very real.

My own tears fell as I held this little girl who was living my worst nightmare. She'd felt the loss of her parents. I wasn't just crying because of her loss, I was crying because any one of us could be next if I didn't rescue the pack.

Ellie cried until she had nothing left. I continued to hold her until Cole tapped me on the shoulder. "Amber. Ellie will be okay with Luna Faye, will you come with me for a minute?"

I didn't want to leave Ellie, but Cole was kind with his words, and I trusted Faye to take care of her. I let go of the little pup and followed Cole into a separate room. Caleb was in there getting his ankle examined by Beta Lauren.

"How is he?" Alpha Cole asked.

"He'll be fine, and it's healing properly, but it will be another day or two before he's fully recovered," Lauren said as she wrapped his ankle with an Ace bandage.

"What happened to you?" I asked. Caleb remained silent.

"I'm sure he will tell you when he's ready," Cole said.

Caleb looked up at us. "How is Ellie?"

I shook my head and whispered, "Her parents died; I failed them." My chest felt tight with remorse.

"No, you did not," Cole said, making me look at him. "You were tasked with keeping those kids safe, and that is exactly what you did."

I snapped. "I failed, Cole. Michael is in surgery, and Ellie is suffering the loss of her parents. All because I failed my pack!"

Caleb tried to move, but his ankle was getting wrapped. "You didn't fail; this was an impossible situation, and you had more than one obstacle in your way. Amber, you are still fighting. That isn't a failure."

"Amber, you have been there for everyone." Cole's words were soft when he asked, "How are you doing?"

Really? When has that question ever failed to trigger a meltdown or receive an honest answer?

For me, it was as if my mouth had filled with cotton. I couldn't say anything. Even though I wanted to respond, the words wouldn't come out. Instead, my breathing became erratic, and tears rolled down my face unbidden, like a faucet being turned on. When I tried to speak, my mouth felt glued shut, and I started gasping through my nose. All I could do was make sounds.

"Breathe, Amber," Cole said, and soon Caleb was in front of me.

"Amber. Look at me. You are not a failure; I am right here with you."

I tried to focus on him, but I no longer felt in control of my emotions. My crying got so bad that I had to close my eyes. The force of squeezing them shut hurt and gave me a headache, but I couldn't open them.

Suddenly, I was in Caleb's arms as he spoke my name, and his scent soothed me. It reminded me of mountain pines right after spring rain. I leaned against his chest as he held me in his lap.

The longer Caleb held me, the calmer I felt. I continued to cry, but I could breathe again. My eyes relaxed, but were now so tired from the force of being squeezed closed that my eyelids felt heavy and didn't want to open. I held onto Caleb as if he were a lifeline.

I felt better after crying like that. My head hurt, and my eyes still felt too tired to open, but I liked where I was with the scent of the woods. It was as though I was in the Sacred Forest.

"It's been a long, exhausting day; lay her down on the bed and let her get some rest," Alpha Cole said. Caleb tightened his hold on me, and I squeezed his shirt. He didn't let go.

I'm not sure when I fell asleep. Still, with the comfort from Caleb holding me after my meltdown, driving all the way here from Telluride, nearly getting arrested, finding Michael in the trap, finding my mate in a trap, and dealing with Deputy Benson. It was as though my mind needed to shut down for a while.

My dream was odd. I was in a dark room with rock walls lit by a single bulb. The floor was wet, and I was cold—I didn't think you could feel cold in a dream. I didn't recognize this place, but something about it felt important.

Before I could figure out why, it disappeared, revealing the Forest of the Gods at the base of the Lunar Tree.

"Welcome back, Amber," the goddess said.

"Why am I here?" I asked.

"I wanted to speak with you."

"You chose the wrong person."

"Are you sure about that?" the goddess asked.

"I failed to rescue Ellie's parents, I failed Michael, and now he might lose his leg."

"Loss is hard for everyone. Don't dwell on it. Allow yourself to feel it and move forward. As for Michael, failure isn't a destination; make this part of your journey and become stronger because of it."

That just made me angry. "Why should my pack suffer just because of my destiny?!"

The goddess approached me. "My child, your pack would have suffered no matter who you are. It would have been worse, but your father was wise; he downsized the pack, evacuated the elders before the humans invaded, and had you rescue all the children. Now they are safe. Yes, Michael is badly injured, and Ellie lost her parents. That doesn't mean you have failed your pack. Your pack is suffering because a human let his heart be filled with hate and contempt for things he doesn't understand. The wolf who betrayed you has a heart filled with greed. He wants something that will never be his."

"But, why me?"

"I chose you, Amber, because I knew you would rise out of this suffering like a phoenix from the ashes. You are the only one brave enough to do what must be done."

"You're talking about my plan to locate my pack."

The goddess gripped my arms with a gentle firmness. "That is only a small part of it. There is so much more you are meant to do. Amber, have faith in yourself. I chose you for this. Do you trust me?"

"Yes, I do."

She moved her hands to cup my face. Her smile was radiant and her eyes glittered with pride in me I didn't feel for myself. "Good. Once you bring the pups to Shadow Moon, it will be time for you to move on. You know what you need to do. Don't let your fear get in the way."

CHAPTER 33

Amber

I woke up in a room filled with sunlight. The room was empty, and I sat up when I heard a noise in the hall. I got out of bed and walked out the door.

Luna Faye took a food tray from a cart and walked into the room next to mine. I followed her in. Caleb was sitting in a chair beside Ellie's bed.

Luna Faye placed the tray on a rolling table, and Caleb moved it over to Ellie. "Thank you, Luna," Caleb said, then gently shook Ellie's shoulder to wake her up.

Michael was in another bed on the other side of the room, sleeping peacefully with an IV in his arm and his injured leg propped up. I walked over to Michael and stroked his hair, thankful he was okay.

"Good morning, Amber," Faye said.

"How is he?" I asked, not taking my eyes off the pup.

"Dr. Parks said that he was able to save Michael's leg, but he will need extensive physical therapy. He will gain full use of his leg in time, but will have a limp for the rest of his life."

Michael opened his eyes and looked at me. "Amber…" I smiled through my tears, and he cocked his head. "…why do you look like that?" he asked.

I laughed and held his little hand. "You're going to be okay."

"My leg hurts," he said.

Faye walked over and checked his IV. "Hello, Michael."

"I remember you." Michael looked up at Luna Faye. "You brought me ice cream in the middle of the night."

"Shhh, that was our secret, remember?" Faye said playfully. "How is your leg?"

"Can I put it down?" Michael asked.

"We can lower his leg," Caleb said.

He approached my other side and helped Michael with the pillows as I lowered and adjusted Michael's bed. Faye lowered Michael's leg so it wasn't up so high, and he looked much more comfortable.

An alarm went off on Caleb's watch. "Michael, you can have another pain med now, but you should eat first."

"What's for breakfast?" Michael asked.

"Porridge with berries and cream," Ellie said happily. She filled her mouth with the warm cereal and smiled.

Caleb chuckled at the sight.

Michael's face lit up. "Are there strawberries?"

"You can't have cream without strawberries," Luna Faye said as she rolled another table over to Michael and walked out into the hall. He rubbed his hands together, eagerly waiting for her to bring him his food. When Faye returned and placed it in front of Michael, he took the lid off his bowl and smelled the cream and berries.

"This smells way better than your cooking, Amber," Michael said, making Ellie giggle.

"Hey," Caleb protested. He's never had my cooking, so he wouldn't know I was so bad that Greta permanently kicked me out of her kitchen.

"I won't argue with that," I smiled at Michael. Caleb placed his arm on my back, making me jump.

"Will you have breakfast with me?" he asked. "There are some things I'd like to talk to you about." I didn't see any harm in it, and it's been a long time since I'd seen Caleb. Part of me felt like I was dreaming. I couldn't believe he was here with me.

"Sure," I said.

I started to follow Caleb out of the room, but Michael reached for my hand.

"I'm sorry, Amber," he said.

"Michael, you have nothing to be sorry for," I told him. His eyes filled with tears, and he wiped them away with his arm.

"You told me to stay on the porch, and I didn't listen," Michael sobbed. I moved the table away, so we wouldn't spill his food, then I held him as he cried.

"Michael, you did nothing wrong. The Siver Suns put those traps out there to catch us. They are responsible for your injury, not you." I held him until he stopped crying, then he lay back on the bed, and I pushed his tray back to him.

Caleb waited patiently at the door for me. When I approached him, he offered me his arm. I placed my hand in the crook of his elbow and let him escort me to the dining room. We got our food and looked for a place to eat.

"There are too many people in here. Let's go outside," Caleb said.

We took our food trays to a little park nearby and sat on a bench under a tree. The porridge with the strawberries was delicious. I didn't realize how hungry I was until my bowl was empty. Caleb and I didn't speak to each other while we ate. When I looked over, he was finishing his bowl.

"You must have been hungry, too."

He nodded. "I haven't had a decent meal in over a week."

"Why not?"

Caleb looked like he was trying to figure out how to answer. "How are Willow and her rat?" He looked nervous as he placed his bowl on the ground beside him.

"How did you know about that?" I asked. Caleb hasn't met Willow, nor did he know about Ratty. His face grew red, and he set my tray on the ground with his.

"I watched over your cabin from the hillside; Willow found me a few times." He smiled when he said, "She and the other kids brought me sandwiches when they realized how hungry I was. It was more appetizing than the rat on Willow's shoulder."

"Did you try to eat my sister's rat?" I asked, trying to hold back laughter.

Caleb laughed nervously. "Not me, exactly; it was my wolf, Apollo."

"I see; why would he do that?"

"He was starving; the snow kept the other animals in hibernation."

"Why didn't you approach me? We could have used your help to get everyone out."

Caleb shook his head. "Olivia was too territorial for me to get close."

I thought about it and shrugged. "True, she would have chased you off."

"Only because I didn't want to fight her."

"Why didn't I ever see you?" I asked. "Not once did I see a black wolf."

Caleb looked away and ran his hands through his hair. I could tell he was struggling. He stood up, and his eyes welled with tears.

"What is it, Caleb?"

"Do you remember what it was like when we first met?" Caleb sighed, and I stood up to help him. But he paced and shook his hands as he waited for my response.

"Yes, I still feel it." I didn't know where he was going with this, and now I had butterflies in my stomach.

He stopped, took my hands, and looked into my eyes. "Amber, I haven't been able to get you out of my head for the last five years. I always wondered if you were my mate because that has never happened to me." He took a deep breath and stepped closer to me. My heart was pounding.

"I've wondered that too, but…." I looked down, not knowing how to tell him. Caleb's wolf was black, so I knew he wasn't my mate.

Caleb gently lifted my chin, his eyes glistening with tears. "Last night, Apollo confirmed it. Amber, you are my mate."

I pulled out of his hands and wrapped my arms around myself. "That can't be true."

Caleb looked at me in disbelief. "Amber, I wasn't allowed to tell very many people, and that's why I didn't tell you the truth about Apollo."

"What are you talking about?"

He took my hands again. "Amber, what I'm about to tell you, you can't tell anyone. As my mate, you have a right to know the real me."

"Caleb, you aren't making any sense."

Before he could say anything else, I touched his lips. "Look, I have a confession too; I've already met my mate. I met him in the hills by the cabin…." something seemed to click. Caleb had been limping on his right leg. The wolf I helped injured his right back leg.

When Caleb saw my realization, his eyes widened. "You know."

"That you're the White Alpha?"

"Yes, and— did you know who you were when you helped me escape the trap?"

"Yes, but I didn't want to say anything; I knew I had to leave to get help, and I'm still not sure about this whole thing."

Caleb smiled tenderly and tucked a strand of hair behind my ear. "It's a lot to process; I think it took me almost a year to accept."

At least I wasn't completely crazy. The air between us crackled with the magnetism of our newly formed bond. I reached for Caleb almost without realizing what I was doing.

He wrapped his arms around me as he drew me closer to him. My heart raced when he leaned down. Caleb's lips were soft against mine, and I held him close to me. The kiss was too short, and I wanted more; when Caleb broke the first kiss, I pulled him back for another. He held me tighter, and I wrapped my arms around his neck.

When he broke the kiss, I laid my head on his shoulder and sighed with contentment. Caleb's heartbeat picked up as he continued to hold me. "I've wanted to do that for the last five years."

I smiled. "Me too."

"Are you mad at me for not telling you the truth about Apollo?" he asked.

I pulled away, but stayed in his arms. "I don't know; I understand why you didn't tell me. When I told Olivia about finding out my identity, she didn't believe me and we got into a fight. Looking back, I'm glad you waited."

Caleb kissed my forehead. "Would you be angry if I told you there was more, I needed to confess?"

"Like what? I mean, it's not like you're some spoiled playboy prince. That would be bad." I'd meant it as a joke, but I was surprised when Caleb's body tensed.

"Why would being a prince be bad? Aside from everyone wanting to use you to gain power and privilege."

I thought that was odd. "Caleb, I've heard the stories about the Alpha Prince, and I am so thankful it's not you."

Caleb's Adam's apple bobbed. "You don't believe those stories, do you?"

"I don't have anything else to go on. Why is it so important to you?"

"Your dad didn't tell you anything?"

"Sure, he vouched for him, but my dad and the king are like brothers. My dad wouldn't say anything bad about his son. But where was he? We were visited by the king and the queen several times, but never by the prince. Not even when we went to court against Bradley Larsen over my feud with his daughter. Or that time…." I trembled as I wiped a tear from my eye as I remembered three years ago when my life was at its worst. I still couldn't talk about the crash without shaking. King Verrick went to war against Bradly Larsen on my behalf. He won, too. The king also won against the human that caused my crash.

Caleb's eyes hardened. "Would you have preferred the prince instead of me?"

"I didn't care about his title. Our packs have been allies for at least ten years, and he couldn't even be bothered to help a small mountain pack. Allies don't abandon each other like that."

"It wasn't abandonment. Being the Alpha Prince comes with responsibilities that no one could possibly understand.

It's a bit selfish of you to think he should have been there. What about me?" Caleb asked.

Any warm fuzzy feelings I had disappeared. I pulled out of Caleb's arms. "I am not selfish! You were there for me. During those months, we talked every day and even video-chatted every night. Caleb, you were at college, getting ready for graduation, but you still made time to take each of my calls and listen to me when I needed you."

Caleb's defenses cracked, and he pulled me back for another kiss. This kiss was chaste, but I felt his love and urgency.

"Ahem," someone cleared their throat behind me. "Sorry to interrupt."

Caleb pushed me away, and his eyes were wide with shock. "Dad!"

I turned and saw King Verrick Norwood standing there with an amused look on his face. I immediately placed my fist over my heart, bowed my head and knelt before the Alpha King. Caleb then knelt next to me.

"I'm glad to see you two taking a moment together, but unfortunately, we have a lot to do," said King Verrick.

"I didn't know you were coming today." Caleb's jaw was tight, and he sounded distressed.

The king placed his fist over his heart, letting us up. "Zane called me yesterday, so your mother and I left early this morning to get here before you left for Wyoming. It's been seventeen months since we've seen you, son."

He approached us, putting his hand on my shoulder. The king's green eyes were warm and kind. "Amber, I'm so sorry for everything you are going through. I promise we will find your pack."

I looked between him and Caleb and saw the resemblance. How did I miss it before? My chest felt tight, and my hands felt numb. My head spun, as I looked at Caleb.

"The king's last name is Norwood. You told me your last name was…. No…. Your last name isn't Dawson. Is it?" I asked him.

Tears filled my eyes, and Caleb reached for me as he his voice shook. "I am so sorry I didn't tell you. My real name is Caleb Verrick Norwood… Alpha Prince."

I took a step back, pulling my hand out of his. "You've had five years to tell me this truth. The secret about your wolf I understood. This was different, why hide who you are? Now it makes sense why you kept defending him. I feel so stupid."

King Verrick narrowed his eyes at me. "I'm confused, Amber; if you didn't know Caleb was the prince, who did you think he was?"

I locked eyes with Caleb, "I don't know who he is." Then I walked away. I stopped just past the king, and over my shoulder, I added, "I am not selfish."

CHAPTER 34

Caleb

"Amber, wait! Let me explain!" I shouted, but she ignored me as she walked away without looking back.

I glared at my dad. "Your timing sucks. Couldn't you let us have at least five more minutes so I could tell her the truth?"

He gave the, 'you know better than that,' look. "I think she said it pretty clearly, son. You've had five years to tell her you were royalty. Why didn't you?"

My shoulders slumped with the weight of the truth. "I don't know. When Ben Barrio tried to challenge you for the throne, mom instructed me to keep my identity a secret. Amber got to know me without the title and everything that comes with a crown. I felt free. When it was over, I was afraid my title would be all she saw once I told her the truth."

You underestimate her.

My dad echoed my wolf. "You might have been surprised. Give her time, Caleb. This will all work out. How did she react to Apollo?"

"Better than I expected. Amber understood why I kept him a secret. So why can't she accept my title?"

My dad put his hand on my shoulder. "It isn't your title that scares her. It's that you didn't trust her."

I picked up the breakfast trays, then my dad and I walked towards the packhouse. I couldn't look at him; I was too weighed down with shame.

When we walked in, I set the trays down on a counter by the kitchen. My mom was nearby talking with Luna Faye and Beta Lauren. She walked over, hugged me, and I melted in her embrace. There is something irreplaceable about being in your mother's arms. Though I had enjoyed my freedom in Utah, I missed my parents more than words can describe.

I cried, worrying about what might happen between Amber and me because I was too cowardly to tell her the truth.

"Shhh, I know," my mom said. I let go of her, and she wiped my eyes like I was eleven years old again.

"How do I fix this?"

My mom just smiled. "It's hard to say at this point. Don't give up; you will know when the time is right."

Lucas walked in with the Ellis twins. "What did you do to Amber?" Kade asked.

"I don't want to talk about it." I noticed Lucas had taken off his sweatshirt. "What happened to your hoodie?"

His face turned red as he ran a hand through his hair. "I gave it to Amber. She needed it for her cousin."

Piper pointed to the front of the packhouse. "Amber looked like she was ready for a fight when she left."

My heart dropped into the pit of my stomach. "She left?" My heart was pounding in my chest, and I could feel the start of another headache.

"Amber took the truck to lead Cole and a team down to Telluride. They'll be back tonight with everyone from the cabin," Lucas said. I took a deep breath. She's coming back.

"We have our mission, remember?" Kade asked.

Lucas checked his watch. "We need to leave, too if we want to be in Wyoming before dark." I nodded, still a little dazed by the morning events.

"We will be here when you return," my mom said.

My dad approached us. "Shadow Moon is in a suitable location for rescuing Forest Moon. Once Amber brings the pups back from the cabin, we can begin the search for the pack."

Kade looked like he wanted to say something but didn't.

"What is it, Kade?" I asked.

"Nope. If my dad hasn't said anything, then neither will I." He looked at his twin sister, and Piper shook her head.

"Same."

My dad narrowed his eyes at them. "Why not?"

My mom placed her hand on his arm. "Honey, you know Zane wouldn't keep it from you if he didn't have a good reason."

My dad put his arm around her. "Why do I feel like this is something I would object to?"

"Ask my dad," Kade responded.

Lucas looked at his watch again. "We need to leave; Jason is meeting us in Rock Springs."

"Fine, let's go," I said. I wouldn't have any more time with Amber anyway, and who knew how much time Rose had left.

"Your warrant to search Julius's pack and blank arrest warrant are in the file I gave Lucas along with a pack directory. We would have started with Rebel Moon if we had thought she was with a wolf pack," my dad said.

"She was kidnapped by humans. Don't be too hard on yourself, Alpha," Lucas said. My dad smiled sadly.

He shook his head and smiled. "William knew Rose was going to bring tragedy to the pack. That's when he started to downsize. She has a lot of good in her. William confided in

Rose our biggest secret. He also told her she had something to do with it and gave her a choice." Tears filled his eyes as he recalled his memories of Rose Baxter. "She didn't hesitate. Rose would not be a pawn for another alpha. She accepted Ian as her mate, then told William she would stay and fight. When I met Rose, I was very impressed with her integrity."

"We'll bring her back," I promised, then turned to my friends. "Let's go."

In unison, Lucas, Kade and Piper responded, "Yes, Alpha."

"Good luck," my mom told us. We gave her a hug, then walked out the door and got into the jeep.

We were halfway to Rangley when Lucas asked, "So, how likely is it you will get rejected?"

I didn't care that he was driving. I punched his shoulder hard enough to make him swerve, then began rubbing my temples.

"Ow, hey," Lucas said.

"It's a valid question if you think about it, Caleb," Piper said from the back seat.

"You can't afford to be rejected," Kade added. None of my friends except these three, and now Jasper, knew the truth about Apollo being the White Alpha.

"I know," I sighed. "I'm praying Amber forgives me."

Have faith in our mate.

The rest of the drive to Rock Springs was quiet, except for the checklists and typical banter on a road trip.

I sighed. "The chopper would have been faster."

"My dad's using it at the moment."

I turned to look at Kade. "Why is it down in Telluride?"

"Something about Amber's plan to locate her pack." Kade stopped himself before he could say more. I tried to get him to tell me, but he refused, claiming he'd already said too much.

Lucas stopped at a small grocery store. While the rest of us waited for him to return with our food, I felt a pain in my chest. Lucas came out with a bag of fruit and beef jerky in one hand, and the other had our usual travel snacks of cereal treats, chips, licorice, and drinks. I started to rub my chest as Lucas got in. He pulled out an apple and handed me a container of blueberries.

Kade grabbed a bag of licorice. "Caleb, are you okay?"

Keeping my hand on my chest, I opened the blueberries. "I'm fine. It's probably just stress."

Lucas swallowed his bite of apple. "Eat, those should help."

It was strange; my favorite snack didn't interest me. I left the cereal treat in the bag and focused on the fruit in front of me. One blueberry eased my tension. I finished the container and felt more focused. The drive up to Rock Springs was better, and the pressure in my chest eased. I wasn't so on edge, and the conversations were more pleasant. Kade's phone rang, and I had a terrible feeling as he answered it.

"Okay…. Yeah… thanks, Dad."

"What's going on?" I asked.

"Olivia and the pups just left the cabin," Kade said. Lucas visibly relaxed as he continued. "Cole has everyone, and they got out of Telluride without a problem."

He was holding back. "Kade…"

He reached into the bag and handed me another container of blueberries. "Here, eat these first."

I didn't like the way he was evading my question.

"Tell me," I growled. When he relayed Zane's message, I lost it.

"What?!" I hardly noticed that Lucas had pulled over. My heart felt like it was going to explode. Everything around me seemed to fade away. Kade's and Lucas's voices were distant as my ears rang.

CHAPTER 35

Amber

Isaw a red shadow in the bushes as we approached the cabin. I sent a mental warning to Olivia.

"Be nice to Alpha Cole and his team."

"What took you so long?" Olivia sent back.

The bushes shook and Olivia walked out fully clothed. I got out of the truck and hugged her. She cried on my shoulder until I broke away to reach into the truck for the hoodie I demanded from Lucas. I shouldn't have talked to him that way. He wasn't the one who'd lied to me.

Olivia took the shirt and held it up to her nose. Her shoulders relaxed, and the tears in her eyes radiated her gratitude. "Thank you, Amber," she sniffed as she hugged it.

The cabin door opened, and Ryan ran out to meet us. I hugged my brother as we heard the other car doors open and close. Alpha Cole Shepherd and his Beta, Mitch Dawson, got out and approached us. Their warriors got out and patrolled the perimeter of the cabin with Cole's Gamma. My face must have given away my concern because Alpha Cole smiled and placed a reassuring hand on my shoulder. "It's all right, Amber; Zane called us last night. The traps on the hillside have been cleared."

I nodded and then looked back at Ryan and Olivia. "Is everyone ready to leave?"

"Yes, what took you so long?" Ryan asked.

"It's a long story. I will tell you when we get back to Shadow Moon."

"Or on the way," Olivia said.

"I plan to use the truck for cargo, so we need to get as much as we can out of the basement." I said.

"Except for the weapons, those go with Jeff," Alpha Cole said. His gamma, Jeff Carson, is a police officer in Grand Junction.

The five of us walked into the cabin, and Willow tackled me, nearly knocking me to the ground.

"You're back!" Willow shouted, "what took you so long?"

As Josh walked over carrying Alice he asked, "How is Michael?"

I took Alice from him, and she smiled and head-butted me, mouthing my cheek. I giggled and stroked her little head. She pulled her head away and smiled at me.

"Michael is going to have a long recovery, but he gets to keep his leg."

"That's a relief," said Olivia as she put the hoodie on. Ratty came running into the room, and Cole jumped back as Willow left me and chased the rodent.

"You've been living with rats?" Cole asked.

"Just the one, that's Ratty," I said.

Cole looked confused, but Mitch started laughing. Willow came back into the room with Ratty perched on her shoulder. Cole wasn't sure what to think about the rat. Mitch tried to pet him, but Willow warned him away.

"Careful, he bites. Ratty doesn't like grown-ups."

Olivia gave her a knowing look. "Lately, he doesn't like anyone. He's bitten Josh twice, you once, and this morning he bit Tyler."

Willow looked guilty. I knelt with her. "Willow, you know why he's acting like this, don't you?"

"He's not happy here anymore," she mumbled.

"He's a wild animal. Ratty needs to go live in the forest. He'll be happier there," I said.

Cole knelt in front of her. "Hi, Willow. Do you remember me?"

She nodded. "You brought us cookies."

He laughed, and Ratty began squeaking at him. Cole looked at Ratty, and his eyes glowed a light blue. "Silence," Cole ordered, and the rat was quiet.

Willow sniffled, and tears fell from her eyes. "I don't want to let him go; what if something happens to him?"

I stroked her hair. "Do you remember what we talked about?"

She nodded. "It's better for him to live in the forest so we can honor the web of life."

"Would you like us to go with you to set Ratty free?" Cole asked. Willow cried and started hiccupping. I gave Alice to Mitch and picked up my little sister.

Ratty moved onto the top of my head. "Don't get comfortable up there," I told him. Ratty just chittered and squeaked at me. Olivia, Ryan, Cole, Mitch, Josh, and the other pups walked out with us as we walked up the path and over to the hillside.

I set Willow down, and she took Ratty off my head and held him close; he didn't try to bite her this time. He was his usual sweet self.

"Goodbye, Ratty, I'll miss you," Willow cried. The other pups came over to pet Ratty and said their goodbyes to him, then, Cole and I walked with Willow a little farther, and she set Ratty on the ground.

The rodent didn't know what to do at first. He turned to look at Willow, then looked back at the hillside. "Go on, you need to live and be happy," Willow said as tears ran down her face. Ratty scampered up to Willow before he ran off into the grass. Willow cried on my shoulder as I carried her back to the cabin.

We kept Willow busy by having her help Josh with the checklist. Olivia was doing better around the warriors. She didn't seem so anxious about being this close to men. I think it helped that she was wearing Lucas's hoodie. The scent of her mate was helping. Now, I just had to get them in the same room.

Since the mattress had been disposed of at Shadow Moon, it was easier to load the boxes and supplies into the truck. Olivia had an odd smile on her face as we loaded the first aid kits. "You're looking better."

"Knowing how close we are to leaving and getting our families back has helped." I gave her a knowing look, and she giggled. "And the hoodie helps. Thank you."

Cole had a few of our rifles from the basement and was loading them into the third SUV. "Is that everything?"

I closed the tailgate and wiped the dirt off of my hands onto my pants. "I think so. Let's do one more run-through."

Olivia and I walked through the cabin; inside my dad's desk, I found his old journal. I picked it up and held it close. I opened the drawers and pulled out anything that looked useful. I found a brown, leather-bound book my dad kept with all the packs, their alphas, and locations. He also had notations on each one. I took it, too.

We walked into the kitchen and put the dishes away in the cupboards. We took the food out of the pantry and the fridge. The basement door was open, so we walked downstairs.

The once-full shelves were now empty. Olivia went over to the empty freezers, unplugged them, and propped the doors open with rags.

I checked the secret compartment, and everything was still intact. I went through the weapons and noticed a bag I didn't recognize. When I pulled it out, I saw some familiar books that belonged to my Aunt Vikki. I closed the bag and took it with me, then, closed up the secret compartment and replaced the rug.

"What is that?" Olivia asked.

"I'm not sure exactly," I replied. It wasn't a lie; I knew the books belonged to my aunt, but that's all I knew. We walked back up the stairs and outside. I put the bag in the truck and the books from my dad's desk into my crisis pack.

Olivia smiled at me. "I'll ride with you."

Cole pointed to where one of his warriors was struggling with Tyla and Tyler, who were screaming from the SUV. "Actually, Olivia, I need you to help me with the pups. They need an adult they trust riding with them."

She sighed, then looked at me as I shrugged. "Ellie was terrified of him until this morning."

"I guess we can catch up when we get to Shadow Moon," Olivia said. I hugged her and watched as she got into the SUV with Cole. Everyone pulled out and drove down the hill.

I looked back at the cabin; it had kept us safe. I closed my eyes and whispered a quiet prayer. "Thank you, Goddess, for looking after us. Keep us safe as we move on to a new shelter."

We will be with you.

I got into the truck, drove down the hill, and out of my territory. Then, I pulled onto the 145, and took the roundabout to go west. Sometimes, when you think everything is going well, it isn't.

Blue and red lights flashed in my rearview mirror just past the roundabout. I could take off; it was only me this time, but that wouldn't solve my problem. I pulled over and waited.

My palms were clammy as Deputy Benson approached my door with his gun raised. "Get out of your vehicle."

I went to do as Benson said. "Keep your hands where I can see them," he ordered. I lifted both of my hands. "Get out now."

"What about my seat belt?" I asked. Benson opened my door and reached across my body to unclip my seatbelt. I stole a glance at the other man on the other side of my truck. He had blue eyes and strawberry-blonde hair. He also pointed his gun at me. I was trapped.

Benson grabbed my hair and pulled me from the truck. It hurt, and I had to put my hands over his just to keep him from ripping the hair from my head. Instantly, Benson had me on the ground. He let go of my hair, placed his boot on my back, and aimed his gun at my head. His partner ran over, pulled the keys from the ignition, and threw them into the grass.

"Rookie, cuff her," Benson said. His partner put his gun away, and the sting of the silver cuffs was so intense that I nearly lost feeling in my hands. All I could feel was the burn of the silver on my wrists.

Benson moved away with his gun still pointed at me, and the man he called 'Rookie' picked me up by my hair and my wrists. It hurt my shoulders to be pulled up like that. Benson lowered his gun and got in my face.

"You don't have your agent friend here to help you. Did you think I would forget the way you humiliated me? There's no escape for you now. I'm taking you straight to the boss."

I wasn't going without a fight. I struggled to get free. "You took my family!"

Benson sneered. "That's right, and you'll join them."

I spat on him and tried to turn my body to get out of the Rookie's grip, but he outsmarted me and I ended up face-down in the dirt.

"Pick her up," Benson ordered. The Rookie picked me up again, and I struggled to get my body into a position to escape. I was stronger than both of them, so it was a fight to control me. The Rookie had a firm grip on my hair and had me pinned against the car.

"I'm not fighting her all the way to Silverton," Benson said, as he went around the car to get something out of his glove compartment.

"What are you going to do?" the Rookie asked.

"This here is yellow wolfsbane and chloroform." Benson was doing something up front, but I couldn't see what it was. I continued to struggle, but I wasn't getting anywhere. "She will be in a cage like all the other mutts by the time she wakes up. That's the only place these monsters belong."

Benson took the lid off a bottle while I unsuccessfully fought the Rookie, then he came over with a sour-smelling cloth that made my nose hurt. I tried to turn my head back and forth to avoid the wolfsbane. But the Rookie held my head still so Benson could hold the cloth over my mouth and nose. I continued to fight, but the fumes gave me a headache and made me dizzy. There was a sharp pain in my shoulder and my veins burned before it all went dark.

CHAPTER 36

Zane Ellis held the binoculars to his eyes as the helicopter flew over the Forest Moon territory; he watched Amber drive away and followed her out of town, where he knew Deputy David Benson was waiting.

He watched as the two officers struggled to get Amber into the police car. He was proud of the fight she gave them until they subdued her and threw her into the back of the vehicle. The helicopter continued to follow them as they turned onto the highway.

The deputy's car drove south at Ridgeway and was followed by two SUVs. When it passed Ouray, a group of motorcyclists pulled up behind the police car. Eventually, several other trucks and SUVs pulled behind Benson's car as the bikers surrounded it.

Zane watched as the police car suddenly stopped, and the bikers circled Benson. He couldn't hear what was going on.

The bikers pulled Benson from his car and shoved him to the ground. There were so many people that Zane wasn't able to see exactly what was going on. He didn't know who the bikers were or why they would force Benson to pull over.

The other cop fought with two of the bikers, but he surrendered quickly, and the bikers left. It was very suspicious and all he could do was watch helplessly from the sky.

The other cop picked Benson off the ground and helped him into the back before climbing into the driver's seat. Hoping that Amber was still with them, Zane continued to follow the police car until it drove down a dirt road that led to an old abandoned mine. When the car parked, he saw the two officers get out of the vehicle.

Zane smiled. "Got 'em."

INSIDE THE MINE

A few minutes later, guards escorted the two officers to a small corridor. A man dressed in black looked up from his desk as they walked in. "David Benson, what are you doing here? Who is this?"

Owen Murdock was known for quickly gaining favor with Charles Balor; he was in his mid-thirties and ranked much higher than most men his age. There were few that Balor trusted more than Owen.

They were standing in a corridor that Owen used for his office. It was dank and lit by little fluorescent lights along the wall. The two officers stood at attention as the guards left the corridor.

"This is our new Rookie, we had another wolf for you, sir," Benson said.

Intrigued, Owen put down his pen and leaned back in his chair. "Where is it?"

Benson looked at the ground. "I'm not sure. We were ambushed, and she disappeared."

Owen didn't handle failure very well. He hated it when things weren't controlled and in their rightful place.

Footsteps came from the corridor's entrance, and an older man appeared. He wore an expensive business suit and black leather dress shoes. His short, gray hair and green eyes looked dark in the dim light. He walked with a crooked gait because of his prosthetic leg. It was Charles Balor.

"What is going on, Owen? I thought these men were posted outside that cabin in Telluride," Balor asked.

"That's what I was about to find out." Owen eyed the two men. Then he turned to the Rookie.

"What about you? What did you see?" Owen asked. The one Benson called Rookie had bruises all over his face, and he looked to Benson for a clue about what to say. Benson was so nervous that the Rookie thought the older cop would wet himself.

"The wolf got the better of him," the Rookie said.

"But not you?" Owen asked.

"Sir, Benson made sure I followed his orders. He wouldn't listen to anything I suggested."

Owen stood up and approached him. "Why should he? He's your senior officer."

"But he failed to collect fifteen loose werewolves; most of them were children. He had weeks to move in on the cabin but failed to act. I wouldn't make that mistake," the Rookie said.

Owen laughed. "I like you." Benson looked over at the Rookie, who had just lied and betrayed him. "You see, Rookie, I have been asking David that same question for weeks."

"You never did give us a straight answer, boy," Balor said to Benson.

Tears welled in the deputy's eyes, "B… But… I… I…"

Owen held up a finger to silence Benson's stuttering so Balor could continue. "You had the manpower. Why did you hesitate? Now you show up here empty-handed, abandoning your post." Balor shook his head at him, then returned his attention to Owen. "Do with him as you see fit."

"Yes, sir," Owen said, as Balor left the room. "Well, Rookie. Do you have an answer for me?"

"I have a theory..." the Rookie began, but Benson interrupted him.

"Please, sir, if you give me another chance, I will bring them to you."

Owen said nothing. His face was expressionless as he opened the bottom drawer of his desk and pulled out a black box. He opened it, revealing what was inside. He put on his black gloves, pulled out the ornately engraved pistol, screwed on the silencer, and aimed it at the two men.

"I can't decide; do I kill you both or just the incompetent one?"

"Please, give me another chance. I know where the girl went," Benson pleaded.

Owen aimed his gun at Benson's head. "You've failed me too many times already," he said, then pulled the trigger, the sudden noise making the Rookie jump. Benson's lifeless body dropped to the ground as Owen lowered his gun and addressed the Rookie.

"I no longer care about the wolves in the cabin. For all I know, they're gone. I need you here. Do you think you can handle these many werewolves?" Owen asked.

"Yes, sir."

"Good. Get your new uniform, and the warden will tell you where to go next. You're dismissed."

The Rookie left the room and walked through the cold, dark tunnels of the mine. He arrived at a tunnel with rows of electrified cages and a single wolf inside each one. It was the Forest Moon Pack.

SNEAK PEEK AT BOOK 2

SECRET

Caleb

I couldn't control my breathing. My hands were trembling, and my chest was tight. Apollo kept whining, but there was nothing I could do. Deputy Benson, a man who abused his badge, arrested Amber. We'd done everything we could to keep her and the children safe. Lucas Barnes, my Beta, touched my shoulder to calm me down. A strangled growl escaped my chest. "Where is Jasper? Have him follow Benson."

Kade Ellis was sitting in the back seat with his twin sister, Piper. Lucas was in the driver's seat next to me. We had pulled over on a highway near Rock Springs.

Kade lowered his head and sighed. "Jasper flew the helicopter with my dad as they tracked Benson. Something happened to the deputy's car, and they lost track of Amber. They followed the car to a mine in Silverton but didn't see Amber exit the vehicle."

Tears stung my eyes, my head was pounding, and now my chest was so tight I thought I was going to pass out from lack of oxygen. "Then where is she?"

Kade's brow wrinkled with worry. "They don't know. My dad didn't give me details."

Amber's last words still haunted me. "I'm not selfish." The last time I saw her, she was upset with me. I didn't blame her. I hadn't been the mate she deserved.

What kind of man calls his mate selfish? We were arguing, and I'd lashed out. Now, I may never see her again. I got out of the jeep and staggered to the ground. A scream ripped from my chest as my friends came out to support me.

Kade knelt next to me. "Caleb, try and hold it together."

Piper placed her hand on my back. "We'll find her."

Lucas was in front of me, forcing me to look at him. "Caleb, what did you feel?"

I shook my head. I couldn't tell if there was a disruption in the bond or if this was all from my guilt. "I'm not selfish," Amber's words repeated in my head over and over.

"The chest pain… I think it was my bond with Amber."

"I'm calling your dad." Lucas grabbed my phone from my pocket and pressed the button for the king. Kade and Piper were still with me. Lucas put the call on speaker.

"Caleb. Son? Are you there?"

"Yeah," I sighed.

"Amber is alive. That is all we know right now. Her siblings and her cousin all say she's alive. How strong did you feel it?"

"I thought it was heartburn at first. Apollo was whining, but I figured that was because of the fight."

"That's good news. You have a bond with her, even if it's small. Have hope, son. We will find her, I promise you. Now, try to stay focused so you have good news to tell Amber when you see her again."

I nodded. There wasn't anything we could do at this point. I was too far away to help anyone.

"Lucas," my dad said.

"Yes, Alpha."

"Stay with him. I don't want the two of you separated. Give me updates every hour."

"I will, if you will."

My dad was silent and then chuckled. "Deal."

Lucas ended the call and handed me back my phone. I took it before standing up. I gave Lucas a hug. He's always had my back.

Even though my wolf, Apollo, recently confirmed that Amber was my mate, I have been in love with her for the past five years. I used our six year age gap as an excuse to stay away from her until she came of age. By the time she did, I was so caught up in my life in Utah, and the lie, that the truth frightened me. I should have seen her three years ago, when she needed me most. I should have been at her graduation and invited her to visit my pack. Most of all, I should have told her the truth and not lied to her about my royal blood.

We won't get anywhere if we dwell on the past. It's best to hope for the future.

Who are you trying to convince?

Apollo whined. He was just as miserable.

Lucas placed his hand on my shoulder, making me look at him. "We'll find Amber. I promise. Right now, we had to focus on Rose Baxter. Amber will never forgive us if we choose her over her friend."

He was right. I'd made a promise, and I intended to keep it. Rose needed to be our priority, even if everything in me was screaming to shift and run back to Colorado.

9 798889 454103